SAMSON AND
AMISH DELILAH

SAMSON AND AMISH DELILAH

Thomas Nye

CrossLink Publishing

CrossLink Publishing
1601 Mt. Rushmore Rd, STE 3288
Rapid City, SD 57702

Ordering Information:
Quantity sales. Special discounts are available on quantity purchases by corporations, associations, and others. For details, contact the "Special Sales Department" at the address above.

Samson and Amish Delilah/Nye —1st ed.

ISBN 978-1-63357-168-6

Library of Congress Control Number: 2019931161

First edition: 10 9 8 7 6 5 4 3 2 1

This is a work of fiction. Names, places, and events are either the product of the author's imagination or used in a fictitious manner. Any resemblance to actual persons, living or dead, or actual events is purely coincidental.

To my only son, Dallas.

May this book help you find your true Delilah.

Love, Dad

Contents

Preface

It may seem unlikely that an Amish girl would have the name Delilah. However, there really are Amish girls with that name. In fact, my stepmom taught at an Amish school and one of her students was named Delilah. I am still friends with that Delilah, and when I told her about this book, she smiled.

This novel was not written as a children's book. It is my conviction that this story, though it deals with tough subject matter, is suitable for teens. Some parents may have a stricter standard than mine. You might want to read this novel before passing it on to a young person.

CHAPTER ONE

To Find the Right Girl

D ave sat alone in the corner booth of a small diner. He pulled soft layers of sugary-sweet cinnamon roll loose from its thick center and dipped them in his coffee. Each bite melted in his mouth. He studied an Amish waitress as she flittered about the restaurant. He couldn't imagine why a young, attractive woman would be willing to wear Amish clothes.

He examined her apparel. She wore a bright blue dress that curved slightly with her outline and reached almost to her ankles. It fluttered as she walked, crisp and clean, and was highlighted by a pleated white apron tied in the back with a bow. Her dark hair, obviously pulled back into a bun, peeked out from under a white head covering. A few delicate strands that had come loose added an adorable feminine touch.

The waitress's petite form scurried about the restaurant checking on tables like a hummingbird visiting a cluster of flowers. Nothing in her demeanor or appearance indicated the possibility of fame. In fact, she went about her work in such a way as to draw very little attention to herself. He doubted that this could be the girl he came looking for.

"Hello—my name is Delilah," she said when she reached his table. "Our other waitress had to leave, so I'll be your server. Would you care for some more coffee?" Her voice lilted like a song.

Dave felt tempted to tease her and say, "Hello Delilah, my name is Samson." Instead, he bit his tongue and tried to be as mature as possible, fearing people wouldn't respect him if they recognized he was only twenty-three. "Yes, more coffee please, and if you don't mind, I'd really like another one of those cinnamon rolls. They're amazing, where do you get them?"

She wrinkled her nose as she smiled. "We make them."

"We?" Dave asked. "Who is we?"

"My mother, my sisters, and me."

He rubbed his stomach. "You women have some kinda special talent."

"I . . . see," she answered. Her eyes sparkled and cheeks flushed, and then she hurried away, disappearing through a swinging door. Every time someone passed through that doorway, a clamor of kitchen sounds and the smell of bacon briefly wafted out. He glanced at his surroundings. His booth looked like an antique made of solid oak. The small restaurant was full of oak booths and could have been beautiful had the walls not been covered with cheap imitation-wood paneling. Dave imagined how much better the place would look if someone simply painted the walls and tossed the red-checkered gingham tablecloths in the trash.

A few moments later, Delilah reappeared, dishcloth in hand, and stopped at a table directly across from Dave's booth. He tried to conceal how carefully he was studying her every move. He watched as she engaged in a friendly conversation with a woman who was with her two adolescent daughters, both dressed in skin-tight volleyball uniforms. The girls held out napkins, pleading with the waitress for her autograph. Delilah wrinkled up her nose again with a slight smile, just as she had when Dave complimented her family's cinnamon rolls. She scribbled on their napkins, and the woman and her daughters stood to leave, admiring their autographs and giggling. Delilah quickly cleared away their mess and wiped the gingham-checked tablecloth clean. Within minutes, she breezed over to Dave's table with his coffee and roll.

He tried to sound nonchalant as he questioned her. "I couldn't help but notice those young girls asking for your autograph. What was that about?"

"Oh nothing, it's just silly." She waved her hand toward the table left by the girls, as if pushing away any compliment.

Dave raised one eyebrow. "Really, nothing? Can you give me just a little hint about it?"

She tilted her head and blushed. "Have you heard about the famous Amish girl from Indiana?"

Dave gave her a wide-eyed, questioning look, attempting to draw out more of an explanation.

"Well, there is a best-selling novel about an Amish girl named Delilah. I guess people all over America are crazy about her." Her lilting voice, and lips that curled into a smile as she talked, interested Dave as much as her words. "At first everyone thought this Delilah was a made-up character. Then, the author told some news people that there is a real girl named Delilah, and he didn't make her up after all."

"No kidding?" Dave tried to pretend he didn't know anything about it. "What is it about her that everyone likes?"

"Don't ask me; I'm not much of a reader. I just work here at DJ's Diner and keep busy at home when I'm not here."

"That still doesn't explain why those young girls wanted your autograph," Dave reminded her.

"I . . . see." She wrinkled up her nose, and her lips returned to that slight smile before answering. "Well, my name is Delilah, and they think that I remind them of the girl in the book."

"Oh, that must feel really good to get all of that attention, right?"

"Not at all," she said, and her dark eyebrows straightened. "I think the whole thing is silly."

"Why did you sign your autograph then?"

"They asked me to do it, and I didn't want to hurt their feelings. It doesn't cost me anything to write my name. If they want it, they can have it, but I do think it's silly." She looked Dave in the eyes as if to confirm he understood.

When their gaze locked, Dave remembered something his dad used to say: "If you want to be sure you've found the right girl, don't look at her eyes, look *into* them."

Dave allowed himself to peer deeply into Delilah's eyes, and his heart skipped a beat. He perceived something profound in them. He wasn't sure if he saw pain or sweetness, wisdom or innocence. He couldn't pull his eyes away until she blushed, turned abruptly, and began toying with the ribbons that dangled from her white head covering.

She poured a little more coffee in his cup and said, "I'd better check on my other tables."

"Oh, sorry, I didn't mean to keep you from your work."

When she walked away, Dave covered his mouth and spoke into his hands with an excited whisper, "She *is* the one!"

He tried to grasp what it was that he saw in her eyes. He couldn't put it into words, but he instantly knew that this was the type of girl books are written about. He didn't know if he felt attracted to her or if she just constituted a curiosity for him. Regardless, he felt something strong. He wanted to talk to her, ask questions about her life, about her feelings. He suddenly wanted to know how this Amish girl lived, what she thought about, and what she dreamed about.

However, he tried to push back those thoughts and focus on his job. He could make a lot of money by locating the girl his boss hired him to find. Dave savored the rich coffee aroma that rose with the steam from his cup. He tugged a soft piece of cinnamon roll loose and dipped it into the dark liquid. Once again, a perfectly baked cinnamon-sugary bite melted in his mouth. *Oh my—and can that girl bake!* he thought. A touch of brown-sugar icing stayed on his fingertips, and he couldn't resist licking it off each one. He scrolled through the files on his laptop and found the Amish novel, *Samson and Delilah*. He tried to find a section describing Delilah, but he struggled to use his laptop without getting the keys sticky. Delilah appeared and handed him a few extra napkins.

"You'd better keep your hands clean or you'll ruin your little machine," she said.

Dave laughed. "Do you mean my laptop?"

"I guess. I mean, do you call it that because it's small enough to hold on your lap?"

"Yeah, I guess that is why," Dave answered, and then he ventured a new question. "So—Delilah must be a rare name? No wonder those girls thought you were the real Delilah."

She didn't make eye contact as she used her dishcloth to wipe off the empty bench opposite him while they talked. "It's not that rare. There are a lot of Amish girls with that name. In fact, there are two of us working at this restaurant."

"What?" Dave forgot to conceal his surprise. He had hoped there were only a few Amish girls in the whole world named Delilah so it would be easy to find the right one. Realizing his eyebrows were giving away his anxiety, he lowered them slowly and tried to sound casual, "Is the other Delilah working here right now?"

"No, but I do think she'll be coming in later this afternoon."

Dave gazed at her over the rim of his coffee cup. "I would've thought there would only be one or two Amish girls in America with the name Delilah."

"Nope—there's a lot of us." She wrinkled her nose with another smile as she straightened, keeping her focus on Dave's coffee cup. She exchanged her dishcloth for a coffee pot that sat on an empty table nearby. While pouring Dave another cup, she asked, "Are you from around here?"

"No, but I went to college over in Rapid City, which isn't far from here," Dave said. He attempted to look into her eyes again, but she averted her gaze. He didn't want to scare her off. He made a mental note not to look into her eyes too often.

"I know where that is. I've been to Rapid City to go to a chiropractor," she answered sheepishly.

"Not Dr. Hatcher?" Dave asked, allowing his eyebrows to rise again.

"Yes," she exclaimed, "we call him Bob! Do you go to him too?"

"Yeah, he knew my dad from when they were in college together," Dave explained.

"It sure is a small world then, huh?" Delilah said before hurrying off to pour coffee for another customer. Dave stuffed the last sticky-sweet bite of cinnamon roll into his mouth and continued reading from *Samson and Delilah* on his laptop.

> *Delilah was not the type of woman who caught a man's eye by her stunning outward beauty. A loveliness emanated from deep within; a sweetness per-*

fectly combined with practicality and a caring heart
revealed by every kind act in her busy day.

He scrolled back to the first chapter to see what it said about her eyes.

Her eyes, coffee-colored, with just the right amount
of cream and sugar.

Dave finished his coffee and closed his laptop. *Huh,* he thought, *I looked into her eyes, but I forgot to check what color they were.* He left a five-dollar bill on the table to make a good impression on Delilah and then stopped to pay the woman at the till.

The cashier popped open her register with a ding. "Was everything okay today?"

"More than okay. I loved the cinnamon rolls and your coffee here is great too!"

"Give the credit to Delilah," she said, nodding toward the Amish girl. "She gets here at six a.m. and starts our first pot of coffee. She and her sisters make the cinnamon rolls fresh every morning before she comes into work."

Dave winked at the cashier. "I bet the guys are coming out of the woodwork to ask her out?"

The older woman rolled her eyes. "Nope—men aren't that smart. Of course, the non-Amish guys around town wouldn't look at her twice. I've asked her about Amish boys, and she said they've never asked her on a date."

Dave shook his head. "They should notice her for her cinnamon rolls if nothing else."

His tab paid, Dave stepped outside and took about twenty steps beyond the front doors of the restaurant before he heard a woman's voice calling after him. "Wait—please wait!" Delilah shouted and ran toward him waving a five-dollar bill. She puffed to catch her breath. "You forgot this on the table."

"I didn't forget it—that's a tip."

"*Un fa shdendich*, that's too much. Your bill was only five dollars." Delilah continued holding out the money, her eyes searching his face.

Dave pointed in the direction of his hometown. "I'm from a bigger city. People leave tips like that sometimes. Please don't be offended. I thought the coffee and rolls were amazing, and you were nice enough to answer my questions."

"I've only had one other customer give a big tip like that before." She gazed off as if remembering. "He was a really kind older man and told me that it was like tithing for him, a way to give to God and others at the same time."

"That sounds like something my dad would've said." Dave put a hand on his heart. "Think of it that way from me too."

She wrinkled up her nose and smiled. As she walked away, Dave heard her mutter, "Un fa shdendich."

He was still grinning as he turned around and bumped into an older man. Dave gathered himself. "I'm sorry—I didn't see you there."

"You need to pay better attention to the world around you," the old man said.

Dave nodded politely. "I'm sorry. Do you know that girl that I was just talking to?"

"That Amish girl?" he growled. "She's a waitress at DJ's restaurant, I think."

"Don't you go there often?"

"Every day," the old man said.

Dave cocked his head. "And you don't know that girl by name?"

"Those Amish girls all look the same to me. Why, do you want to ask her out?" The old man laughed at his own joke.

"I just thought she might be a local celebrity." Dave raised his eyebrows to get a response out of the older guy.

The man stuck out his chin and shook his head. "There is no such thing as an Amish celebrity. That's the last thing an Amish person would want. They don't believe in it."

CHAPTER TWO

Another Delilah

D ave sat on the bed in his dimly lit hotel room and read from his paperback copy of *Samson and Delilah*. He searched for clues and wrote notes about the distinctive traits of the true Delilah.

He jotted down *Un fa shdendich, a strange word Delilah uses, often as an expression of surprise.* Pronounced *Un fa shdendie.*

He read on. A moment later, he scribbled *She wrinkles up her nose with every smile and waves away compliments.*

All the descriptions fit the waitress at the diner, but he still couldn't be certain. He reminded himself that those might be common mannerisms among Amish young women. After all, he hadn't talked to very many. Though he had grown up in a community inundated with Amish people, he had always ignored them, just like the locals in this town. He read a section where Delilah gave a buggy ride to a little girl who wasn't Amish. He smiled when the Delilah in the book said, "I . . . see."

This has to be the same girl! he thought to himself. He gathered his pencil and wrote *She often says, I . . . see.* He drew an asterisk, followed by *She separates the "I" from the "see."*

Every few minutes he caught himself thinking about her eyes. He couldn't explain it, but there was something so unique, so deep, and so mysterious about them. Dave replayed his conversation with her in his mind, comparing her with the girl in the book until he fell asleep.

A deep rumble stirred him enough that he dropped the pencil that had been resting loosely in his fingers as he slept. A troubling dream worsened as locomotive sounds intensified. He dreamt that he was on a set of railroad tracks. A train whistle blew, and he lifted his head enough to see a bright light coming straight toward him. A beautiful woman with long dark hair slumbered on the tracks, between him and the train, just out of reach. He tried to scramble toward her, but his head felt thick with drowsiness, like a drunken man. He couldn't make his hands and feet do what they should. He fell to her side and tried to shake her awake. When she awoke, her eyes were full of fear. She struggled to get away from him more than from the train. The rumbling grew to a full crescendo. The train whistle blew again. She screamed.

This time the deafening blast of the train's whistle jerked Dave's head up with a snap. He awoke from his dream and clamored to his feet, yanking open both curtain panels. The blurry mass of a speeding locomotive rattled the windows and shook the hotel's foundation.

He shouted, "Un fa shdendech! Who builds hotels twenty feet from railroad tracks?"

Dave slumped back onto his bed in a cold sweat. His mattress jostled with the rumbling of the locomotive, probably just as much as seats on the train did. After rubbing is eyes, he shook his head, trying to recover from the nightmare. He looked over his notes, straining to read from a jiggling notepad. Finally, the clicking of wheels and the rumbling of train cars subsided. An oversized clock on his hotel room wall clicked off seconds with a clatter that rivaled the steel wheels of the train. He watched as its red second hand moved methodically uphill toward twelve.

"Ten to twelve," he announced to himself. He stood up, glanced in a mirror next to the clock, and straightened his hair. He took a moment to examine the progress of his beard. Short, wiry hairs that matched the color of those on his head, covered his jawline from ear to ear. He smiled, pleased with his success in growing a chinstrap, even though the hairs were sparse in places. At 1:00 he decided to revisit the diner and get a bite to eat—and hopefully get a chance to meet the afternoon Delilah, just to rule her out for sure.

Dave stepped out of his hotel room and drew a breath of fresh country air. The world outside seemed bright and sunny compared to his dark room and terrible nightmare. He studied the view of Falls, Wisconsin—a picture-postcard small town with two-story brick buildings lining Main Street. Only a few antique stores, the diner, a gas station, and a tavern constituted the business district on Main, which came to a T in front of the Carriage Inn. The hotel's proprietors no doubt gave the Inn that name to capitalize on Amish tourism. Dave leaned against a lightpost and watched a horse pulling a buggy through downtown Falls. The horse stopped at the hamlet's only stoplight. A semitruck roared through the intersection, causing the horse to rear up. As soon as the eighteen-wheeler passed by, the horse calmed down and waited for a green light before resuming its trek down Main Street.

Victorian-style houses painted in rich colors with ornate trim lined a hillside behind the brick buildings downtown. Maple trees lined the streets and large oaks surrounded the houses on the hill, looking picturesque in every season.

Off to the far right, Dave noticed a huge water tower with massive blue letters reminding the citizens they were in Falls. To the left, a waterfall fell over a twenty-foot ledge and flowed under a bridge. That landmark, no doubt, gave the town its name. Beyond the falls, a large lumberyard clamored with activity. Although the sawmill buzzed and whined all day, the buildings looked outdated and only a small portion of the yard appeared to be in use. Dave guessed that trains used to stop regularly in Falls during the logging industry's glory days. He imagined that every time a locomotive rumbled past, without even slowing at intersections, its whistle functioned as a painful reminder to the locals that those good days were over.

Dave listened to the roaring sound of falling water merge with whines from the sawmill as he walked along the sidewalk. He followed the same route the buggy had traveled a short time before. An Amish girl in a blue dress hurried past storefronts ahead of him. He watched her closely as she crossed the street and entered a low building where buggy horses were tied. Dave leaned against a mailbox and studied her as she untied her horse and backed it out toward the street. He felt positive it was Delilah, his waitress.

Two little girls worked a lemonade stand directly across the street from the diner. Remembering that the Delilah in the book was always willing to give buggy rides, he decided to test this girl and quickly took two five-dollar bills from his wallet and tossed them on the lemonade stand table. "I'll buy two cups of lemonade for five bucks each if you kids will do me a favor."

The older of the two girls squinted at him. "What's that?"

"See this buggy coming up the street?" Dave pointed toward Delilah. "Ask the Amish girl driving if you can have a buggy ride."

The younger girl poured two cups of lemonade and pushed them toward him while the older girl placed the money in a little box. The girls eyed him suspiciously as they headed toward the buggy.

"What's the matter?" Dave asked.

"We ask her for a ride every day, and she always gives us one."

The girls climbed into the buggy and waved at Dave as the horse clip-clopped past. Delilah's smiling face came into view behind the girls' waving hands. He took one sip of his ten-dollar lemonade, and it was so warm and sour that he spit it out. He dumped both cups in the bushes and headed toward the diner.

Blue lettering painted on a large storefront window spelled out DJ's Diner. Dave pushed open the heavy wooden door that jingled an attached bell as he walked in. Everyone inside stopped talking and eating long enough to stare at him until he found his way to a stool at the lunch counter. He sat down, and everyone resumed their conversations.

A much larger crowd found their way into DJ's over the noon hour. A skinny Amish girl in a lime-green dress handled the lunch counter. "Are you Delilah?" he asked.

She smirked at him and shook her head as though annoyed. A pleasantly-plump Amish girl stepped through the swinging door of the kitchen, and the skinny waitress said, "That's Delilah over there."

Dave sank his teeth into a thick cheeseburger. He decided to give it three stars. Nothing about the burger seemed as original or unforgettable as the five-star cinnamon rolls on the breakfast menu. He watched the plump Delilah make trips in and out of the kitchen. She seemed friendlier than the skinny waitress in the green dress, but he never once saw her wrinkle her nose with a smile. Both Amish girls worked hard, scrambling out of the kitchen with platters of food and hustling back in with empty plates.

Nobody seemed to notice either of them as they efficiently kept the kitchen doors swinging.

Sizzling sounds came from the kitchen with every swing of the door—likely french fries or breaded mushrooms bathing in a vat of oil. Dave didn't bother to ask questions of the other Delilah since she couldn't fit any of the descriptions in the book. After his meal, Dave stopped at the cash register to pay his bill. A woman with hair so black that it looked fake took his money.

"Who's DJ?" Dave asked.

She lifted one finger in the air as her cash register dinged. "That's me, Delores Johnson." Her red-checkered gingham apron matched the tablecloths and curtains and should have been a dead-giveaway she owned the tiny diner.

Dave nodded. "Okay, nice little restaurant you have here, especially the breakfast menu. Can I just ask one little question though?"

"Sure, what's that?"

"Have you had anybody from the media stop in here and ask about Delilah?"

DJ shook her head. "Which Delilah? I have two of them working here."

"The morning waitress that makes the cinnamon rolls."

"Why? What would they want to know about her?" DJ let her jaw drop.

"Don't you know about the Delilah craze going around our country?" Dave asked.

Delores covered her mouth that had been hanging open before she answered. "Yes, that famous Amish girl from Indiana."

Dave leaned on the counter and spoke in a low tone. "Nobody knows who she is. We just know that Samuel VanRokel wrote a novel based on a real-life Amish girl. There are a lot of people searching for the real Delilah, and when they find her . . . let's just say, her life will never be the same again."

DJ's eyes got wide. "It never crossed my mind that it could be one of our Delilahs. My Amish waitresses told me that the book was about a worldly Amish girl from Indiana."

"I know it's surprising, but I think there's a slim chance it's the morning waitress." Dave winked at the older woman. "If you care about Delilah, do what you can to protect her identity. I think it should be her choice about whether or not everyone knows who she is." DJ nodded in agreement as he continued, "Meanwhile, if anyone comes in here looking for an Amish girl named Delilah, show them the afternoon waitress. I think they'll know it's not her and head on down the road."

She continued covering her mouth in disbelief.

Dave headed for the door and then turned back. "What do you think about her eyes?"

"They're brown?"

"Eh—yeah—anything else?" he asked.

The middle-aged woman gave Dave an annoyed expression. "What else is there?"

He shrugged. "I don't know—I just thought I'd ask."

Dave left DJ standing frozen in shock and headed back to his hotel room to make a quick phone call. He sat on his bed because it was the only piece of furniture in his tiny room, other than a TV on a stand. A computerized voice answered his call. "*Humans* magazine. You have reached the office of Chief Correspondent Charlie Rose. Charlie is either on the other line or out of the office. After the beep, please leave a brief message and your name and number. Charlie will get back to you as soon as possible."

Dave listened for the beep. "Hello Charlie, this is Dave. I think I may have found the girl!"

He ended the call and tossed his cell phone onto crumpled blankets. He fumbled with the remote, trying to find something on TV. Within minutes his phone began to chirp. Dave scrambled to find his phone and simultaneously shut the TV off. His finger found the mute button as he answered the phone.

"Hello, Dave here."

"Dave, this is Charlie Rose! Where are you?"

"I'd rather not say where I'm at until I talk to this girl."

"Listen, Dave, I'm paying you a hundred thousand dollars to find this Delilah. I have the right to know where you think she is!"

"You haven't given me a dime yet," Dave sneered at the phone. "If I give you a lead, you'll figure out who she is, and I'll never see a penny."

Charlie let out a sinister chuckle on his end of the phone line. "You're as smart as your daddy! Keep me updated and find her quick. I've heard through the grapevine that *People* magazine is on her trail. The *New York Times* has a full-time staffer searching for her. And CBS has a manhunter on the prowl too!"

"Wow—you'd think the girl killed somebody," Dave said.

Charlie growled out, "Some people would kill to find out who she is. There are millions of dollars to be made in endorsements and magazine covers."

Dave scratched his chest. "Okay Charlie, I'll probably know by tomorrow."

"Call me the second you find her!"

The phone went dead, and Dave realized the conversation had ended. His focus returned to the outdated hotel TV. An NBC news lady interviewed a teenage girl with a scarf on her head. The girl was wearing a plain-colored dress and looked almost Amish. Dave frantically pressed buttons on his remote to unmute the sound while he thought to himself, *Oh no! Maybe someone else found the right girl?*

As he increased the volume, the girl's voice became audible. She didn't sound Amish. Rather, she sounded like any modern high schooler. "Oh gosh, we all fell in love with Delilah. She is such a sweet person and a great role model for girls in this day and age."

The news lady nodded. "Good point! And what would you say to her if you ran into the real Delilah?"

"All I would be able to get out is, 'Un fa shdendich!' " The girl's hands went to her cheeks as she shouted the saying, obviously beside herself at the thought of meeting Delilah.

The news lady faced the camera and explained, "Un fa shdendich is an Amish saying that Delilah uses often in the novel. Girls can be heard using this strange phrase in malls and high schools all over America! This is Katie Korver, reporting live from Des Moines, Iowa."

"What a crazy world!" Dave said out loud in his tiny hotel room. He picked up his copy of *Samson and Delilah* and started reading where he'd left off before his nap. His phone chirped again. Dave looked at it and saw the word *Mom*. He let out a deep breath, rolled his eyes, and tapped the screen to answer.

"Hello Mom."

"Hi David," she said. "Did you make it to Falls okay?"

Dave looked at his phone and smirked. "Yes, I'm here. Why wouldn't I make it okay?"

"David, I was just asking. Did you find that Amish girl yet?"

"I think I did. I haven't asked her about revealing her identity though. I'm trying to figure out how to say it. Do you have any advice for me?"

His mother moaned. "I told you before you left that no Amish girl will want all of that fame. You should have read *Samson and Delilah* before you headed up there. Then you would know what kind of a girl this Delilah is *and* a little more about the Amish."

"Well, I'm reading it now."

"Why would you want to bring trouble on that poor Amish girl?" she asked.

"Mom, I'm not bringing trouble on her—I'm doing her a favor! *And* I'm going to ask her for permission before I tell anyone. Besides, maybe she'll love all the attention. All the girls I know take selfies and post them on Facebook daily. Girls love attention."

"Not Amish girls. Not this Delilah. If you had read the book, you would have known that. All you are thinking of is the money."

"Oh Mom, you worry too much. You know that I want to start my own restaurant. I have half the money I need in savings, and if I can get Delilah to agree to meeting the press, I'll have the other half. This girl is my golden ticket."

"David, don't think of her that way. I know how much you want your own restaurant, but please don't get what you want at someone else's expense."

"That's why I'm going to ask her before I tell anyone." Dave rolled his eyes, knowing his mother couldn't see him. "Most guys my age would just rat her out. At least I'm nice enough to ask her first."

"Hopefully you don't expose her to publicity by just going up there. Some of those paparazzi types might figure out what you're up to and follow you."

"I know. I'm trying to be careful—so they don't get the money instead of me," Dave said and laughed.

"Well, ask her nicely, and then get out of there before anyone figures out where you are."

Dave let out a long breath, trying to be patient. "Okay Mom, whatever."

"One more question," his mother said. She hesitated, giving away her reluctance to ask what she knew she shouldn't. "Do you think this is the Delilah you used to know?"

"Mom, please don't bring that up." Dave lifted his free hand in exasperation. "No, it definitely isn't, and this Delilah made it clear that there are a lot of Amish girls out there with the name Delilah. I'll never find that one again. I'm only here because I need the money."

"Oh David, some things are more important than money."

"I need to get going, Mom."

"Okay, call me when you know more."

Dave rolled his eyes. "Okay, see ya."

CHAPTER THREE

Teenage Delilah (flashback)

The first Delilah Dave ever met wasn't dressed in Amish clothes. In fact, she was at a swimming pool. Dave had been in high school at the time, and the teenage Delilah he'd known back then was the polar opposite of the morning waitress at DJ's Diner. During his high school years, Dave's friends always teased him about how picky he was. He didn't have a girlfriend for much of high school—but not because the girls didn't like him. Dave pretty much had his choice of girls at school. He stood 6' 3" and served as the captain of his basketball team his junior and senior year. There were cute girls around town and nice girls he admired because of how sweet they were, but none of them were the girl of his dreams. But then, one fine summer afternoon between Dave's junior and senior year, he saw her.

Nate, Dave's best friend, begged him throughout the summer to go shoot hoops at the park almost every day where teenagers from three nearby towns frequently met up. Dave enjoyed himself once he got there, but he wouldn't have felt the need to go if Nate hadn't talked him into it.

On the afternoon Dave met the teenage Delilah, he and Nate were playing a game of HORSE on the small basketball court near the pool. As usual, Dave let his buddy take the lead on purpose. After Nate made a few buckets and Dave allowed himself to miss a few, then he'd start trying. Every time someone missed a shot the other made, they had to accept a new letter. The first player to spell HORSE lost the game. Dave had let himself fall behind to HOR and Nate only had an H.

"Alright, Nate, I'm done playing around!" Dave said, his voice raspy because of a summer cold. He shouldered his buddy and scooped up the ball, dribbling past Nate. Then Dave rose up and threw down a dunk with authority. "There—now you have an O."

Nate tried to dunk but got stuffed by the rim.

Dave recovered the ball and headed all the way back to the picnic area. He stood on a table for his next shot and it dropped with a swish. "There, now we'll both have HOR."

"I might make it," Nate said as he tossed up an airball.

With a chuckle and the ball in his hands, Dave charged to the chain-link fence of the swimming pool. He pounced off the side of the springy fence for a very long trick shot. A few girls in the pool whistled as he made the move, and it threw off his trajectory. The ball ended up on the roof of the bathhouse, stuck behind the backboard.

Nate jawed his buddy, "Great shot Mr. Basketball! Now you gotta climb up on the roof and get my basketball *or* forfeit the game. And buy me a new ball."

The girls in the pool area laughed. Most of them were class-mates from Dave and Nate's high school. Dave stuck out his tongue in a teasing way, and a few girls whistled in response. That moment, someone caught his eye—a dark-haired beauty he had never noticed before.

"Watch this, girls!" Dave shouted with a hoarse voice as he leapt onto the chain-link fence and began climbing it like a cat. This wasn't the first time he had climbed to the roof to recover basketballs, so he knew he could do it. He puffed and grimaced as his fingers gripped the fence. Near the top, he had to hold on with his hands while his Nike shoes searched for a toehold in the mesh. He bit his lip as he maneuvered from the top bar over onto the bathhouse roof. Once he stepped onto the shingles, he took a moment to lift his hands up in a victory stance. Most of the girls cheered. Dave searched for the brunette and found her. She floated in the water on her back and smiled at him. He did a double take. She appeared to have no swimsuit on at all. Her long dark hair floated around her, and beyond that, everything else blurred under the surface of choppy water in the same skin tone.

Dave didn't mean to stare, but he did. She returned his gaze and slowly flailed her arms and legs as if tantalizing him. He forced himself to look away from her for a moment and gathered Nate's basketball and dropped it through the hoop from above.

"There, Nate. Come up here and make that shot or you'll have an S."

The girls all cheered.

Nate argued, "It wasn't your turn."

"Okay," Dave called back, "you go ahead and shoot. If you miss, then I'll take my turn from up here!"

While Nate chose his spot, shot, and made a bucket, Dave searched the pool for the brunette. She had moved to the ladder and began to climb out, her eyes still on him. He watched her long, dark, soaking wet hair cling to her body. Her hair reached to the bottom of where her swimsuit would end, if in fact she was wearing one. Dave, so focused on the girl, didn't look where he stepped. His long leg dipped into the valley of the roofline, and he tumbled headlong onto the shingles. Fortunately, and unfortunately, the backboard caught him at the waist. It was good because he didn't fall off the roof, but it was bad because it stung like a knife and left a bruise that he wore for a month.

Dave began his descent from the roof, ignoring the pain. He carefully maneuvered onto the fence and then down one fingerhold at a time until he stepped onto the concrete court. He picked up the ball and searched the area around the water for the brunette. He finally spotted her, laying on a reclining chair. With her hair falling over her shoulders, her body became visible and he spotted a tan, one-piece suit. It disappointed him slightly, even though he knew she surely would be wearing a swimsuit. However, he wasn't disappointed at all about how beautiful she looked in her tan suit, or about the smile on her face.

Dave tried to focus on the hoop for his next shot, but the brunette's dark eyes distracted him so much that he missed again.

"Haha," Nate yelled, "now, you've got an S!"

Nate grabbed the ball from Dave's hands and made a simple free throw. It suddenly occurred to Dave that Nate might beat him with the brunette watching. He bit his lip and prepared for his final shot. Dave had a lot of experience making free throws during critical moments of big games. However, nothing he could remember had ever unnerved him as much as this girl. He glanced in her direction just before he shot. She rearranged her legs and ran a hand through her long hair, her dark eyes still on him. Dave shot before he meant to, and the ball rimmed out.

"I beat you!" Nate yelled. "You've got a HORSE to go along with that hoarse voice!"

Dave picked up the ball and slammed it on the concrete court in frustration. He looked back toward the brunette and she was gone. He hurried to the chain-link fence, locked his fingers through the wire and searched the area.

Nate dribbled the ball behind him. "What are ya doing?"

"I'm looking for that girl."

"What girl?"

Dave turned to face his buddy. "Didn't you see that gorgeous brunette in the tan swimsuit?"

Nate shook his head and continued bouncing the ball. "Come on, Dave, let's get out of here and go get some pizza."

"I'm not going anywhere until I find out that girl's name," Dave said. He took a seat near the exit of the bathhouse and watched the door like a cat staking out a mouse hole. He ran his hand over his hair to be sure he looked his best. Short, bristly hairs met his fingers, reminding him of his buzz cut. A few weeks ago, the whole basketball team shaved their heads in support of their assistant coach who had been battling cancer. Dave loved the idea at the time.

He turned to Nate. "Quick—let me borrow your hat."

"No—I'm not giving you my hat! What's the matter? Don't you think you look cute enough for that girl?"

Dave stood up and paced for a moment and then sat back down. He glanced at his own arms, noticing how tan they were. During the past few weeks he had been working for his uncle, doing lawn care. He hoped his tan would take the edge off the appearance of his buzzed head.

Nate sat on his basketball and laughed. "I've never seen you like this."

"I wish my voice wasn't so raspy right now," Dave said with a wheeze.

"She'll think it's cute," Nate said with a laugh.

A moment later, Dave's dream girl emerged from the bathhouse, barefoot, and wearing a pair of tight jeans and a white blouse. Her long dark hair flowing around her, still wet. She had a friend with her, but Dave didn't notice even one thing about the other girl.

"Are you okay?" she asked. Her voice had a mysterious quality about it that he couldn't place. His mind sorted through possibilities and concluded that she sounded European.

"I'm fine! Why?"

She smiled and said with a lilting voice, "It looked like you took a hit when you almost fell off that roof."

Dave winked at her. "It would have been your fault if I fell."

She wrinkled her nose. "How could it have been my fault?"

Nate stood behind the girls and smirked. He tossed the ball to Dave, attempting to distract him or humiliate him further. Dave caught the ball and dribbled it. He looked at the basketball while he explained. "Because that tan-colored swimsuit made it look like you were skinny-dipping from where I stood on the roof."

"It did?" her eyes gave away her surprise at his words.

"Yeah, it did!" He winked again. "What man wouldn't about fall off the roof with a doll like you skinny-dipping in the public pool?"

She quickly recovered, saying, "Bathsheba was probably wearing a tan swimsuit when King David looked down from his rooftop and thought he saw her bathing nude!"

Dave laughed hoarsely. "What is your name, girl?"

"Delilah. What's yours?"

"If you're Delilah, then I'm Samson," he said, the smoothness of the improvised pickup line surprised even himself.

Nate interrupted, "Hey, girls, did you see me beat Samson in HORSE a few minutes ago?"

"From what I saw, I could beat him," Delilah said with a coy smile.

Nate laughed. "Oh—Samson—that girl just dissed you big time."

"Okay, little Miss Delilah, you go first." Dave palmed the ball and handed it to her.

She smiled at him with flirtatious eyes and took a shot from where they stood. The ball sank directly into the hoop. "Your turn Samson."

The ball bounced right back to Dave. He picked it up and didn't take his eyes off her while he flung it over his shoulder and it swished. "How about that?"

"It hit the front of the net but didn't go through," she teased and scrambled around him, elbowing her way to the ball before he could get it.

As she bent to pick it up, he grabbed her waist and she squealed while he spun her in a circle. He rushed to the ball while she tried to regain her balance. Dave got to the ball first and slammed it through the rim with a dunk.

Delilah stood with her hands on her hips. "Da-hang it—that wasn't fair." Her long dark hair flowing in the breeze. She pulled a few strands from her open mouth and tossed her head to send the mass of silky hair behind her.

Dave spun the ball on his fingertips. "What should I do to make it fair?"

"Get me up on your shoulders."

"Okay," he said, and motioned a circle with his finger. "Turn around."

She laughed and faced away from him. He stopped to look at her long hair for a moment. She held her arms out like a little girl and he scooped her up by her waist and hoisted her over his head and onto his shoulders.

"Whew—that was fun! Now give me the ball," she ordered.

Dave held her knees and she locked her bare-feet behind his back. He lifted the ball with the toe of his shoe, letting it bounce. He took a hand from her knee long enough to dip down and grab the ball. He handed it up to Delilah and carried her toward the net.

"A little closer," she commanded, her voice giving away a smile.

He looked up and watched her dunk the ball. She raised both arms and called, "Woo-hoo! I believe I just beat Samson in HORSE!"

Dave said, "I'll teach you something about horses!"

He trotted off with her riding on his shoulders. His motion fell into a lope, and she held onto his head with one hand and imaginary reins with the other.

"Giddyup, Samson," she called.

He circled around until they came to a sandy area with playground equipment. He feigned being out of control, and she held onto his head with both hands.

"Easy boy, easy there, Samson," she lowered her voice as though trying to calm a wild horse.

He kicked and spun a little until they both fell into a heap in the sand, laughing. He sat up and gazed at her. Her dark hair tumbled in waves around her face and shoulders as she lay there giggling.

"Hey there, Delilah," he said, reaching a hand to help her up.

"Hey there to you, Samson," she echoed, clamoring to her feet. She brushed off the sand and walked away.

He enjoyed watching her graceful motion for a moment and then realized she wasn't stopping. He ran to catch up. "Hey there, Delilah. Are you coming to this park on Friday night? A bunch of us are planning to play sand volleyball. Do you and your friend want to come join us?" Dave nodded toward Nate, who had been talking to her friend while Samson and Delilah played around.

"I'll try to be here," she said. Her chocolate-brown eyes flirting with his.

Dave watched as she and her friend walked away. He smiled when he saw her turn back to see if he was still watching. The girls locked arms and giggled together.

Nate pushed Dave's shoulder, knocking him out of his trance. "Wow—what is *up* with you?"

Dave lifted both hands. "What do you mean?"

"You see some strange girl at the pool and within minutes you two are acting like you've known each other for years," Nate explained. "I've never seen you act like this, and we've been buddies our whole lives."

"She is the most captivating female I've ever met. I hope my cold clears up and my hair grows out a little before Friday."

Nate shook his head. "Oh man, you're pathetic!"

CHAPTER FOUR

Not a Date

A cock-a-doodle-do rang out in the early morning light of Falls, Wisconsin, interrupting Dave's sleep. The rooster's crow repeated until Dave started to get annoyed. He slowly remembered that he had set a cock-a-doodle-do as the ringtone on his cell phone alarm. It seemed like a funny idea before he fell asleep, but he didn't even crack a smile when it crowed at 6:00 a.m. He turned the alarm off and took a quick shower, determined to get to DJ's Diner before it got too busy.

The tiny restaurant smelled of bacon and eggs and buzzed with activity when Dave walked in. He took a seat at the same booth he sat in a day ago. A bright red-checkered gingham table-cloth glared up at his half-shut eyes until he got himself situated and opened his laptop on the table. An Amish girl popped out of the kitchen and Dave's heart skipped a beat.

Delilah stepped to his table and spoke cheerfully, "Are you back for coffee and another cinnamon roll?"

"Yes, I sure am. Only, this morning I think I'd like some bacon, eggs, and toast to go with it." Dave looked up at her and gave a slight smile, trying to hide how happy he was that she was wait-ing his table again. He noticed those delicate, loose strands of her dark hair waving ever so slightly around her face. He wanted to stare at them but forced himself to act uninterested in her as a woman. He came up with something benign to say. "Being out here in farm country seems to be giving me a bigger appetite."

Delilah giggled as she held a pencil to a notepad. "And what brings you out to farm country?"

"Funny you ask," Dave said, trying to sound professional. "I work for a magazine and I'd like to ask a local Amish girl a few questions about this Delilah craze. Would you be willing to talk with me when you get off work today? I could take you out for lunch somewhere."

"Un fa shdendich, are you kidding?" She dropped her pencil and stooped down to retrieve it as it rolled under Dave's feet. "There is no way in the world I could be seen alone with a guy like you!"

"No disrespect ma'am," Dave said as he leaned under his booth to get the pencil. Their hands touched, and they both took hold of the pencil at the same moment. He tried to engage her eyes as they both rose up holding opposite ends of the pencil. He pulled it from her grip, wiped it off on his shirt, and handed it to her. Her mouth curled with a smile as she took it. Dave repeat-ed himself, "No disrespect ma'am, but it seems to me the locals here don't even notice you Amish girls. What would anyone care if you had lunch with me? I mean, it's not like it'd be a date." Dave was talking with his hands and tipped over a glass of water. Delilah quickly mopped it up with her white apron.

Dave held his hands out of her way. "I'm so sorry about that. I'm a little clumsy."

"It's fine," Delilah assured him and giggled. "So—you weren't asking me on a date, but in this one-horse town it would look like it. Nobody notices us Amish girls if we're behaving. As soon as one of us steps out of line, the whole community starts talking." Delilah's cheeks flushed red as she smoothed out her wet apron. "English people seem to know the Amish rules better than we do. I don't know why, but there's nothing people enjoy more than seeing someone with a standard, fail to keep it."

Dave nodded. "That's sad but true."

Delilah held her pencil to her pad again as if she wanted to end the awkward conversation. "What kind of eggs did you want?"

"Over easy and white toast," Dave said.

She jotted it down and hurried off to the kitchen. Dave stared at his laptop even though it wasn't turned on. He thought about how dumb he must have sounded. *"It's not like it'd be a date."* *What a terrible choice of words.* He intended to avoid making her feel stalked. However, nothing could be worse than asking a girl out and then saying, "It's not like it'd be a date." Only one other time in his whole life had any girl rendered him tongue-tied so quickly.

This girl intimidated him because she represented a huge amount of money, free for the taking, if he didn't screw up. Dave wondered if part of nervousness might be due to the fact that he found her attractive and intriguing. *No, it's just the money*, he convinced himself. He tried to think of how he could have a conversation with her alone without compromising her reputation.

Moments later, Delilah swooped back over with a full cup of coffee, setting it carefully in front of him. A wonderful aroma rose as he took a sip. She didn't utter a word, but she hesitated for a moment, looking at him out of the corner of her eye as if trying to figure him out. When she walked away, he tried to hide behind his small laptop, peering at her over the top of the screen. He wanted to watch her every move without anyone noticing.

Delilah floated around the small restaurant like a shadow, quickly waiting on every table, completely unnoticed. Locals filled most of the booths. They all talked loudly about sports and farming. A great deal of gossip could also be heard, coming from tables occupied by men and women alike.

Dave continued scrutinizing his waitress and simultaneously remembered his conversation with his mom. He considered momentarily if she could be the girl he once knew. Her voice had a familiar ring. However, Dave had concluded that all Amish girls speak with that same lilting voice. *This Delilah is definitely the girl in the book,* he thought to himself, *but I'm positive she is not the girl I knew in high school. They are as different as night and day.*

Delilah stopped by again and set a huge cinnamon roll in front of Dave. "I didn't know if you wanted this roll with your meal or as a dessert?"

"Now that it's here, I won't be able to keep myself from eating it," Dave said.

Her smile was momentarily accompanied by her trademark winkled nose. "Are you going to turn on that little computer machine or just stare at the blank screen?" She walked away before he had a chance to think up an answer.

Dave pulled apart his cinnamon roll, dipped a piece into his coffee, and stuffed it in his mouth. His eyes rolled back with pleasure. "Oh wow, these rolls are unbelievable," he moaned as he flipped on his laptop and pulled up his electronic copy of *Samson and Delilah*. He scrolled down through a few pages, searching for a section he read yesterday and thought about reading it to Delilah.

Delilah whisked by and set down a plate with eggs, bacon, and toast in front of Dave. She spoke quietly. "If you really feel like you need to talk to me alone, there is a way." She glanced around as if wanting to be certain nobody would overhear her. "I will head out the back door at one thirty. You could be waiting at the picnic table out back, and I would be willing to answer a few questions."

"Perfect, thank you so much. You won't be sorry you talked to me," Dave said, keeping his voice as low as hers.

"I . . . see," Delilah answered, just as the Delilah in the book always did, and headed off to wait other tables.

Dave smiled to himself and mouthed the word, "Yes," emphatically, though under his breath. He enjoyed his delicious breakfast even more now that he'd secured his chance to speak with Delilah alone.

She stopped back by and asked, "Is there anything else I can get you?"

"Yeah, I'd like one of those cinnamon rolls to go, please."

"Okay!" She wrinkled her nose and headed off to get his roll.

Dave left her a five-dollar tip again, then stopped to pay his bill. "Please, take my word for it. There will be people from the media here at some point." He gave DJ a sincere look. "Do your very best to keep them from finding out about the morning waitress named Delilah. Otherwise, she might lose her privacy completely."

"Okay, but this is all really exciting for us!"

He nodded. "I've been offered a lot of money to find her, and I plan to give the real Delilah financial compensation when I find her."

DJ leaned close to Dave and whispered, "I don't think Amish people want anything to do with the media, but if she is the right Delilah, you may be in luck. Her family has had lots of struggles with medical bills, and they could use the money."

"Oh good!" As soon as the words left his mouth Dave realized how shallow he sounded. "I mean—good that she might be willing to talk to the media, not that they have medical bills." Dave glanced at DJ, and her face flashed disgust. He quickly added, "I'm going to leave it up to her. If she wants to keep her privacy, she will have to go into hiding for a while. Please help me give her that choice by not telling anyone about her."

Boredom set in after Dave got back to the hotel. He read from his paperback copy of *Samson and Delilah* until his eyes got heavy. He let the book rest on his chest while he took another short nap before lunchtime. Once again, deep rumblings vibrated the mattress as a locomotive approached Falls. Dave lifted his head and saw the same beautiful woman sleeping on the tracks between himself and the oncoming train. He tried to yell but nothing came out. The clickety-clacking sounds intensified, and he crawled toward the woman. His arms felt thick and useless, his head drunk with sleepiness. When he got to her, he attempted to wake her but fell onto her. She screamed as she woke up, trying to get away from him. The train whistle blew a deafening blast and Dave woke up in his hotel room, listening to the clatter of train cars jostling past his window.

"Un fa shdendich!" he shouted. He sat on the edge of his bed in a cold sweat and his book fell to the floor. With his head in his hands, he poured over ways to explain to the girl that he didn't fall on her on purpose. He tried to think of how to explain himself to the police. Slowly, he came to his senses and realized he had been dreaming and didn't need to explain anything to anyone. He picked up his copy of *Samson and Delilah* and studied the cover for a while. He fell back onto the bed and stared at the ceiling while he thought about the book and Delilah's eyes.

At 1:15 Dave left the hotel and strolled casually down the alley behind DJ's Diner. His heart pounded, but he restrained his excitement, trying to appear calm and cool. He took a seat at a picnic table behind the restaurant. While he waited, he pondered about whether his excitement came from the possibility of making money or getting another chance to look into those mysterious eyes again.

Exactly at 1:30, Delilah stepped through the back door and stood by the table.

"Won't you sit down?" Dave asked.

She spoke curtly, "I'm on my way home. Please ask your questions quickly."

"Okay," he said, wondering if she might be feeling stalked. He had planned to make small talk with her and possibly gaze into her eyes but decided he'd better get straight to the point. "I have good reason to believe that you are the Delilah that everyone in the country is talking about."

She placed one hand on her stomach as she giggled. "Un fa shdendich, that's ridiculous."

"No, believe me," Dave said, and lifted both of his hands for emphasis. "I knew the author of *Samson and Delilah*, and he told me about this restaurant and you. In fact, I came here with him one time, and I'm quite sure you were our waitress."

"I don't remember meeting any great author here."

"Samuel VanRokel wasn't ever famous during his life. He was just an ordinary middle-aged man with gray hair and a short beard. His book became a best seller after his death."

"I think I might know who you are talking about," she answered, looking up and off to her right as though recollecting. He was a really nice man, and he always called me by name. Few people actually do that," she added. She stood looking at Dave and then at her feet intermittently, as though trying to take it all in. Suddenly, she waved her hand as if to dismiss his story.

Dave tried to look Delilah in the eyes, attempting to assure her of his sincerity. "I've been offered one hundred thousand dollars to find you and tell *Humans* magazine where you are."

At those words, Delilah sat down, facing away from Dave on the other side of the picnic table. She didn't look up as she muttered, "I . . . see. Are you going to tell them about me?"

"I'm going to let you decide. I think Samuel VanRokel would have wanted you to make that choice."

She twisted at the waist, just enough to glance at Dave. "Please, don't tell anyone about me." Then she turned her back on him again.

"Okay, if that is what you want. However, before you make a final decision, just let me add a few things to think about. I would be willing to give you twenty-five thousand dollars."

She twisted at the waist quickly and narrowed her eyes at him. "Why would you do that?"

"Because, I want at least some of that money," Dave confessed, "but, my conscience won't let me tell anyone about you without your consent."

Delilah stood up and turned to face Dave as if studying his genuineness. "What's the other thing I should think about?"

"I think you should consider what an important role model you've become to girls all over America. There are not many positive influences out there. Most movie stars and singers are wild girls covered in tattoos and piercings. It'd be good for young women across the country to see a clean, modestly dressed girl as a role model."

"I'm not any kind of a model," Delilah said emphatically, pushing a hand toward Dave as though refusing his compliment.

Dave let his hand slap the rough, wooden table. "The world thinks you are, whether you like it or not." He paused to let that sink in. "The question here may be one of time. People from other media outlets are searching for you, and they're better at finding who they are looking for than the police. I'm here to tell you that you can reveal your identity through me, and I'll give you twenty-five thousand dollars. Or, you'd better find someplace to hide until this all blows over."

Delilah turned slowly and started to walk away. She stopped and muttered, "I'd like to ask my dad what he thinks before I decide."

Dave's heart sank as he felt his chance at the money slip away. He frantically struggled to think of an angle he might toss at her to change her mind. "How old are you?" he asked.

"I'm twenty-two, but I still live at home." She stopped walking even though she didn't turn back.

"This could be your chance to leave the Amish. You are old enough—you don't need your dad's permission," Dave said.

Delilah turned to face him and glared. "I like being Amish— and I want my dad's opinion," she answered ardently and walked away.

Dave clunked his knuckles against his forehead and said to himself, "That was dumb."

His hopes sank as he watched her dark dress disappear into the alley. Suddenly, it occurred to him that his disappointment had more to do with losing her respect than with losing the money. A moment later her blue dress reemerged from the shadows. After taking a few steps toward him, she asked politely, "Would you mind coming over and talking to my parents this evening?"

Dave stood up. "I'd *love* to! What time, and how do I get there?"

"After chore time. We live on the farm just under the water tower. You can't miss it. Just head for the tower." She started walking away again.

Dave called after her, "When is chore time?"

"Come over around dusk," she said and disappeared into the shadows between buildings.

Dave hurried back to his hotel and called Charlie right away. "Hello Charlie, this is Dave. I found some Amish girls working at a restaurant, in a location that I thought might be right. There is a Delilah that works the afternoon shift, but it's unlikely she is the one in *Samson and Delilah*." He convinced himself he wasn't lying because there was a Delilah at the restaurant who wasn't the girl from the book.

"How many Amish girls are out there with the name Delilah?" Charlie asked.

"I know!" Dave nodded. "You wouldn't think Amish people would ever name a girl Delilah. Odd as it may seem, it turns out that it is a fairly common name for them. Who knew?" Dave heard Charlie groan on the other end of the phone connection. "Don't worry, Charlie, I haven't given up on this yet. I'll get back with you if I make any progress."

"C'mon Dave, I'm counting on you. You should have as good of a chance to find her as anyone."

"I'm trying. I'll keep in touch," Dave said.

"Okay, that's all we ask." The phone clicked and Dave knew Charlie had ended the call.

Dave spent his afternoon reading while laying on a towel beside Falls Community Pool. He hoped to work on his tan in his spare time. In high school, Dave found summer employment working for his uncle's lawn care company. He'd always had such a dark tan that people asked about his nationality. When he took off his shirt in the pool area, he felt he looked as white as a ghost.

Children splashed and played nearby. Dave had to work to keep his paperback copy of *Samson and Delilah* from getting soaked in the spray of their playfulness. As he breathed in the scent of coconut oil and chlorine, he envisioned Delilah's eyes—something he had done every few minutes since he first looked into them. He wished he could sit at a table across from her and gaze into them until he could completely analyze what he saw.

Despite the squeals and laughter of children splashing in the pool, Dave began to read from his book and the story drew him in. He couldn't help but smile when he read about Samson helping Delilah elude paparazzies that were bent on taking her photograph. He laughed out loud while reading a chapter that focused on Delilah's little brother named Earl. He bit his lip as the plot thickened and Samson helped Delilah and Earl escape to the home of their relatives in Iowa.

Dave kept turning pages, completely engrossed in the book, until a child near him jumped into the pool sending a splash of cold water onto his back. The sensation snapped him out of the storyline long enough to consider that maybe he had been laying in the sun too long.

He pulled on his shirt and gathered his book and towel., Shadows of nearby trees sloped across the pool where bright sunlight had been shining when Dave first opened the book. A redheaded woman and a set of toddler twins with orange hair sat on beach towels a few feet from him. He remembered a teenage boy and girl were sunbathing there when he let himself become absorbed by the story of Samson and Delilah. He left the pool area as quickly as possible, hoping to avoid a sunburn.

Dave stopped off at a convenience store on his walk back to the hotel. While he was paying the middle-aged attendant for a fountain pop, he noticed a magazine cover with a half-dressed actress. He said to the cashier, "It sure would be funny if they found that Amish girl and put her on a magazine cover."

"You mean that girl from Indiana?" the lady asked. "They can't seem to find her."

Dave raised an eyebrow, "They don't know where she is. Maybe she lives in Wisconsin?"

"She couldn't be from Falls. None of our Amish girls are pretty enough to be the one."

"Actually, that's not true." Dave narrowed his eyes at the homely cashier. "If you read the book, you'll know that the real Delilah isn't striking at first—it's her personality that makes her a leading lady."

"Our Amish girls don't have much personality either," the middle-aged woman said, and fell into a coughing fit. "I need a cigarette," she wheezed as she brought her cough under control.

Dave left the convenience store shaking his head. He strolled through the quaint town of Falls, heading to his hotel with Delilah on his mind. He took time to watch buggies pass by and to listen to the pleasant clip-clopping sound on cobblestone streets. The sound reverberated off the brick buildings as they passed. Dave felt hot and uncomfortable by the time he walked down the hall that led to his hotel room and unlocked his door. He peeled off his shirt and twisted to look at it in the tiny bathroom mirror. He pressed a fingertip to his red shoulder, and it left a white fingerprint.

His phone chirped, and he knew instantly it would be his mom.

"What does she want now?" he asked as he looked at his phone, trying to decide if he should answer.

"Hello."

"Hi David, it's Mom. How's it going up there in Wisconsin?"

"Okay, I guess. I'm almost positive that I found the right Delilah. I talked to her a little, and you were right about her not wanting attention, but I think she might want the money."

"David, you have probably put her in a bad spot. If she takes the money and lets them take her picture, she'll be in trouble with her church. If she turns you down, she'll wish she would have taken the money."

Dave paced the floor. "I think she'd end up enjoying all the attention once she gets used to it."

"She would probably get shunned by her church and family if she does," his mother contended.

"I'm still not positive that this is the girl, but I'm going to her parents' house to talk to them this evening. I've been reading a chapter from the book about Delilah's little brother. If she has a younger brother named Earl, then I'll be positive I've got the right one. There just can't be two families in the world with a Delilah and an Earl."

"Is there any chance she could be the girl who used to live in Indiana?" His mother made an obvious effort to ask a touchy question in a discreet way.

Dave lifted his free hand in frustration. His back stung with the sudden movement. "Ouch!"

"What happened," his mother's voice sounded panicked.

"Nothing, I'm just a little sunburned."

"Oh David, get some aloe vera for that right away!"

Dave just mumbled.

She repeated her question. "Could this be the girl you used to know?"

"It seems really unlikely, Mom. I don't feel like she seems familiar at all."

"Well, be careful with her feelings, David. She may remember you."

"Mom!"

"I'm sorry, David, I just know how women feel."

"It's not the same girl, I'm almost positive." Dave studied his back in the mirror and rolled his eyes. "I really need to get going now."

"Alrighty. I love you, David," She said.

"Okay, talk to you later, Mom."

"Bub-bye."

CHAPTER FIVE

A Little Mishap

E ven though it would be hours before dusk, Dave decided to drive past Delilah's farm to be sure he could find it. He didn't want to be late, and there seemed to be nothing else to do in a town the size of Falls. Most of the traffic seemed to be pickup trucks. An occasional buggy rolled quietly along the shoulder of the road.

Massive green tractors and other farm implements sat like monoliths in a John Deere sales lot just below the water tower. Dave popped on his sunglasses as he drew near the tower, hoping to conceal his identity should Delilah happen to be outside when he passed her home. His car, a Mustang, surged up the final hill. As soon as it rounded the crest, Dave saw a few Amish girls working between the rows of a large garden. His heart rate sped up when he caught a glimpse of Delilah. She and her sisters wore dresses in pastel shades of blue, lavender, green, and yellow. The girls looked like Easter eggs partially hidden in rich green foliage. Big white buckets seemed to be placed strategically throughout their work area. The girls appeared to be picking produce and loading it in the buckets. Dave looked away when they waved in his direction, hoping Delilah wouldn't recognize him.

A little Amish boy ran out of the house and down the steps toward the garden. He held onto his big straw hat with one hand while his little legs churned forward. Dave chuckled to himself at how cute the little guy looked with suspenders hiking up his trousers that were already too short. It surprised Dave, when the little boy took notice of the passing car and stopped running long enough to wave at him. Dave gave the little guy a smile and a friendly wave in return.

Only a little paint clung to the weathered wood of their huge old farmhouse. Dave shook his head and spoke aloud in his car, "Good. These people are as poor as church mice. There's no way they'll be able to turn down the money I'm gonna offer them." He laughed and turned up his radio. One of his favorite songs happened to be playing. "Money, it's a gas—grab that cash with both hands and make a stash!" While the singer crooned, the sound of change dropping and of a cash register clunking open and shut kept rhythm with the drumbeats. Dave's body shifted involuntarily in time with the music until he accidentally rubbed his back on the seat. He shot forward and yelled, "Ouch—my sunburnt back!"

A buggy came into view as he left Delilah's farm. It slowly made its way up a hill ahead of him. Dave couldn't pass, so he followed behind, watching the horse's hooves thump the road under the buggy. He glanced out his side window at another Amish farmstead that sat right next to the road. Cows and horses grazed together peacefully in a lush green pasture. A large white barn stood close to the road with doors wide open and bursting at the seams with hay. The buggy crept along so slow that the farm dog outran it, barking excitedly. Dave had time to examine everything thoroughly. A little Amish girl with a lime-green dress worked a hand pump, filling a bucket with water. She seemed to be around three years old and appeared quite serious about her job. She stopped pumping the handle long enough to smile and wave, first at the people in the buggy ahead of him and then at Dave.

A middle-aged man with a graying beard drove a team of massive work horses away from the barn. The man also took time to wave at the folks in the buggy and at Dave. Teenage girls in Amish dresses crouched between rows of vegetable plants at this farm as well. They all stopped working long enough to give a friendly wave to the passersby. Dave was completely mesmerized by everything he saw. He studied the massive farmhouse, square and white. Breezes turned the windmill and caused a row of Amish dresses to a dance on a clothesline. White fenceposts, outbuildings, and gates were edged with brilliant purple flowers that made the structures look even whiter. Suddenly, the buggy in front of him veered to the left. Dave thought it was turning into the Amish farm lane, so he set out to pass on the right but quickly realized the road curved sharply ahead. He felt the front right corner of his car lurch forward and then downward.

Dave experienced a strange sensation as one side of his car sunk lower than the other. He could feel the momentum of the situation propelling him toward disaster, and yet, there wasn't anything he could do to stop it. The balance of the car had already shifted enough that his efforts to stop or turn proved futile. All he could do was hold on and watch how everything would unfold. As if in slow motion, the front of his car dipped toward the bottom of the ravine, and he helplessly watched his Mustang hood plow into the muddy bank that rose up on the other side of the ditch.

He sat still for a moment until he realized that he hadn't died and apparently wasn't even injured. After revving his engine multiple times, he concluded his wheels were spinning uselessly. He unbuckled his seatbelt, pushed in the emergency brake, and climbed out of his passenger-side door. After scrambling out onto the road and assessing the situation, he realized he needed a tow truck to pull him out. Then he remembered that he had left his cell phone in the cup holder. He looked through the window to see if he could reach it without getting back in. A voice startled him.

"Did you forget something in there?"

Dave turned around to see who spoke and realized that an entire Amish family stood in a semicircle, looking at him, all of them blond except the father.

"Yes, my phone is in the cup holder," Dave explained. "I need to call Triple A and get a wrecker out here to pull my car out of this ditch."

The man with a long graying beard shook his head. "There's no need to bother Triple A. We'll pull you out with our horses."

Dave grimaced and said, "This Mustang is probably a lot heavier than a buggy. I doubt horses can pull it out."

The man folded his arms and nodded toward a team of black horses. "Beula and Stan can pull you out of there easily."

"Okay," Dave shrugged, "I guess they can give it a try."

Once he got situated in the driver's seat, even though he sat leaning sideways, he put his car in neutral and gave the Amish man a thumbs-up to indicate he was ready. The massive horses lurched forward impressively, muscles rippling in their hindquarters. Dave looked at his dashboard and a thought popped into his head. *I left the emergency brake on.* It was too late. He felt the car lurch upward. He thought about reaching for the brake release, but it took both hands to hold onto the wheel as the big horses yanked his car up out of the ditch. They continued forward until Dave's Mustang sat a short way within the farm lane.

Dave climbed out and said, "Wow, those horses are amazing!"

The Amish man stepped off his cart and scratched his beard while looking at Dave's Mustang. "Did you put your car in neutral before we pulled you out? It looked like your wheels were dragging, not rolling."

Dave felt his face flush hot. "I had it in neutral, but the parking brake was on. I didn't think of it until your horses were already on their way. Was that bad for your horses?"

The Amish man laughed heartily. "Well, it would have been a lot easier for them without the parking brake."

The whole Amish family got a chuckle out of what their dad said. Dave stood beside the huge horses. He looked at their large hooves and heavy-boned legs. One horse snorted and rubbed its large head against the other's neck. A fly buzzed around them for a moment and then landed on the near horse's belly. The horse lifted one of its massive hooves, scaring the fly and Dave as the heavy foot clomped back onto the ground.

"These are some big horses," Dave exclaimed.

A blond boy that appeared to be around ten, helped his father unhitch the team from the cart. "We have a bigger team in the barn."

Dave shook his head in disbelief. "You have a team that's bigger than these?"

The Amish man with a long beard clucked to the horses. They stepped out obediently, and the man said, "Come on back to the barn with us and see them."

Both horses clomped past the house, leaving a hoofprint behind with every step. Dave couldn't get over how big they were. They dwarfed the Amish man as he followed behind their massive hindquarters.

As Dave caught up, the Amish man pointed to the smaller of the two horses. "This mare, Beula, is the mother of this other horse, Stan. One of our neighbor's horses got in with ours, and the next spring Stan was born.

"Oh wow!" Dave exclaimed. "Do you mean this was a free horse?"

The man stopped driving his team and narrowed his eyes at Dave. "No, I wouldn't say it that way. This little mare wasn't even two years old at the time, way too young. It almost killed her when she had this colt. Our neighbor offered us a large sum of money to reimburse us since he failed to keep his horse on his own property."

Dave nodded that he understood. "It turned out pretty good that you ended up with such a nice colt out of the deal?"

The man continued driving his horses toward the barn as he explained, "It stunted this mare's growth. She is the last of a line of horses that have been in our family for years. We had high hopes for her. She's never been able to have another foal after that. And this one she had is a crossbreed."

Dave swallowed hard and replied, "I'm sorry that happened."

Fresh scents of livestock and grains greeted them as Dave followed the man and horses inside the barn. His eyes adjusted enough to match the smell of fresh hay with a stack of dark green bales. The man drove his horses into a dark walkway and called, "Whoa!" Beula and Stan froze in place. He laid the driving lines behind them and turned to Dave. "My name is R. Duane."

Dave reached to shake hands. "My name is Dave."

R. Duane looked at his hand for a moment then shook it. "My first name is Richard but there are three Richard Millers in this community, so everyone calls me R. Duane."

"Nice to meet you," Dave said. "I'd be happy to pay you for pulling out my car."

R. Duane smiled in a friendly way. "No, it didn't cost us anything."

Dave heard a sound behind him and glanced over his shoulder. Two massive black horses stood a few feet behind him. Dave jumped and heard a chorus of laughter. His eyes adjusted enough to see the young boy standing between the huge horses. The rest of the family gathered behind the horses, each watching Dave as if looking forward to seeing his reaction.

"Those are the biggest horses I've ever seen!" Dave said.

The boy grinned from ear to ear. "They are only three. They'll fill out more over the next couple of years."

Dave reached to pet one of the horses on its nose. It shied away, and the boy said, "Whoa." He seemed too small to hang onto the giants, but he didn't show any fear. Dave touched one horse's arched neck and smoothed a hand along the muscle. "My dad used to have riding horses, but they were a lot smaller than these."

"Do you ride?" the boy asked.

"I have." Dave shrugged. "I might have been more interested if my dad would have had horses like these."

The entire family laughed.

R. Duane stood next to Dave and took the lead ropes from his son. "Let's take them out into the light where Dave can see them better."

Dave backed out of the way while he led them outside. A row of teenage girls stood near their mother, all smiles in their dark Amish dresses. The boy who had been holding them and a younger brother stood beside their dad, watching Dave to see what he'd say. Dave tried to think of something intelligent but all that came out was, "Someday, I'm gonna own a team of horses like that."

They all laughed again.

R. Duane said, "We'd better let you try driving a team and see."

Dave's eyes popped open in surprise. "I don't think I could drive this team of three-year-olds."

"I didn't mean this team." R. Duane chuckled. "You could try your hand at the team that pulled out your car. Beula and Stan are more the type to try on."

"Oh, that'd be fun," Dave said, hiding the fear that grew inside his stomach.

R. Duane handed the huge colts back to his son and headed into the barn to retrieve his slightly smaller horses. The boy led the massive team to a small corral and turned them loose. R. Duane reemerged from the shadows driving Beula and Stan. Dave tried to steady his shaky hands as he watched R. Duane hitch the team to a wagon. The Amish man and his sons climbed aboard and waited for their visitor to follow. Dave took his place, standing with them near the front of a seatless wagon.

R. Duane handed the lines to Dave. "Go ahead. It's about the same as riding a horse, only you're a little further back."

Dave clucked, and the horses surged forward, causing him to lose his balance and fall, pulling on the lines. Both horses stopped again, and the little boys reached out to help Dave back onto his feet. R. Duane's wife and his daughters all giggled. Dave shook off his pride and balanced himself better. He clucked again. This time he stayed on his feet when the team started off. R. Duane pointed to an open gate and Dave drove the horses through. One of the boys reached up and applied a little pressure to one of the driving lines to keep the wagon from hitting a fencepost as they passed through the field entrance.

Dave didn't try to hide his smile. He could feel the power of the horses in his driving lines and under his feet through the wagon. He began to feel comfortable with the horses and turned them toward the open field. R. Duane made a kissing sound and both horses surged into a quick trot. Dave braced himself better, and only needed a little help from the boys to stay on his feet. He drove the team in a wide circle and headed back toward the gate, where the women all stood, smiling, as if watching a funny show.

He slowed the horses by leaning back on the lines and maneuvered them through the gate and called, "Whoa." Both horses stopped instantly, almost dumping their driver over the front of the wagon. R. Duane and his boys caught him and helped him down.

Happy to be on solid ground again, Dave let out a sigh. "That was fun!"

"You did good!" the ten-year-old boy said.

Everyone around the circle nodded in agreement.

R. Duane asked, "Are you from around here?"

"No, I'm from Goshen, Indiana."

"Really?" he asked in surprise. "Who's your family?"

"My mom's grandparents were Amish."

"Did they leave the Church?" Duane's wife asked with concern.

"No, they died." Dave wished that he hadn't been so blunt.

R. Duane's face showed sympathy. "What were their names, we might have known them."

"Jonah Hershburger was my mom's grandpa. Her dad was Menno."

"Oh, no way!" R. Duane exclaimed. "I know your grandpa. He's a carpenter, isn't he?"

Dave nodded with surprise. "Yes. But he's gone now. He died a few years ago."

The kind Amish man placed a hand on Dave's shoulder. "He employed a lot of young Amish men over the years. He's well respected among the Amish and gave a lot of carpenters a good start."

"Thanks," Dave returned a sincere smile to show how much the words meant to him. "I was always pretty close to my grandpa."

Duane's wife spoke to one of her daughters in Pennsylvania Dutch. The twelve-year-old sprinted toward the house in bare feet and a long dress. A few moments later she returned with a baggie full of cookies and handed them to Dave.

"Thank you so much for pulling out my car. For the cookies." He held up the baggie. "And, most of all for letting me drive a team of horses!"

They all gave him a friendly smile and waved as he drove away.

On his way to the hotel, Dave's phone vibrated. He tapped the screen connecting his phone to the Mustang's Bluetooth for a hands-free conversation. Dave smiled as he did, happy for a chance to talk to his best friend, Nate.

"Nate—how are things in Indiana?"

"Kinda boring around here with you up in Wisconsin. Me and the guys are gonna go watch a movie tonight. Have you heard of *Ready Player One?*"

Dave shook his head. "No. What's that about?"

"It's a good one about the future. These guys' whole lives are wrapped up in playing a virtual reality game. It becomes an epic battle with some corporate big shot who's in the game for money. I hear it's awesome!"

Dave passed a buggy. "I'm having my own virtual reality game up here in Falls, Wisconsin. Only this one took me *way* back in time." After a moment of silence, Dave shouted, "Hey, I think I found that girl I was telling you about. If I can get her to agree to it, I'll be making some big bucks!"

"Don't ask her!" Nate shouted back. "Just tell your boss where she is and let him take over. He doesn't care what she thinks."

Dave ran a free hand through his hair. "I can't do that. My mom would kill me if I ratted out this Amish girl."

"Aw man, you're crushing on this girl! Because I know you're not worried about what your mom thinks." Nate laughed. "Is she the girl you knew back in high school?"

Dave sat up further in his seat and winced as the seatbelt rubbed his sunburn. "No!"

Nate's laugher grew. "What's with you and Amish girls?"

"C'mon Nate, you know I'm not interested in Amish girls. Besides, I didn't even know the girl I met in high school was Amish until after she moved away."

Nate snickered. "Yeah, you thought she was a classy European woman."

Dave growled, "Don't say anything bad about that Delilah or I'll come back to Indiana and give ya a fat lip!"

"Okay," he said in a sinister voice, "if you don't care about this girl, rat her out."

Dave let out a chuckle and thought about how friendly that Amish family had been to him, and how sweet Delilah's eyes were. "I might," he mumbled.

"I gotta go," Nate shouted into the phone. "The guys are here to pick me up."

Dave heard a click and he drove back into town alone.

CHAPTER SIX

The Water Tower Farm

D ave could see the water-tower from his hotel, and it wasn't hard to navigate his way back to Delilah's family farm. He passed through the edge of town and noticed rows of soybeans rolling in waves. One other Amish farm separated modern houses and Delilah's home. The water tower stood like a colossal tree in a field behind a white barn. It wasn't as close to the house as it had looked at first. However, it seemed odd to have such a massive, modern-day fixture looming over an otherwise perfectly old-fashioned scene.

Dave wasn't sure where to park his car. His heart rate sped up as he stopped near their hitching rack and stepped out. He couldn't see anyone around at first, so he awkwardly meandered in an open area between the barn and other buildings. A mutt-looking farm dog trotted up and began to sniff Dave's pants. A loud rumbling noise came from behind a long building with mesh over the windows. Reddish-brown chickens behind wire screens watched with wide eyes as Dave approached. They clucked and fluttered away when his footsteps passed the low windows. Dave followed a worn dirt path toward the ever-increasing roar of a motor and found a little Amish girl of about ten years old checking on an engine with a spinning wheel.

Dave pointed at the machine and spoke over the sound, "What does that do?"

The little girl cupped her hands and shouted through them. "That's our egg belt. This motor turns a belt that helps us gather eggs." The little girl's Amish dress showed signs of wear and sported a few smudges and stains. Her face reminded Dave of Delilah's, only younger, and with blond hair. "My sisters are inside finding eggs and putting them on the conveyer belt." She tucked a long strand of loose hair back inside her bandana.

"Oh, I get it!" Dave shouted, "are they about done?"

"Really close," the girl called over the motor noises. "Not more than a half hour." She motioned for Dave to follow her and they headed inside. The little girl clicked on a headlamp positioned just below her headscarf and cast a hazy beam of light through the chicken dust. A few Amish girls appeared like shadows walking through a multitude of reddish-brown hens. They were reaching in among chickens and gathering eggs. The girls set them carefully on the conveyer belt that ran through the middle of the building.

"Is there anything I can do to help?" Dave asked above the cackling of chickens and a rattling conveyer belt.

"You could sweep this walkway if you want, we have to do that every evening," Delilah said.

She handed Dave a push-broom and pointed up the long walkway. Dave started at the end and when he came to where the girls were working, they each stepped carefully over his broom in turn, so he could sweep under their bare feet. Delilah's lips curled into a smile as she stepped over the broom and met eyes with him. "Just sweep all the debris off to one side at the far end," she instructed. "My little sister will haul everything away from there."

Dave smiled at her and nodded that he understood.

He pushed the broom with a swoosh. Chickens fluttered and fanned out ahead of him in a circle as he made his way through the flock. A few feathers swirled around him in the cloud of dust he created with his swish, swishing. He finished his job about the time the girls finished gathering eggs.

A brilliant sunset lit up the sky behind a huge farmhouse. A perfectly manicured garden seemed out of place next to a house that was gray and peeling. They all took turns pumping water from a hand pump while each sister washed her feet. Dave watched, and then followed the group of weary workers who were silhouetted against the glowing sky. Their wet, bare feet pitter-pattered up a wooden ramp that sloped onto their porch and on inside. Dave noticed that there weren't steps and wondered if it was an Amish tradition. He followed the string of Amish girls through their dark living room and into a brightly lit kitchen. Fantastic smells grew rich and savory as they approached. A hissing sound emanated from the lantern as it burned brightly.

An Amish man with a salt-and-pepper beard sat at one end of a long oak table, and he smiled at Dave and said, "Have a seat." He pointed to an empty chair at the opposite end of the table. Dave did as he was told. The girls left for a few moments and came back wearing clean dresses, and instead of headscarves, they had white Amish coverings. Everyone crowded around benches on either side of the long table and sat quietly, all eyes on Dave. Nobody made any kind of introductions and Dave felt uncomfortable about it. He quickly surveyed the large, hollow-feeling room. Only a few small rugs lay like islands on an otherwise bare hardwood floor. Lime-green walls were void of decorations except for a hanging Scripture verse that read: "Therefore shall a man leave his father and his mother, and shall cleave unto his wife" (Genesis 2:24).

Dave glanced at the Amish girls surrounding the table. Something about their eyebrows made the sisters all look alike, even though a few were blonds and a few brunettes. Delilah seemed to be the oldest of six girls. They all gawked at him, their pretty eyes wide, as if they had never had an outsider at their table before. Each girl met his gaze as he looked from face to face, and each one in turn looked away bashfully. Only one boy locked eyes with Dave, a little guy seated next to Delilah. He looked cute in his suspenders and bowl-cut hair. His dark brown eyes were similar to Delilah's, although they weren't as mysterious, just very expressive.

Dave noticed a unique cleft in the boy's chin and while he studied it, the little boy pointed a chubby finger toward his mouth. He tilted his head and showed Dave that he could wiggle one of his front teeth with his tongue.

"What's your name?" Dave asked the little boy.

He smiled and said, "Earl."

Dave instantly knew for sure that he had found the right Delilah.

A middle-aged woman with a swath of gray hair showing under her Amish covering brought a few more plates of food over and laid them on the table. The older man, with a full chin-beard, bowed his head, and all the others followed his lead. After a short silence, he cleared his throat. Everyone opened their eyes and passed the plates. The meal seemed odd to Dave. They passed a platter of homemade bread, freshly baked and clearly the source of the wonderful aroma. Then a bowl overflowing with garden lettuce, already doused with what Dave guessed to be homemade dressing. Delilah handed him a bowl of boiled sausage encased like brats. He took one but wasn't sure how they planned to eat them. He stabbed his with his fork and took a big bite before realizing that the others were putting their sausages into their bread, rolled up like a hotdog bun, and lathering on a fluid they got out of a mason jar.

"What is this?" Dave dared to ask.

Earl wrinkled his nose and said, "Ketchup!"

The girls giggled as if amused that a little boy had to explain what it was. Dave put some on his bread and rolled it up like the others were doing and took a bite. "Oh wow—this ketchup is really good."

Everyone smiled but nobody said anything. They passed around a plate with tomato slices on it and a plate with homemade pickles. The children all took generous helpings and Dave took quite a few himself.

"These pickles are amazing too!" he said.

All the sisters eyed each other and snickered among themselves.

Finally, their mother replied, "That's just the way my mother always made them. She taught me, and I'm teaching my daughters to do the same."

The younger girls and little boy were so quiet and well-behaved that Dave didn't know if they were nervous about having a stranger in their house or if Amish children were just always like that.

Delilah's dad asked, "What do you do for work?"

"I just finished college and I've been looking for a job."

"Here in Falls?"

"No, I went to college up at Rapid City, and I have been looking for work down near my home in Indiana. I live in Goshen."

"Oh really?" Delilah's dad seemed surprised. "Are you Mennonite?"

"No, but my mother grew up Mennonite. We go to a non-denominational church."

"What was her maiden name?" the older man asked.

"Hershburger. Her dad was Menno, and her grandpa was Jonah."

"Jonah Hershburger? I believe we are related to you then," her dad said, his face revealing how pleasant he might be if a strange man weren't there to ask something about his daughter. "My wife's grandmother was a first cousin to a Jonah Hershburger from Goshen."

"You can't be serious?" Dave stopped eating even though the food was scrumptious. "I guess that is pretty distant, but I can't believe we are related!"

The girls all looked at each other and smiled. After that, everyone around the table seemed more relaxed. They were all as genuine and kind as Delilah. Their wide-eyed expressions revealed that they had nothing to hide and assumed the best in Dave. That is, except for her dad, who still seemed quite suspicious.

Delilah's dad wiped his mouth with a napkin and set it down. "What are you doing here in Falls?"

Dave met eyes with Delilah. Her gaze surprised him, and he couldn't look away from her sparkling, dark eyes for a moment. Then he suddenly realized how that might seem to her father, and he quickly asked, "Didn't Delilah tell you?"

She shook her head with a coy smile. "I thought I'd let you tell him."

Immediately, it seemed as if the ceiling and walls were closing in on him with a silent pressure. Her sisters gobbled up their food as if time would soon run out. Her mother coughed nervously into her napkin, and nobody looked up. Dave's face heated, and the temperature of his sunburned back rose a few degrees. He pondered Delilah's expression. The more he thought about it, the more certain he felt that her parents assumed he came to ask if he could date Delilah. His mind raced. He tried to think of what he should say to clear up the confusion. He started to stammer out, "I . . . I . . . wanted to."

Delilah waved a hand. "We can talk to my dad and mom alone after we eat."

Dave loosened his shirt collar around his sunburnt neck. Her words added to the confusion. When he originally smelled the food that sat before him, he planned to savor the delicious meal.

Instead he gulped down large mouthfuls and chewed nervously, and later, he didn't remember eating any of it. The perceived awkwardness of his presence only made Dave eat faster, in the hope that would speed up up his opportunity to explain himself to Delilah's dad. He feared that the truth about how infatuated he was with their daughter and sister might be clearly visible to everyone. He fully intended to conceal that fact.

"Let's bow and thank the Lord for what we have just eaten," Her dad blurted out.

Everyone bowed for silent prayer. Dave used the moment of silence to prepare a speech.

When he opened his eyes, Dave saw Delilah's dad giving him a death stare. "We will go out and have our conversation on the porch."

The rest of the children stood up and began to gather everything off the table. Dave waited for Delilah's dad to stand up, but he didn't. Instead, he pushed his chair back from the table and began to roll toward the doorway. All at once, Dave realized the older man was in a wheelchair.

The little boy jumped onto the wheelchair footrests as Delilah's dad maneuvered through the house using his hands to power his way. Dave walked behind, drawing in a deep breath. The small boy took on the appearance of an Amish farmer as he pretended that he stood behind a team of horses and called, "Giddyup," to them. He shook his imaginary lines and pulled them to one side as his dad turned the corner. Dave felt like laughing at the cute scene until he saw how sober Delilah and her mother looked as they followed.

Soft evening breezes met them on the porch, and Dave was happy for something to cool the sweat off his forehead and his hot sunburned back. Delilah's dad spoke to the boy in words Dave couldn't understand. The little guy jumped off the wheelchair and drove his imaginary team of horses back into the house.

Things grew awkwardly silent. Dave looked around the porch, wondering if he should sit down. He decided to reach out a hand to shake Delilah's dad's, and said, "My name is Dave, and may I ask yours?"

The older man reached out to shake. "I'm Virgil."

Dave turned to Delilah's mother. "And your name?"

"Lucille."

Virgil motioned toward a porch swing. "Please, sit down."

As Dave sat, the swing floated back and forth. Delilah timed the motion of the swing, and at the right moment sat down beside him. The swing gained momentum, and they rocked without speaking. Flowering bushes lined the porch edges and graced the occupants with a sweet scent. From his swinging seat, Dave looked upon the large garden, barely visible in the moonlight. He could make out neat rows of growing vegetables. He noticed that the outer edges of the plot had been thoughtfully decorated with bright flowers. Beyond the garden, white pasture fences glowed by the light of the moon.

At the bottom of the hill, a section of the highway that lead into town curved close enough they could watch cars and trucks go by. Lights from the John Deere sales-lot illuminated each vehicle as it passed. A cow, grazing near the garden fence, let out a long mournful bellow while Dave tried to decide how to begin his explanation.

"I thought Delilah had told you about me already," he said, and then wished he had worded it more carefully. He glanced at Delilah and she smiled at him again. "Okay, this is probably not what you are expecting to hear from me, but the reason I'm here in town has to do with your daughter." He winced at his choice of words again and rushed to blurt out a better sentence. "Have you heard of the best-selling novel *Samson and Delilah?*"

"No," Virgil said matter-of-factly.

Dave glanced at Lucille and she shook her head.

"Well, there is a novel about an Amish girl named Delilah. You probably know that people all over America love to read books about the Amish." He looked at Delilah's parents and they both nodded. "This novel, *Samson and Delilah*, has sold about a million copies, and everyone fell in love with the main female character named Delilah." He checked to see if they were tracking. They both nodded, and Dave pointed to a newspaper that lay on a stand nearby. "The author explained, in a newspaper interview, that there is a real Amish girl named Delilah that he claimed to have based his book on. She is a waitress in a restaurant he frequented. He said that she is very kind, full of faith, and always doing good deeds. Now, after reading the book, everyone in the country wants to meet Delilah."

Virgil turned his chair to face Dave. "Will the author tell them who the real girl is?"

"He can't. He passed away about a year ago," Dave explained. "Since I knew the author, a magazine called *Humans* approached me and offered me a lot of money to find the girl. From everything the author told me, I had a pretty good idea that Delilah was from this town. Everyone else thinks she is from Indiana, since that is where the author lived."

Virgil's forehead wrinkled. "What makes you think that our Delilah is the one?"

"Well, if you read the book you would be sure of it yourself." Dave held out a hand in Delilah's direction. "He describes a girl almost exactly like your daughter. She smiles like her and uses the same expressions, like 'un fa shdendich.'"

Delilah wrestled with her fingers on her lap. Lucille's mouth hung open.

Dave shook his head. "And I've already observed how your daughter treats others. She is honest and kind just like the Delilah in the book. After seeing her eyes, I'm ninety-nine percent sure your daughter is the one the world is dying to meet."

Virgil glared at Dave. "What's this about her eyes?"

"Oh—I mean she looks like the girl described in the book. That's all I meant." Dave glanced at the man in the wheelchair and pitied him, not because of his wheelchair but because his face went white with those words.

Delilah's mother had been quiet most of the evening. She opened her mouth to speak and then shut it.

Dave watched her for a moment and then said, "Lucille, please tell me what you are thinking."

"I was just going to say that if they want to meet her, I don't see what the harm in that would be."

"Okay, that is really a nice way of looking at it," Dave said, "but, let me clarify what that will be like. A few news crews will probably show up here in town. They will probably flock around your daughter, taking pictures and . . ."

"Wait," Lucille said, "did you say pictures?"

"Yes, they will want pictures of her for magazine covers and newspapers. There'll be film crews wanting to interview her, and she would most likely be invited to be on TV shows like, *Ellen* or *Jimmy Kimmel.*"

"Un fa shdendich!" Delilah gasped. "Please, don't tell anyone about me then!"

Lucille's eyes widened as she held a hand to her mouth.

Virgil gripped both wheels of his chair. "No, we wouldn't want that at all."

"Are you sure?" Dave lifted his first finger. "Remember, I've been offered one hundred thousand dollars to find her, and I'd be willing to give you folks . . ." he thought for a moment and upped his earlier offer. "I'd give you thirty-five thousand if you give me permission to tell them where she is."

"We don't want to keep you from getting all that money, Dave, but this would be completely against everything we believe in," Virgil said.

"That's why I didn't tell anyone about Falls and DJ's restaurant. The author respected Amish people and their beliefs, and he would want me to protect your privacy."

"Did he make a lot of money off that book, then?" Lucille asked.

"Not really," Dave explained. "The book didn't get big until after his death. The publishing house made a lot of money, and so did bookstores and Amazon. That's how it is in America these days, it's a marketing world, and everyone is out to grab a slice of the pie."

"Thank you for asking us before telling other folks about our daughter. That was really nice of you," Lucille said. Her eyes showed genuine gratitude.

Dave folded his arms and shook his head. "Well, it's not over yet. I won't tell anyone where Delilah is, but I'm also here to warn you. These magazine and newspaper crews are good at finding people. If you don't want any attention, you'd better think of changing a few things."

Delilah leaned forward. "Like what?"

"For starters, I'd give Delilah a nickname and go by that for a while. If anyone hears of a Delilah, they will ask questions." They all three looked at each other in shock. Dave continued, "You had better quit working at the diner for now. That is another giveaway as to your identity."

Delilah's eyes looked troubled. "I can't quit working there, it's my only job, and we need that income."

"We can make do without that money." Virgil shook his head and set his jaw. "We don't want all of this evil to surround you. We'd better take Dave's advice."

Lucille turned to face her husband. "Maybe we should send her to stay with my sister in Iowa for a while?"

Dave gathered himself and stood up from his swinging chair. "That might be for the best."

Delilah stopped the swing's motion by skidding her bare feet on the wooden floor. "Please, don't leave yet," she pleaded, "I feel like we really need your help right now. We have so many questions and no one to help us figure this out."

"I will do whatever I can to help you and your family. I'll give you my phone number . . . Oh maybe that won't help."

"We can call from one of the community phone booths," Delilah said as she stood and grabbed a pencil and pad off a table near her dad. "Please do give us your number and your address."

"Okay, I will. Unfortunately, I should probably stay far away. People know that I was close to the author, and if they see me here, it will make them suspicious. I should leave town as soon as possible."

Virgil pointed past the garden toward the section of highway illuminated by the John Deere sales-lot. "Look, what are those odd-looking dishes on top of those vans on the highway down there."

"Oh no!" Dave stepped to the edge of the porch. "That's the NBC news vans, and they are no doubt here because of you, Delilah. I'd better find a place to hide my car. If they see it in front of the hotel, they'll know they're in the right town."

Delilah stood near Dave to get a better look at the news van. She turned to face him. "Do they know you?"

"No, but they would see my license plates and know I'm from the same town as the author. Believe me, these people are good at what they do."

Dave and Delilah turned back toward Virgil and fell silent, waiting for his advice.

"You can hide your car in our barn if you feel you should," Virgil said.

Dave put his hands on his head as he thought out loud. "Okay, maybe I'd better. Maybe I should sneak down there and get my stuff and leave town tonight?"

"Do you have a lot of things in the hotel room?" Virgil asked.

"Just a few suitcases and my computer, things like that."

"You could take one of our buggies down and get everything and bring it up here," Virgil suggested.

"I grew up around horses, but I've never driven a horse and buggy before."

Virgil looked at Delilah. "You can drive him down there. Take Earl along with you so he can help Dave get his things."

CHAPTER SEVEN

Buggy Ride

Dave guessed that five-year-old Earl was more of a chaperone than a helper. They quickly hitched up a horse and headed down the hill toward town. There was just about enough room on the buggy seat for two people. Earl half sat, half stood between Dave's jeans and Delilah's Amish dress. They all three, out of awkwardness, stared at the horse trotting ahead of them. Streetlights illuminated the inside of the tiny vehicle and highlighted Delilah, who bit her fingernails. The pace seemed incredibly slow to Dave, even though the road sloped downhill from Delilah's home into town.

Dave looked at Delilah and nodded toward Earl. "Does he know English?"

"A few words of it," she said, "We Amish don't teach our children English until they start school. Earl won't start kindergarten until next fall."

"Next fall," Earl repeated and smiled, his crooked loose-tooth in the middle of his grin. His five-year-old voice rang out a long string of words in his Amish language. Delilah's voice seemed to lower an octave when she replied in her native tongue. Dave enjoyed listening to their foreign words and guttural German sounds.

Delilah translated in her singsongy, higher-pitched English. "Earl wants me to tell you about his horse."

Dave leaned back and looked down at the little Amish boy. "Earl has his own horse?"

Earl nodded, his dark brown eyes twinkling with the glow of streetlights.

Delilah laughed. "Well, let's just say he is the only one who wants the horse." She put a hand on Earl's shoulder. "I just bought Thunder, this horse we are driving, a few months ago because my old horse, Maggie, was getting so slow that I could almost walk to town faster than her. Earl is our little horseman. He begged for us to keep Maggie. He rides her, and if we aren't in a hurry to get somewhere, we'll hitch her up and let Earl drive."

Dave patted Earl's other shoulder. "You show me your horse when we get back to your house."

Delilah spoke in Pennsylvania Dutch, but Earl already had a big smile and started nodding his little straw hat-covered head.

After that they rode in silence. Their buggy wheels rumbled into the sleepy town where only an occasional car met them on the road. A few porch lights glowed in the dark gaps between street lights. Thunder's hoofbeats echoed off buildings until they pulled up at the town hitching rack and Delilah called, "Whoa." Dave glanced over and realized little Earl had fallen fast asleep, leaning across Delilah's lap. Falls Bank and Trust stood a short distance from where they were parked. Flashing lights on a huge sign announced the time and temperature intermittently. *Flash*— 10:14—*Flash*— 68⁰.

Delilah stood, rocking the buggy on its springs. She hoisted Earl up to where she had been sitting. "I'll help you get your things."

"I can get them myself, it's not that much."

She climbed out and tied her horse. "I don't mind. We can get it all in one trip if I help you."

Dave nodded at the sleeping boy. "What about little Earl? He may wake up while you're gone."

She gave a knowing smirk. "Nope, once Earl is asleep, a tornado couldn't wake him."

Dave climbed out of the buggy with a laugh. "Alrighty then, let's hurry."

They slipped like shadows across the road and hurried into the hotel. Dave led her into his room and grabbed clothes that were laying on his floor. He quickly shoved everything into a large suitcase.

"Can you toss those shoes into that duffle bag?" Dave asked as he unplugged his laptop and headed into the bathroom for his toiletries.

"Un fa shdendich, how many shoes do you have?" she called from the other room.

"Oh, I'm kinda obsessed with Nike basketball shoes. It's my thing."

"I . . . see!" she said in her distinct way.

In only a few moments they had all his things gathered. Delilah needed both hands to haul the heavy duffle bag loaded with shoes, Dave followed her down the hall with his suitcase, laptop and backpack.

She waved a hand. "It smells like cigarette smoke in here."

"Yeah, all hotels smell like that," Dave answered.

When she opened the door, Delilah stopped and said, "Some people are out there."

Dave leaned closer and whispered, "Maybe we'd better go out the other door."

Just as he spoke there was a flash of light. It took a few moments for them to regain their vision. When they did, they realized that a man with a huge camera was standing in the hall. He flashed another photo before Dave pushed open the door and Delilah followed him down the steps and past the small group of people in the parking lot. Dave tilted his head to hide his face and Delilah followed close behind. They hurried across the road toward her buggy. Delilah flopped his shoe bag onto the buggy's floor and set about untying her horse. Dave tried to fit his suitcase inside her little buggy and finally had to stand it upright on what was left of the tiny floor.

"I'll have to hold Earl," she said, "I didn't know you would have so much stuff."

He watched as Delilah climbed in, stood on his shoe bag, hunched over, picked up sleeping Earl, and situated herself carefully in one corner. Dave had to crawl over his suitcase. He let himself fall into the little bit of space that was left inside, which stung his sunburn. His legs lopped awkwardly across hers.

"Sorry about that, it's a little crowded in here," he said as he did his best to retract his legs and fit them into a tiny open gap. All their legs were still pressed into a heap. She only giggled.

"You are going to have to drive," she said, passing her leather driving lines over to Dave.

"I can't drive a horse!"

He could see her matter-of-fact expression. "It's either that or hold Earl."

Dave looked at Earl, who seemed stocky for his age. The little boy was sound asleep in a thick ball on Delilah's lap. "Okay, I'll try driving."

Delilah made a kissing sound and her tall, dark horse charged out of the parking lot with its head held high. "You'd better hold Thunder in a little tighter," she instructed.

Dave worked hard to get a better grip on the leather lines and drew them in against his chest. She laughed as her horse plowed through the front yard of a dentist office and came out a gravel drive on the other side. Somehow the big horse ended up heading the right way down an empty road. Once on an open straight-away, Dave had a chance to play a little with handling driving lines and figuring out how to keep his horse on the right side of the road. A big smile came over his face until Delilah spoke. "It looks like those camera people are following us!"

Dave turned to glance out the tiny window between Delilah and himself. He could see a van with a huge dish on top, closing in behind them.

"Watch out, Dave!" she yelled.

Dave turned back to see Thunder veering into an oncoming car. Dave yanked on his right line and Thunder made a sharp turn onto a small side road.

"That worked out nice," she said. "But you'd better hand me those lines."

Dave gladly turned Thunder back over to her. He watched Delilah as she held a little sleeping boy and found a way to maneuver enough to drive her horse better than Dave had done. Thunder's hooves rumbled hard as Dave glanced out the tiny window again. "They are right behind us!"

She shrugged. "I think I can lose them."

They rounded another corner and headed into a small park. Thunder pulled the buggy around playground equipment, past picnic tables, and charged onto a walking path.

Dave felt his heartrate double. "What are you doing?"

"There is a little footbridge up ahead that crosses the creek. They won't be able to follow us in that van, and they won't be able to keep up with Thunder on foot."

Dave thought it sounded like a great idea until he saw the bridge. He glanced out the tiny back window. The van with a dish jerked to a halt when they came to the sidewalk. Men jumped out and started to run after them, big cameras in tow. Dave looked ahead just in time to see a narrow bridge without railings stretch over a creek. Thunder's hooves pounded like a hammer on the wooden boards as he charged onto the bridge. Only water was visible on either side of the tiny buggy as Delilah drove her horse over it.

Dave heard a man's voice rising in a yell. He didn't realize it was his own until they had made it across the bridge and Thunder charged through a field and raced away from the running men.

Earl sat up and rubbed his eyes. "What happened?"

"We just crossed Murphy's Bridge," Delilah answered.

Earl said a whole sentence in Dutch and lay back against Delilah, resuming his slumber.

Dave chuckled at the little boy and looked at Delilah. "What did Earl say?"

"He was mad that I didn't wake him up. He loves to cross that bridge in a buggy."

She headed her horse uphill toward the water tower. As Thunder slowed, she asked, "How did the camera men know that was us?"

"They didn't. They just wanted a picture of Amish people. That's the way media people are. The bad thing is that if any of them recognize me in that picture, they might guess that it was you with me."

"Well, they have their picture now. Maybe they will go home and leave me alone?"

Dave shook his head. "We could only wish they were that nice. They will hound you for weeks trying to get more pictures, and then they'll start begging you to do an interview. Once they know that it is you for sure, they won't give up until they get what they want."

Delilah's face sagged. "I . . . see, what am I going to do?"

"You mentioned earlier that you have relatives in Iowa. You may want to go for a visit until this all quiets down."

She nodded. "Yes, we'd better go inside and talk to my parents about it."

***

"News people took a picture of us at the hotel," Delilah told her parents as soon as she entered the house.

Lucille's jaw dropped. "Did they know who you were?"

"I don't think so," Dave answered for her. "They just love to take pictures of any Amish people. But I'm afraid that some of them might notice me in the picture and figure out that Delilah was with me."

Delilah's dad wheeled his chair closer. "Will that be the end of it then?"

"Unfortunately, it's just the beginning. If I were you and didn't want my daughter on the cover of magazines and newspapers all over America, I'd send her off to visit some relatives in another Amish community."

"That is a good idea," Virgil said. Delilah and her parents spent the next ten minutes discussing what relatives they had where and who would be the best for her to stay with. Finally, Dave interrupted. "Now that I've done more damage for your family than good, I should probably get going. I think I'll head back to Goshen tonight."

Delilah's mother dropped her dishtowel. "Are you driving to Goshen?"

"Yeah," Dave nodded, "that's where I'm from, and I'd better get away from here before I cause you more trouble."

"We have relatives near Goshen," Lucille said, "Would you be willing to give her a ride. We would pay you."

"Sure—she could come along. I wouldn't take any money from you for it though. I'm heading that way, and it's the least I can do to help."

Virgil held up his hands. "Would you be willing to wait to leave until tomorrow morning. We'd rather not send her off at this hour."

"I completely understand," Dave said. "There's no reason I can't leave in the morning."

"Oh, thank you so much," Delilah's mother said. She hurried off to make things ready for the trip.

Dave stepped closer to Delilah and whispered, "Do you trust your boss, DJ?"

"Oh yes, we have worked for her for years."

"Good, I mentioned some of this to her. I asked her not to say anything to anyone about you, and she said she wouldn't."

"I'd better go talk to her tomorrow morning and tell her that I'm going to be gone for a while," Delilah said.

"After what we saw in town tonight, you'd better let me go talk to her. I'm afraid that you wouldn't know how to handle those wild media people if you ran into them. I'm a little more experienced with that."

"I think Dave is right, Delilah," Virgil interrupted. He can take the cinnamon rolls down to DJ's in the morning."

Delilah lifted a finger as though remembering something. "He'd better not take his car."

"He can take a buggy," Virgil said. "Earl can go along to help with the horse." His words ended the discussion.

Lucille touched her ten-year-old daughter on the shoulder. "Elsie, show Dave where our guest bedroom is." As they were going up the steps, Lucille called, "We usually leave with the cinnamon rolls at 5:30, I will wake you around 5:00."

Dave's eyes widened. "Okay . . . thanks."

Delilah's little sister set the lantern down on a dresser. "When you don't need the light anymore turn down this wick, like this." She turned it until the flame flickered and then back to full light again.

He watched her close. "Okay. I think I can do that."

Alone in the tiny room, Dave glanced at his surroundings. Everything seemed neat and tidy. The walls were bare, except for a calendar with a Bible verse: "Awake thou that sleepest, and arise from the dead, and Christ shall give thee light" (Ephesians 5:14).

Dave barely finished getting ready for bed when his phone vibrated. He looked at the screen and tapped it to answer the call.

"Mom, I've got to be quiet," he whispered into the phone. "I'm staying in an Amish home tonight."

"In Delilah's parent's home?"

"Yes, I talked to her parents about the whole thing and they don't want her to be found."

"I told you they wouldn't," she said.

"I know, I know." Dave sat on the bed and ran his fingers through his hair. "Things went worse than I expected; a bunch of media people showed up in town tonight. I told her family that I was heading home to Goshen and they asked me to bring Delilah along. I guess they have family not too far from us."

"You'd better not take money from them," his Mom scolded.

He rolled his eyes. "I won't. I told them they didn't need to pay me." Dave stood up. "Maybe there is still a chance she will change her mind and decide to let me introduce her to Charlie Rose."

"David, give up on that money! You'd better not hound that poor girl while she's riding in your car."

He paced the floor. "Wow, Mom—really? I know what I'm do-ing— I'm a grown man."

"But, I'm a woman—with Amish relatives. I know how she'll feel about it."

Dave didn't answer.

His mother cleared her throat. "You should ask her if she remembers you."

He hissed between his teeth, "Mom—it's not the same Delilah."

"Why don't you ask her?"

"She doesn't show any sign of recognizing me if she is," Dave said.

"David—you have changed so much in looks. You've matured a lot and now you have hair. Back then you had your head buzzed. And you were always so suntanned that people asked where you were from." She snickered.

"I'll ask her a few questions before I drop her off," Dave promised. "I don't want to make our drive awkward by bringing up a bad topic. But for right now, I gotta go, Mom. I'm going to shut my phone off for tonight to save power. They don't have any place to plug it in here."

"I love you, David."

He nodded and rolled his eyes again. "Okay. Good night, Mom."

Dave tossed and turned, unable to fall asleep. The Amish bed wasn't the issue. He nestled into its soft mattress and drew in a fresh scent of clean sheets. He thought, *Ooh, that's right, these sheets were probably flapping on the clothesline today*. His tight and tender sunburned skin radiated heat in his T-shirt. He pulled it off, and the sheets created a cooling effect. At one point he felt himself float off to sleep for a second.

Suddenly, as if someone nudged him, his eyes popped open and he imagined a pile of money sitting in front of him. He mentally worked through scenarios, trying to think of a way he could get the money without hurting Delilah and her family. His eyes blinked and fluttered shut for a moment. Delilah's face appeared. Her nose wrinkling as she giggled. Dave's eyes opened again, and he realized he had a smile on his face. He tried to clear his thoughts and sleep. He drifted into a dreamlike state and could see Delilah's dad wheeling his chair through the house with Earl standing on the footrests. Dave's eyes peeled open like slits. The room was so dark he couldn't be sure if his eyes were open or shut. A guilty feeling pressed on his chest while he tried to ignore it and fall asleep.

He finally slipped away into a dream, only to be awakened by a clap of thunder that shook the bed under him. Dave startled, and his quick movement stung his sunburned back. Every time he started to drift off, he dreamt he could see Delilah running from camera men, or that she gave in and posed for photographers. They crowded around her, telling her where to stand, what angle to hold her head, and asking her a barrage of questions.

A bright light, another clap of thunder, and subsequent rumbling sounds woke him again. He got up and dug through his suitcase for his Kindle. It almost seemed as if Samson and Delilah called to him, pleading with him to finish reading their story. A blue glow lit up his tiny room as the words jumped out at him. Beads of sweat dripped from his brow, and he wished he could open a window, but rain pounded on the pane. He thought about turning his Kindle off, but he couldn't pull his eyes away from the letters on the screen. His heart pounded. His stomach churned. He moaned as he read the final chapter, trying to keep quiet. His hands shook his Kindle, making it hard to read. He had to lay it on the mattress for the last few pages of the book.

At the last word he shut down his Kindle. He let out a long, slow breath that he hadn't realized he had been holding. Dave looked at the dark ceiling and whispered, "Why didn't I read this before I came up to Wisconsin?" He rolled and tossed, trying to fall back to sleep, which stung his back. His mind continually returned to the unbelievable ending of the book.

CHAPTER EIGHT

Déjà Vu

A knock sounded on his door, and a voice called out, "It's after 5:00, you'd better stand up if you are taking the rolls to DJ's Diner!"

"Oh, okay I'm getting up!" Dave sat on the edge of his bed and scratched his head. "Oh, that's right," he whispered to himself, "they are expecting me and Earl to take rolls to the diner."

He got dressed in the faint morning light and stumbled down the steps, almost sleepwalking. Sweet aromas of cinnamon and yeast drew him along, and he followed the scent. He turned a corner, stepping into the kitchen. Columns of sunlight flooded the room, illuminating a tableful of freshly baked rolls and a room crowded with Amish girls. A clattering of pans and utensils fell silent for a moment as Delilah and her sisters all looked up and stared at the intruder.

Delilah's eyes narrowed. "What's wrong, Dave? Don't you feel well?"

"Oh—I'm okay," Dave said and rubbed his forehead. "That storm woke me up during the night."

Delilah and her mother looked at each other for a moment. Her mother asked Delilah, "Did you hear a storm?"

Delilah shook her head. "No, but I think it did rain."

Lucille stretched plastic wrap over a box of cinnamon rolls. "I hope the guestroom was comfortable?" She squinted up at Dave with a worried brow.

"I was very comfortable," he answered. "I'll be fine, as soon as I can get myself awake. I'm not used to being up so early."

Delilah's littlest sister stepped into the kitchen and spoke in Pennsylvania Dutch. Her inflection suggested that she had a question. Lucille and her daughters bantered back and forth with foreign words while boxing up the remaining rolls.

Dave edged near Delilah and whispered, "Could you save a roll for me?"

"I already set two aside," Delilah said, and her nose wrinkled with a smile. "Earl is hitching his horse to the buggy. Take out this box of rolls and send Earl for the rest."

Dave took a firm grip on a large box and headed out the door. He found the little Amish boy and his slightly older sister outside hitching a horse to a buggy. Earl pointed to a trunk-like drawer that stood open on the back of the buggy. Dave could see a few boxes of rolls stacked neatly inside.

Dave set his box on top of the others and looked at the little boy. "Are you about ready to go, Earl?"

"He doesn't speak much English, yet," his sister explained.

Dave tried to make eye contact with the girl. "I don't know how to drive a horse. Somebody who knows English should go with us."

Delilah's little sister let out a giggle. "You are taking our old horse, Maggie. Earl can drive her to the restaurant. He's done it many times before."

Dave lifted a finger. "Oh, I was supposed to send Earl in to help bring out more cinnamon rolls."

They all three headed in and brought out the remaining three containers of rolls. Delilah called after him, "We will be ready to head to Goshen as soon as you get back!"

Dave's mind immediately recalled the ending of *Samson and Delilah*. "Are you sure you don't have another way to get to Indiana?"

Delilah poked her head back around the screen door, her eyes wide. "Why? Don't you want me riding along?"

"It's not that . . . I just . . . didn't know if your parents want you traveling with a man you don't know."

"We are related to you," she said, walking toward him confidently. "My dad said he believes God sent you to help us."

"We aren't that closely related," Dave replied as he climbed into the buggy.

Delilah's mouth hung open as if shocked by his words.

Earl called to his horse, "Maggie!"

The horse lurched forward, jostling the buggy and Dave fell back into his seat beside the little boy and his back screamed a reminder to go easy on the sunburned skin. Maggie let out a groan and sauntered down the hill leading into town. Dave's mind revisited the story he read last night and the part where he and Earl took a buggy ride to town together. It wasn't playing out word-for-word. Every scene did not correspond exactly with the book. Yet, the general storyline matched way too closely. He breathed a sigh of relief that Delilah's parents wanted him to take her to

Indiana, because, in the story, they went to Iowa. The old horse drifted toward the center line, and Dave had to restrain himself from taking the driving lines from Earl.

Dave nudged the little guy. "Do you drive the buggy right up to DJ's to deliver the rolls?"

Earl spoke a few foreign words and looked at Dave as though he had just asked a question.

Dave shrunk down to look in Earl's eyes. "I'm sorry, but I didn't understand a word you just said."

"Almost there," he said in English.

"Okay, good."

Earl nudged Dave and pointed to his own mouth. The little boy wiggled his loose tooth with his tongue and smiled as if proud of it.

Dave nodded and half laughed. "That tooth is about ready to jump out of your mouth."

Earl chuckled from his belly and repeated, "Jump out."

A rooster began to crow. Dave and Earl looked at each other in surprise. The sound seemed to come from somewhere within the buggy. Suddenly, Dave remembered his cell-phone alarm. He pulled it from his pocket and stopped the annoying crowing. Earl watched closely and chuckled again.

Maggie pulled them down Main Street. She seemed to know where they were going. The old horse turned into the alley behind DJ's, near the place where Dave had met Delilah to talk.

Earl called, "Ho!"

Maggie lurched to a stop. Earl climbed down from the buggy and took a tray of rolls, heading toward DJ's back door. He kicked the door three times and it opened. DJ leaned out and gave a start when she saw Dave instead of Delilah.

"Earl and I brought the rolls down this morning," Dave explained. "Delilah is going to have to leave town for a short time, until this whole book thing blows over."

DJ didn't speak. She helped carry in the cinnamon rolls and gave Earl an envelope, apparently with money in it for the rolls. She smiled at little Earl and told him, "Thank you."

Dave stood and waited for DJ to acknowledge his words, but she ignored him. "Excuse me," Dave tried again. "Virgil and Lucille wanted me to tell you that Delilah won't be able to come to work for at least a few weeks."

"Yeah, thanks to you," she said with a sound of disgust in her voice.

Dave leaned one ear closer. "I'm sorry, what did you say?"

"Don't play dumb around me anymore. I know what you are up to."

Dave held his hands up in surprise. "I came here to warn Delilah that the media world was coming."

DJ raised the corner of her lip as if to snarl at him. "You told me yourself that you were going to make a lot of money telling everyone where Delilah was. I hope you enjoy getting rich at her family's expense." She hesitated enough to glare at him. "Now you plan to get her out of town before anyone else gets a picture of her."

"I'm sorry you think that is what is happening here, but that's not completely true." Dave tried appearing innocent by making eye contact. He could see that DJ was not interested in having a conversation with him. He turned to Earl. "We'd better get going before all the news people show up."

Earl gave another mysterious reply in his Amish tongue, and they climbed into the buggy. He clucked to his horse and they clip-clopped out of the alley and on down the main street of town. Dave looked out of the back window and he could see activity near the news vehicles and hotel. "Make your horse go as fast as she can!"

The little boy wrinkled his nose and shook his head. Dave assumed Earl didn't understand. He reached over and shook the lines and made a kissing sound. Earl laughed and did the same.

Maggie continued with the same slow pace heading uphill toward the water tower.

When Maggie finally drew near Virgil's farm, Dave contemplated getting out and walking because he was sure it would have been faster than Maggie's trot. His heart began pounding when he saw Delilah standing by the barn where they had hidden the car last evening.

She called to her brother in Pennsylvania Dutch. Little Earl jumped from the buggy and ran into the house. "We have everything loaded in your car. All we need to do is slide open the doors and drive away. Earl went inside to tell our dad good-bye, and then we will go."

Dave had been heading toward the barn, but he stopped short at her words. "Is Earl coming with us?"

Delilah nodded. "My dad thought it would be best."

Lucille was standing near the barn wringing her hands. She looked at Dave with pleading eyes. "We talked about it this morning, and we think it would be better if Delilah was with our relatives in Iowa. I know it would be a little bit out of your way, but could you drive her there instead? We'd gladly pay you."

"Oh, Iowa." Dave stopped and looked at his Mustang. "I guess we could make that work. But I won't take any money from you."

"Thank you so much. After you drop Delilah off, you can stay the night with my sister's family there before you head home to Indiana." Lucille smiled and thanked Dave again.

Little Earl came running toward them, holding onto his black Amish hat to keep it from blowing off in the breeze he generated as he ran. He stopped and pointed to the Mustang emblem on Dave's trunk and said something in Dutch.

"Hurry and get in, Earl," Delilah said as she held the door for him.

Dave had been getting ready to slide open the big barn door, but he stepped back and raised his eyebrows. "Are your parents sure they want Earl to come along?"

"Is that a problem?" Delilah asked.

Dave remembered what he had read during the night. He recalled the part about an accident and ambulance ride. He attempted to remind himself that *Samson and Delilah*, being fiction, didn't have anything to do with reality. However, it seemed like tempting fate to bring Earl along since the book mostly consisted of a road trip with an Amish girl named Delilah and a little Amish boy named Earl. He also knew it made sense to send her little brother along so Delilah wouldn't be alone on the road with a single man. It wouldn't seem right if he suggested they went without a chaperone. He shrugged. "I guess there's no reason Earl couldn't come along."

Dave experienced a strange sensation as he watched Delilah help Earl into the Mustang. He could feel the momentum of the situation propelling him toward disaster, and yet, there wasn't anything he could do to stop it. The balance of events had already shifted enough that his efforts to turn them back were futile. All he could do was to hold on and watch how everything would unfold. Unfortunately, everything that had transpired so far mirrored the book thoroughly, and he feared how it would end. When he put the last of his belongings in the trunk, a sickening feeling of déjà vu passed through him, having already witnessed Samson do the exact same thing.

"Please take good care of Earl and Delilah," their mother said with pleading eyes. "I don't know how we'll manage everything here at home without them, even for a few weeks."

"I'll do my best," Dave reassured her, quoting Samson's words from the book. He hoped his face didn't give away his own doubts about their safety.

Delilah buckled Earl into the backseat and situated herself on the passenger side opposite Dave. All of Delilah's sisters stood in a clump around Virgil's wheelchair and waved as the Mustang rumbled out of the barn and onto the road toward town. Dave glanced at Delilah, who wore a long Amish dress and black bonnet. Earl seemed to be wearing his Sunday clothes too—black pants and suspenders with a white shirt. He sat quietly in the middle of the backseat with his black straw hat.

The mustang roared up to a four-way stop at the edge of Falls. A CBS News van pulled up on one side and a *Humans* magazine van on the other.

Dave shouted, "Duck, duck, duck!"

Delilah leaned forward and looked beyond the media vehicles. "Where?"

They passed between both vehicles and Dave mumbled, "I meant for you to duck so they wouldn't see you in my car."

"Oh—I'm sorry—I thought there was a duck on the road," Delilah said.

Dave checked his rearview mirror and watched the *Humans* magazine vehicle turn sharply to pursue them. "Hang on you two," he warned, "I'm gonna have to try and lose this media van that's on our tail."

He punched his accelerator, and the Mustang tires let out a squeal. Delilah pressed herself back into her seat and held onto the door with one hand and the armrest with the other. Earl chuckled as they sped over a hill and lost their stomachs for a moment. The highway flattened out momentarily and ran alongside a set of railroad tracks. Dave happened to notice the morning train speeding toward them. He checked his rearview again and realized the *Humans* magazine van was still in hot pursuit. Just then they passed a crossroads, and Dave slammed on his brakes, throwing the Mustang into a spin. He used the momentum to do a donut on the highway. Once the Mustang straightened out again, they were crosswise to the tracks, and Dave accelerated across them, bouncing Delilah and Earl in their seats. The train blew its horn as the Mustang sped away.

"There," Dave said, "those news guys will have to sit and wait for the train. By the time it passes, we'll be in the next county."

Delilah turned her bonnet toward Dave, and he struggled to keep from laughing at her wide-eyed expression.

"Don't worry—I don't always drive like this," he said and laughed.

They wound around some curvy roads and over some Wisconsin hills.

Eventually Delilah asked, "Do you know where you're going?"

"Yeah—I know this area pretty good from when I was in college up here. I don't think those media guys will be able to find me in real life like they do in the book."

Delilah's black bonnet turned to face Dave again. "What do you mean by 'in the book'?"

"Oh—in the book, Samson and Delilah are running from the media too."

She met his eyes and straightened her brow with a troubled expression but didn't say anything. After a long silent spell, Delilah held out a small bag and said, "Here are your cinnamon rolls."

"Oh, perfect! Now if I just had a cup of your coffee."

"I'm sorry, but I don't usually make coffee at home." She watched Dave as he began to devour one of her cinnamon rolls. "Do you want to eat the other one now too?"

"I'd better save it for tomorrow," he said.

She handed him a napkin and carefully unscrewed the lid off a mason jar. "Do you want a drink of milk?" She passed him the jar when he nodded.

He took a big gulp. "Mmm—that's great milk! I suppose its fresh from the cow?"

He noticed her wrinkle up her nose with a smile. "No, from the goat." She took a little sip herself and carefully screwed the lid back on, placing the jar into a container by her feet.

Dave focused on his driving, and Delilah and Earl rode along properly for the first one hundred miles. Awkwardness hung between them. Delilah nibbled at her fingernails. Every time Dave glanced at her, she quickly put her hands down on her white apron and glanced at him out of the corner of her eye. He wanted to ask her a multitude of questions about her life and opinions. However, everything he thought of asking seemed wrong. Either the topic would be too personal or sound like a creepy thing for a single English guy to ask an Amish girl. The longer silence reigned between them, the more awkward his question ideas seemed. A few more miles down the road and she had her hands back to her mouth, biting her nails again. Whenever Dave looked in the rearview mirror, he could see Earl working his loose tooth with his tongue.

Suddenly Earl shouted, "Duck, duck, duck!"

Delilah scrunched down in her seat. Dave looked in his rearview mirror at the empty highway behind them and then at Earl. The little boy pointed out of his side window at a pond.

Dave laughed and said, "Look, Delilah, there are some ducks swimming on that pond."

Delilah giggled and let herself lean back and relax after that. A few miles later, Earl spoke in Pennsylvania Dutch. Delilah and Earl had a short conversation in their own language. Dave, curious about what they were saying, glanced at Delilah and raised his eyebrows.

She took his que and explained, "Earl wants to take his shoes off. I told him that you don't want his bare feet in your car."

"Oh, I don't care. Earl take your shoes off!" Dave looked in his rearview mirror at the little boy's dark eyes. "Tell him to take his shoes off, Delilah. We're gonna be traveling for hours, he might as well be comfortable."

Delilah gave Dave a sheepish grin. "Would it be okay if I took off my shoes too?"

He laughed out loud. "This isn't a fancy car. Please, make yourself comfortable. I don't mind at all."

"Oh good. We don't wear shoes at home. We're both a lot more comfortable without shoes on." Delilah took off her black bonnet as well, placing it carefully beside her. She leaned down and untied her shoes and pulled off her stockings. He noticed her shoes and purse showed signs of wear around the edges as she passed them to Earl and spoke to him in Dutch. The little guy loaded their shoes into a bag beside him on the seat.

After a few more awkward miles, Delilah spoke. "Would you mind if I looked at your book?" She pointed to a copy of *Samson and Delilah* that Dave had tucked under his armrest. The cover peaked out, apparently having slid from its hiding place.

Dave tried to act nonchalant. "Oh—you just want to look at it?" He choked out the words as he tried to think of a way to tell her no.

"I thought maybe I should read a little of it, to see if I think it's about me." She looked at him and their eyes met. Her eyebrows arched up and she asked, "Why don't you want me to read it?"

"It's just that . . . I'm not sure it's about you after all," Dave stammered out.

"What?" Her mouth hung open. "Just yesterday you were certain it is all about me. Why would you take me away from home if it's not about me?"

"Well, I finished reading it last night." Dave winced as he spoke. "I don't think you'll like the ending."

She scrunched up her eyebrows. "Why—what happens?"

Dave searched the highway ahead of him, looking for the right words. "Okay, let me put it this way—I think you *are* the Delilah the world is looking for." He glanced at her face and noted her bunched up brow. "I just don't think you should take the whole story too personally. I mean—it's a novel. The story is made up."

She looked at the cover for a long time, then opened it and started reading. Dave watched her out of the corner of his eye. She kept a straight face for a couple of pages. About midway through the third page, she covered her face and giggled. Dave could see rosy cheeks between her fingers.

He cocked his head. "Do you think that Delilah sounds familiar?"

"Maybe," she said, and her nose wrinkled with a smile. Instantly, as if realizing the nose-wrinkling smile gave herself away, she put her hand over her face and giggled. She spent the next half hour completely engrossed in her reading, turning pages at a steady pace. She placed one of her bare feet against the glove box and wiggled her toes. Dave looked at her foot. She flashed a glance at him and sat up straight, slapping her foot to the floor, as if embarrassed.

"You can put your feet on the dashboard. I don't mind," Dave said.

She waved a hand. "I'm sorry. I didn't mean to put my foot up there. It just happened."

"Don't worry about it. This isn't a new car." Dave felt his seat move slightly, and Delilah turned around, leaning over as she looked at Earl. She spoke a long Pennsylvania Dutch phrase. Her voice was a much lower pitch when she spoke in her native tongue. Everything she said sounded guttural, a mish-mash of grouchy-sounding words. Quite a contrast to her singsongy high-pitched English that was filled with kindness and warmth.

After a while, Delilah's foot was on the dash again, toes wiggling. Dave smiled. She glanced at him nervously, dropping her foot to the floor.

"Put your foot back up there," Dave ordered.

She waved a hand again. "No, I'm sorry about that. I get reading and my foot just goes up there."

"Listen, Delilah, put your foot back on the dash." Dave lifted his own foot and put his Nike shoe against the dash. "I really don't mind. Put your feet up there and be comfortable."

"How are you driving?" she asked, looking at Dave's foot in astonishment.

"I have the cruse control on," he explained. "Now, put your foot back up there and be comfortable," Dave ordered with a smile, and she laughed.

She slowly put her bare foot back on the dash and looked at Dave sheepishly. "Thank you."

Dave alternated between watching the road and glancing at Delilah reading. The thin material of her Amish covering, almost see-through, got him wondering about her hair. He tried to imagine what her updo looked like without the covering. Every now and then little Earl spoke loudly in Dutch. Whenever he did, Dave checked his rearview mirror and witnessed a big smile on the little boy's cherub face, his smile crooked because of the cleft in his chin. Earl worked his loose tooth back and forth with his tongue.

Dave leaned near Delilah. "What's Earl saying?"

She let her book fall to her lap. "He is saying, 'horse.' "

Dave noticed the little boy was sullen and quiet most of the time, until he saw a horse and then he shouted, "Gaul!" and grinned from ear to ear. At one point, Earl said a long row of Pennsylvania Dutch words and Dave interrupted Delilah's reading. "What's Earl saying now?"

"He's asking, 'Where is everyone's horses?' " Delilah explained, and then said a long Dutch phrase to her little brother. She then turned to Dave and said in English, "I told him that those are all English people, and they don't use horses."

Earl spoke in English, "No Amish people."

Wisconsin-style mountains rose up before them. Dave's Mustang raced around a ribbon of road that meandered along wooded hills. His car chugged up over a high point.

Earl spoke in his native language, and Delilah translated, "That was a high mountain."

"Have you been over huge hills like that before?" Dave asked, looking at Earl in his rearview mirror.

Delilah translated, and Earl spoke a long line of happy-sounding words with a big smile.

"This is the first time Earl has been away from home," Delilah answered.

"Look down below," Dave said, pointing over a railing at a stunning view of a valley. "We are going to go down into that deep valley you see there." Dave could see Earl's face and bright eyes in his rearview mirror. The little boy watched everything intently. Slowly, the wrinkles of the Wisconsin landscape smoothed out more and more. The mighty Mississippi River came into view. "Look at how wide that river is." Dave pointed toward a massive body of water that separated Wisconsin from Iowa. Earl spoke in Pennsylvania Dutch, and Dave looked at Delilah.

"He's wondering if that river is too wide for us to cross," she said.

"Tell him no, it's not too wide. There is a big bridge for us to cross up ahead."

Earl leaned forward as far as his seatbelt and suspenders would let him. They neared the huge bridge, and Earl jabbered excitedly. Dave picked out the word *boat* over and over again in Earl's sentences.

Dave winced as they started onto the bridge.

Delilah watched him closely. "What's the matter?"

"I don't like bridges," he answered. "Ever since I was a little boy I've hated them."

"Is that why you shouted when we crossed the bridge at the park?"

He felt his face heat up. "I didn't really shout, did I?"

"A little," she said and wrinkled up her nose with a giggle.

Dave squinted his eyes, hunched his shoulders even though it stung his sunburn, and held one hand to the left side of his face while they headed up an incline and onto the bridge. He tried to focus on the road a few feet in front of the car, holding his breath. Delilah watched him with a smirk. Earl's laughter rose from behind them. Dave began to moan and moved his fingers into a cup shape, shielding his eyes from the view to his left. His moaning grew louder as they passed over the center point.

Delilah shouted. "Dave! You're getting close to the side!"

He moved his hand and grimaced, taking in quick breaths. "I'm sorry, but . . ." He covered his eyes again, still breathing rapidly.

Delilah shrieked.

Earl's belly laugh deepened.

"We've reached the other side," Delilah announced. "Please look up!"

Dave sighed and took a few slow breaths. "That river is too wide. And now, after I drop you off, I'm going to have to cross it again."

His eyes met Delilah's for a moment and then she lowered her gaze, looking at her hands. After examining her fingers, she bit at her nails. Her eyes were like an ocean—or maybe more like a clear lake that he could see into. So much kindness, and yet, a certain type of confidence. As much as he wanted to look into them, he also feared it, afraid that she would be able to see what was within him as well.

CHAPTER NINE

Volleyball with Teenage Delilah (flashback)

The two Delilahs in Dave's life were so different that he wondered if they would get along if they ever met. The teenage Delilah from his high school years burst at the seams with cuteness. Dave never took his dad's advice about looking into her eyes, so he wasn't sure what he would have seen in them.

Both girls had a Disney-princess aura about them. The teenage Delilah from Indiana was a spunky and edgy princess, always quick with comebacks, comical, carefree, and spontaneous. The Delilah from Wisconsin who had been riding in his car was a sweet, self-controlled princess—as serene as a windmill in a gentle breeze and kind to a fault. The teenage Delila had been so outwardly beautiful that he assumed her beauty went all the way through to her core. The Delilah in his passenger seat overflowed with sweetness bubbling out from somewhere deep inside and glowed through all her features.

Dave would never forget his second meeting with the high school age Delilah. She had walked into the park wearing tight shorts and a T-shirt. And, of course, bare feet. Her silky mass of dark hair was waving in the breeze. Dave tried to play it cool and hang out with his buddies instead of running to pick her up and swing her around like he wanted to. He watched her carefully but planned to only seem sort of interested when they crossed paths.

A few guys, from a rival high school of Dave's, stopped her and her friend. One of them stood in front of them, trying to hit on them with a few pickup lines. The other guy circled around like a hyena examining the hindquarters of a pair of gazelles. Dave knew what kind of guys they were. He moved a little closer and tried to hear what they were saying.

"You need to tie all that hair back so we can see your cute outfit," one of them suggested to Delilah.

Dave's own hair bristled.

The other said, "Yeah, no use covering up a beautiful back porch with hanging vines."

"What does that mean?" Delilah asked as she tried to back away from them.

"I mean—that back porch sure has a nice swing!" he said and moved closer.

Her eyes showed fear, and that was all Dave could take. He rushed in and caught Delilah's eye and winked as he got near so she would know something was up. He took her by the waist and swung her around. He dipped his face in her soft hair and whispered, "Pretend that I'm your boyfriend."

He set her on her feet and she gave him a big hug. "Samson, I've been looking for you everywhere!"

He put his arm around her waist casually and nodded to the other guys. "What's up?" he asked but didn't stick around for a response. He led Delilah over to the gang of friends from his own school, looking for safety in numbers. The loser guys ambled off to seek easier prey.

Dave pulled Delilah over to a picnic table. He coughed and tried to clear his voice, still hoarse because of a cold. "Sorry about messing up your chances with those guys, but I don't like them."

"I didn't come here to meet new boys," she said. Her mouth curled into a sweet smile. "My cousin, Katie, and I came tonight because someone invited us to play volleyball."

Katie joined them at the table and asked, "Where are the nets?"

"Just on the other side of that swimming pool." Dave nodded in that direction.

Delilah's cousin, Katie, also had a mass of long hair, but hers was blond. she didn't have as strong of an accent as Delilah, but she had a lilt in her tone as well. The girls' outfits were so similar that they must have picked them out on the same shopping trip. Except that Delilah's natural gifts made her clothes seem twice as expensive. Nate resorted to his regular "flirting with girls" routine that involved telling the poor girl (in this case, Katie) about how amazing he was at every sport. It seemed to be working about as poorly as usual.

Dave focused his attention on Delilah. "I'm so glad you like volleyball. The girls from our school went to state last season, and they're pretty good. A bunch of them come here on Fridays, and us guys give them a little competition."

"They won't mind if we play, will they?" she asked.

"No—anyone can play! And, if they don't like it, too bad. You girls are with us."

"That tall blond girl is Shelby. She leads the state in kills," Nate told the girls.

"What's a kill?" Delilah asked.

Dave explained, "That means she hit a ball that nobody was able to make a play on. Usually it refers to a spike."

Delilah nodded and eyed Shelby.

Nate, Dave, and their basketball buddies all clumped around the new girls and told them stories about last year's basketball season. A few of the guys sipped on beer.

Dave pointed to a cooler that sat partially hidden under some bushes. "Did you want a beer, Delilah?"

She looked at the open cans on the picnic table and shook her head. "No thanks."

The volleyball girls gathered in a semicircle with Shelby in the middle. They all wore their hair in high ponytails because Shelby did. In fact, the girls at Dave's high school watched every step Shelby made because she not only led the state in kills her junior year of high school, but she also could spike a putdown during a conversation with the best of them. She was a long, tall blond with natural good looks. It didn't hurt that her daddy owned a local car dealership and provided her with enough plastic cards that she could wear all the latest fashions. She headed for the nets, and her cluster of girlfriends followed. Shelby was the captain of the team, and she already had a scholarship to play college volleyball. Her long frame and narrow hips gave her an advantage in sports and with the boys.

Dave hoped that Delilah and Katie didn't notice, but the volleyball girls tossed their heads as if they had long flowing hair. They laughed when the new girls stepped into the sand. It seemed obvious they were jealous of how much attention the boys were giving the newcomers.

Dave told his basketball buddies, "Let's give these girls the inside and us guys will be in the front row and the back row. Delilah and Katie seemed pleased to take those positions, and the game commenced. Dave served first, and the volleyball girls set up a play. They worked together like a finely tuned machine, setting Shelby for a big spike. Shelby rose up high and the guys in the front row jumped to try and block her, but it made it through their hands, descending toward Katie. Katie shocked them all by getting under it and keeping the ball alive. Delilah made it to the ball and surprised the volleyball girls by slamming a good hit directly back at Shelby. The ball bounced off her elbow and out of bounds. The guys all cheered.

Dave gave Delilah a high five before he sent over another serve. This time the girls seemed unified in the goal of paying Delilah back. They carefully set a play where Shelby would be free to hit at an angle, slicing between the boys and directly at Delilah. Delilah didn't seem bothered. She not only found a way to ward off the ball but somehow directed it to Dave. Dave tipped it to Katie and Katie walloped it and scored another point. Dave, Nate, and the other basketball guys all laughed this time.

Delilah and Katie had a slightly different style than the girls from Dave's school. They didn't set the ball with their fingers but bounced it to each other. They didn't try to jump above the net and spike like Dave's schoolmates. Instead, they hit it from where they stood. Amazingly, their hits were effective, even though they didn't jump like Shelby. Their placement and top-spin proved quite powerful, and they held their own.

Nate asked loud enough for the volleyball girls to hear, "What high school team do you girls play on?"

"We're not on a team," Katie answered for them both.

"Well, you girls are single-handedly beating our all-state volleyball team."

Dave moved near Nate and mumbled hoarsely, "Careful, man, you're making it worse."

The volleyball girls set up another opportunity for Shelby, and she smashed another directly at Delilah. Delilah dug it out somehow and popped it high enough that Dave bashed a spike right at Shelby, and it bounced off her knee and out of bounds. The guys all cheered, except for Dave.

He looked at Shelby and glared. "Quit it—now!"

"What?" Shelby shrugged, trying to look innocent.

During the next play, Delilah thumped another that Shelby couldn't handle, and the guys all roared. Nate yelled, "If you had these girls on your team, you'd actually win state and not just get there!"

It was a harsh burn, and the guys all chorused, "Ooooohh."

Multiple volleys ensued. The basketball guys and the volleyball girls all had a few moments in the spotlight, but everything centered around Shelby's vendetta to target Delilah.

One powerful spike Shelby shot at her, Dave reached in and deflected it, afraid it might hurt her.

Delilah elbowed Dave and said, "Hey that was my ball. I could've got that!"

When Shelby loaded up again, all Dave could do was watch and hope that Delilah could handle it. Shelby reached the peak of her jump and brought her forearm down with everything she had. The ball shot directly at Delilah with a force that made Dave shudder. Delilah nicked it with her fist, but it ricocheted off, slapping her cheek with a loud smack.

Delilah put a hand to her face and muttered, "Da-hang it."

Shelby's teammates all cheered with a shout that had more to do with Delilah getting hit in the face than about the point they scored. And, it seemed their cheering hurt Delilah more than the ball did.

Dave tried to yell at Shelby even though his voice came out raspy, "I said cut it out!"

Delilah's cheek had a large red splotch, but she bit her lip and got ready for another. Dave looked at her in amazement and then noticed a tear in the corner of one eye.

"That's it!" Dave hollered. He took Delilah by the wrist and pulled her away from the game. The volleyball girls all let out an, "Aww," in unison.

Dave led Delilah to the drinking fountain behind the picnic area and soaked his hand in cold water and gently laid his wet, cool, hand on her cheek. A big tear swelled up in her other eye and fell. Dave pulled her in and gave her a bear hug. Delilah began to sob. He ran his fingers through her hair as he had seen his mother do for one of her Sunday school students. He slipped one hand under the mass of silky hair and patted her on the back while she let out a good cry.

All at once, Delilah wriggled her shoulders free of Dave's arms and pushed against Dave's chest with both hands. "Da-hang it—why did you hug me?" Her face and voice both showing anger.

Dave held his hands up in surrender. "Sorry—sorry—I thought you looked ready to cry and like you needed a hug."

She pulled the bottom of her T-shirt up and leaned down to wipe her eyes. "I didn't want to cry! I was going to be okay until you went and hugged me!"

"I'm sorry, but I thought girls wanted a hug when they are about to cry."

Delilah folded her arms and looked away from him, as if ashamed of her tears. "Don't you know that when a person is about to cry, a hug will push them over the edge. I was trying to keep from crying, and then you went and hugged me!"

"I'm so sorry, Delilah. I didn't know that."

She turned back and shook her head. "I'm not really mad at you, I just didn't want to let that Shelby make me cry!"

"It's all my fault," Dave said with a gravelly voice. "Shelby thinks she owns me. Whenever she sees that I like another girl, she gets mean."

Delilah finally smiled. "She sees that you like another girl?"

He laughed. "I'm not hiding it very well." He leaned in and gave her a gentle push on the shoulder. "And, by the way, you just did what no other girl in the state has been able to do. She slammed her best shots at you, and you were able to handle it!"

She giggled in the darkness. "Really?" She looked over toward the volleyball game and said, "I don't think I can go back there now. Maybe I should see if my cousin is ready to leave?"

"Please don't leave, Delilah! What can Samson do to make Delilah happy again?"

Delilah sat and stared straight ahead for a moment, as if thinking. Then she lifted one hand and pointed. "Is that a Pizza Hut over there?"

Dave looked where she pointed, and he could see the red sign through the park's trees. "Yeah—it is. Do you want us to go over there and get a pizza?"

She gave him a coy smile, barely visible by the park lights. "Would Samson go get Delilah a pizza? I didn't bring along any shoes, and I think it'd be fun to eat pizza out here in the dark."

Dave felt a deep vibration under him, rumbling in the picnic table they sat on top of. "Oh no—here comes the train! The tracks go between the park and that Pizza Hut."

"Can you beat it?" she leaned over and gave him a gentle shove.

The train whistle blew, and the rumble began to build into a roar.

Dave jumped up and started running. He called back, "What kind of pizza do you like?"

"Ham!"

He called, "Wait right there for me! I'll be back in about fifteen minutes!"

Dave ran at an angle, heading for the path that crossed the tracks. The train's headlight appeared, and the engineer pulled his loud whistle again. Dave rushed ahead at top speed and charged over the tracks, completely bathed in brilliant light from the oncoming locomotive.

It really wasn't that close. However, a minute after he crossed the tracks, he felt the rush and power of the train pass behind him. He couldn't help but shudder. The rumble shook the ground and echoed off the Pizza Hut as he hurried inside.

When Dave crossed back across the quiet tracks, he couldn't wait to see Delilah again. Words his dad once told him came to mind: "*A relationship with a woman is like building a fire. If you do things right, and build it properly, it starts slowly but lasts a lifetime. If you get in a hurry, there is a huge flame, but it burns up in a blaze and it's over.*" Dave knew his dad meant for him to take relationships slowly, but with a girl like Delilah, that seemed impossible.

He hurried toward the bench with a smile on his face and a pizza box held up with one hand and a two-liter bottle of pop in the other. His smiled faded as he came to the picnic bench and there wasn't any sign of Delilah. He dropped the pizza and pop on the picnic table and looked around.

Dave called "Delilah!" softly. He didn't want the others to hear him, but he hoped she might. He looked through the dark trees to where the others were still playing volleyball. The sand courts were lit up, and he could see that she wasn't there. More than that, he couldn't see any sign of her cousin Katie either. He pulled a piece of pizza out of the box and took one bite and then threw it as hard as he could. It made a splat as it hit a nearby tree.

"Why did you do that?" a soft voice asked.

"Oh—Delilah—I thought you left."

"No—why would I leave after brave Samson outran a train and risked his life to get my favorite kind of pizza?"

He laughed. "Where were you?"

"Katie and I went over to the restrooms for a moment," she said.

She opened the box and pulled out a slice. He could see her hold it up and take a bite, silhouetted by the light of the volleyball courts. He wished he could see her pretty face better, but her outline proved to be enough to keep him totally focused.

"I brought us a bottle of Cherry Coke, but we'll have to share it. I didn't bring any glasses," he said.

He unscrewed the lid, and it popped and fizzed. She sat on top of the picnic table and devoured a piece of pizza while he watched.

"Aren't you going to eat any?" she asked. "Or do you just throw pizza at trees?"

Dave's laugh echoed in the wooded area. "You are one sassy girl."

She dropped her piece of pizza on the table. "Is that what you think?"

"Yeah—but I like it." He pulled two pieces out of the box and started eating them as one. With a mouthful of pizza, he asked, "Is this pop okay? Or should I sneak into the enemy camp and steal Delilah a can of beer?"

Her silhouette took the two-liter bottle of pop and tipped it high. He could hear her lips suction off the mouth of the bottle and she set it down.

"Thanks for offering—but this is fine," she said and then let out a loud belch.

They both laughed.

"I'm glad you didn't leave," Dave said. "I thought you stood me up when I came back and couldn't see you anywhere."

She pushed on his shoulder. "I would've gave you a hug when I saw how sad you were, but I didn't want to make you cry."

"I seriously was about ready to start crying," he said. "But—it would've been worth it to get another hug outta you."

She giggled and threw her crust at the same tree Dave hit with a whole piece of pizza.

"Don't you like the crust?" he asked.

"I love it!" she paused for effect, "I was just imitating you having a temper tantrum."

He gave her shoulder another nudge, enjoying every touch between them.

She asked, "Why do you and all of your buddies have your hair so short?"

He rubbed a hand over his buzzed head. "I know—it looks goofy, but we all shaved our heads to support one of our coaches that is going through chemotherapy."

Dave took a long drink from the bottle and attempted to match her belch.

She laughed and then said in a whisper, "I like your hair that way, if that's why you did it."

They barely finished their pizza before Katie came over and announced, "It's time to go, Delilah. We'd better get back before my parents start worrying about us."

Dave stood up. "Can you girls come back tomorrow? Saturday evenings are really fun here—there's usually a really big crowd of kids from all over."

Delilah watched Katie for an answer.

"We'll try," Katie said. "But we can't be out too late because Delilah has been staying at my house, and she's supposed to go home tomorrow night."

"Okay—thanks!" Dave held out the pizza box. "Katie, do you want a piece of pizza?"

She took the last piece, and the girls headed off through the trees. Dave watched Delilah's outline as she went. When she got to the lit-up area near the volleyball courts, she turned and waved, as if she knew he had been watching her. When he couldn't see her anymore, he walked over and picked up the piece of pizza he had thrown at the tree, and her crust, and ate them both.

CHAPTER TEN

The Mountain Song

The same road that curved and coiled like a snake in Wisconsin unfurled and slowly became a straight line in Iowa. After gliding over so many rolling hills, at first the wide-open fields seemed to stretch out for miles with only a few farmsteads in sight at any given moment. Delilah read from her book, nibbled on her fingernails and wiggled her toes. Earl watched for horses and wiggled his loose tooth with his tongue.

All at once, Delilah stopped reading, set the book down, and folded her arms. Dave thought she was mad at first. He looked away from the road and noticed a tear trickling down her cheek.

He let her have some quiet time before he broke the silence. "It's almost noon. Would you and Earl like to stop pretty soon and get something to eat?"

"Yes," Earl answered.

Dave raised an eyebrow at Delilah. "Does he understand my English?"

"Not unless you don't want him to," Delilah said, and giggled.

Dave took the next exit and asked, "What would you two like to eat?"

"We brought some food along with us," Delilah said.

"McDonalds," Earl answered.

Delilah chided him in their own language.

Dave guessed what she was saying. He announced, "I'm taking Earl into McDonalds. You can come in with us if you want."

"We don't want to spend the money," Delilah explained.

"Please, Delilah, let me take you and Earl to McDonalds. I'm buying. Earl and I really want a burger."

Dave could see her in his peripheral vision, staring at him as though she didn't know how to respond. After a few moments she waved a hand. "Okay, this one time—but that's it."

Dave gave her a smile and met eyes with Earl in the rearview mirror. "You'll need to put your shoes on if we are going inside."

Earl pulled their shoes out of the bag without Delilah translating and pushed hers over the seat. They both pulled their shoes on quickly and popped off their seatbelts as Dave parked the Mustang. Earl retrieved his hat from the back window and pushed a hand on top, forcing it down till his ears bent under the brim. The little guy's shoelaces dragged on the ground as he stepped out onto the parking lot.

Delilah carefully lowered her black bonnet over her white covering and cleared her throat as she knelt to tie his shoes. "Earl hasn't learned to tie his laces yet. We don't wear shoes often." She took Earl's hand, restraining his excitement as they headed inside.

Dave placed his order right away and watched with amusement as Delilah and Earl studied the lit-up menu board for a long time.

Delilah leaned toward Dave and whispered, "Earl is trying to decide if he wants a hamburger or chicken nuggets."

"Tell him not to worry, I'm going to order both for him."

"We don't get to eat at McDonalds often," She explained. "Could I get a chocolate milkshake?"

"Of course you can. Does Earl want one too?" Dave asked.

Delilah spoke tohim and he answered in Pennsylvania Dutch. She winced. "Could he have a hot fudge sundae?"

"Absolutely," Dave answered. He gave the girl at the counter Earl's order and then looked at Delilah, waiting for her. She leaned close to Dave and whispered, "I'd like two fish sandwiches." Dave smiled and passed the order on to the girl at the counter and added, "Give her a large shake and an order of fries too."

When they sat down to eat, Dave had already popped a french fry in his mouth before he realized that Earl and Delilah were sitting with their hands under the table looking at him quietly.

Dave put a few fries back. "Oh, yeah, I guess we need to pray."

Earl had already taken off his hat. He and Delilah bowed their heads and prayed silently.

Dave prayed within his heart, *Dear Lord, please bless these two kind people across from me.* He said "Amen" out loud. They both looked up at Dave and smiled and started eating.

A song came on the radio, and it was so loud that Dave felt self-conscious about it at first. The words to "Ain't No Mountain High Enough" came blaring out of the speaker. By the second verse, Dave couldn't keep himself from singing along. He held up three french fries as though they were a microphone. Delilah and Earl smiled and continued eating while watching him perform.

Delilah ate her two sandwiches right up and most of her fries. When her milkshake was about two-thirds gone, she passed it to Dave. "Oh, please finish this. I can't."

Dave held out a hand in protest. "You can take it with you."

"No, it will be all melted before I could take another drink." She pushed it closer to Dave and nodded for him to take it.

Dave shrugged and took a long drag out of the straw while she watched him.

She smiled and said, "It's good, huh?"

He nodded. "Delicious."

As they headed out, Dave held the door for an older lady.

The lady leaned closer as she walked by. "You have a really nice little family."

Dave quickly corrected her, "I'm just their driver."

Delilah added, "He's our cousin."

"I'm a distant cousin," Dave said.

They headed out to get into Dave's Mustang. Earl hurried ahead and stopped to point at the Mustang emblem again. He jabbered in his German-sounding language.

Delilah smiled and said to Dave, "Earl likes your 'horse car.' "

Dave gave Earl a wink and a thumbs-up and they climbed in. When they were driving down the highway again, an awkward silence returned between the passengers. Delilah sank back into her reading.

Earl broke the tension. "I liked that mountain song." The little boy's accent put such a twist on his words that Dave presumed he was still speaking in Pennsylvania Dutch.

He nudged Delilah with his elbow. "What did Earl say?"

"He likes that song about a mountain that we heard in the McDonalds store."

"Oh, I could play that on my phone if he wants to hear it again." Dave checked Delilah's face for permission.

She asked, "How would Earl hear it on your phone?"

"I have Bluetooth in this car. We can stream it," Dave said and glanced to see her reaction.

Delilah's face went blank. "Blue teeth?"

"I'll show you what I mean," Dave said. He spoke into his phone, "Play, 'Ain't No Mountain High Enough.' " Instantly the drumbeat began. Dave couldn't keep himself from singing along. He feigned singing to Delilah easily, as he really wanted to sing it to her. She turned red and tilted her face away as her lips curled into a smile.

"Is that good?" Dave asked while looking at Earl's face in his rearview mirror. The little man nodded, all his teeth showing with a big grin.

Delilah answered, "Yes, he wants to hear it again!"

They listened to Marvin Gaye sing the same song over and over for the next twenty minutes. By the time they were done, they had gotten almost all of the words down. Dave sang along with Marvin Gaye and Delilah along with Tammi Terrell. Earl sat in the back with his little bowl haircut, smiling from ear to ear.

"I wanna play another song for you," Dave said. He tapped on his phone screen. "Play, 'Hey There Delilah.' " Softer sounding music began to pour out of his car speakers. A tear came to his eye as usual. The song reminded him of the first Delilah he got to know. Dave glanced over at her while the song played, and she was blushing.

She did a double take. "What's the matter?"

"I just got something in my eye, I guess."

It almost felt unfaithful to share the song with another Delilah, and he almost resented her for stealing his affection. Then he reminded himself that the first Delilah would be in another relationship for sure. As cute and outgoing as she had been, boys would be swarming around her like bees to honey.

After things grew quiet again, Delilah asked, "Are you embarrassed to be related to us?"

Dave looked away from the road and focused on her. "Why would you think that?"

She shrugged. "You made sure that woman knew we weren't first cousins."

"Oh, that." Dave cleared his throat. "I don't know why I said that." He felt his ears get hot as her eyes searched him and he watched the road. "I promise I'm not embarrassed of you or Earl," he added. He couldn't say that he didn't want her to think of him as a cousin because he was falling for her like a rock.

Dave drove on for a bit before asking, "I don't even look Amish—do I?"

She giggled and eyed him cautiously. "It's that little beard thingy."

"That's a chinstrap." He pulled on the hairs. "A lot of modern guys are wearing whiskers like this."

It seemed she couldn't keep from smiling. She covered her mouth and giggled out, "It makes you look Amish."

The next fifty miles were spent in competition as Earl and Dave tried to beat each other at shouting "Horse!" when one came into view.

Earl rattled off another long Dutch phrase during a dry spell when they saw no horses.

"What did he say?" Dave asked.

Delilah stopped her reading and set the book down. "He wants me to tell you a story."

"Good idea, Earl. Let's hear it," Dave said and smiled at Delilah.

"It's a story about sheep," she explained, her mouth curling into a grin as usual. "Years ago, before our dad had his accident, we used to have a lot of sheep." Earl bleated from the backseat. Delilah continued, "One time we bought a couple hundred lambs at the sale barn. Our dad was going to fatten them up and resell them. We penned them up in a lot right beside the house. Mom had invited our Bishop and his family over for supper that night." Earl bleated again, and his older sister's face broke into a big smile, but she continued her story. "While we were eating, we had trouble hearing each other because the sheep were so loud."

"Baa! Baa!" Earl sounded from the back.

Delilah was laughing as she finished the story, "We were going to play Dutch Blitz after supper, but our Bishop said, 'We might as well go, since we can't hear a word you are saying!' "

By that time, Earl's variety of bleating sounds were loud, filling up the airspace of Dave's Mustang. All three of them were laughing almost to tears. He concluded they were laughing about how odd it seemed to have a conversation drowned out by sheep, and Earl's effort to imitate that occurrence. Dave, however, laughed at how adorable Delilah acted while telling the story, and at how cute the little Amish boy looked while baaing like a lamb.

When things were quiet again, Dave noticed little Earl's head was nodding. He took the opportunity to ask Delilah about something he didn't want to bring up in front of Earl. "What happened? I mean—how did your dad end up in a wheelchair?"

"A buggy accident," she said matter-of-factly.

"Really, when did that happen?"

"Around the time Earl was born," Delilah answered in her higher-pitched English voice and set down her book. "He was driving down a road near Shipshewana, and a guy in a big truck was trying to pass a tractor on a hill. When he came over the hill, my dad was right there. He hit the horse and killed it instantly, and my dad was thrown out into the ditch." Delilah didn't look at Dave while she told the story; instead, she stared out of the passenger window.

Dave imagined the scene and shook his head. He thought that was all she was going to say, and he didn't dare ask more.

She drew in a long, deep breath. "We Amish don't have insurance. We pay for our own medical bills. Dad was in the hospital for a long time and it cost a lot. We had to sell our farm."

"Didn't that guy driving the truck have insurance?"

Delilah waved a hand. "The man told the police that my dad's horse jumped out in front of him."

Dave shook his head and let out a growl.

Her face twisted in shock. "What was that?"

Dave growled again. "That makes me sick! How could he do that to your family?"

She smoothed a hand over her apron and spoke calmly. "We've forgiven him."

He shook his head and hissed through his teeth. "I can't forgive him. Anyone who brings so much trouble on a kind family like yours should have to pay for what he did!"

She wrinkled her brow and glanced at Dave again before continuing her story. "We are friends with a cop, and he told us that we could get a lawyer and fight it, but we don't believe in that. His insurance payed a little, but we are paying back the rest. Our church helps out too."

Dave glanced up in the mirror and surprised himself with the anger he saw in his own eyes.

Delilah continued with gentle, lilting words. "Mom spent almost all of her time with Dad at the hospital those first months and then she went along with him to rehabilitation." She looked over her shoulder at Earl. "I feel the worst for Earl's sake. He doesn't even know what it was like when my dad could work and play with us. Earl wants to farm with horses, but we had to sell our draft horses after Dad's accident."

Dave revved his engine as he passed a slower-moving car, taking out his frustration on the other driver. "I ought to hire a lawyer to sue that guy and make him pay for what he did."

Delilah stared at Dave. Her kind eyes met his and seemed to pierce his heart. "You need to learn to forgive."

"I don't understand how you can forgive him."

"My grandpa, Earl, was a very wise man and he taught me about forgiveness." She twisted once more to check on the little boy in the backseat. Dave glanced in his rearview mirror and could see little Earl's head dangling as he slept sitting up.

Delilah remained sideways in her seat. "During that time, I really struggled with forgiveness." Her face looked pale as she studied her hands. Her fingers wrestled on her lap. "Grandpa said, 'If you realize that your own sins put Jesus on that cross, then you can forgive others.'"

Dave shook his head. "But you didn't do anything as evil as that guy! He lied about what happened, and it cost your family all that money."

"My sins cost Jesus his life and so did yours," she said. "When you finally see that, you'll be able to forgive others. After all, that man's sins only cost us money."

Dave watched the road for a minute and thought about what she said. He turned back to Delilah and asked. "So, your family doesn't own that farm?"

"No. We had to sell our farm in Indiana." Her face looked pale as she continued. "We rent our house and that chicken building from some relatives."

"Money is huge! Maybe you should reconsider my offer, Delilah." He continued checking her face and the road intermittently. Her head tilted to one side as though she considered his suggestion. He quickly added, "I'd be willing to go in halves with you, girl. I'll split the hundred thousand with ya. This might be a way your family could get out of debt and buy your own place again."

Delilah looked at Dave out of the corner of her eye. "How would my dad feel if I went against everything we believe in to get money?" She looked away. "And besides, it would ruin my life."

"How would it ruin your life?"

She looked Dave in the eyes and he saw sincerity. "I would always be known as, 'That Delilah.'"

Earl smacked his lips, and Dave checked his rearview mirror. The little guy rolled his head the opposite direction. He rubbed his eyes and spoke in his German-sounding language. Delilah gave him a long answer.

Dave turned to Delilah. "What does Earl need?"

"He's fine. He's just saying that he's tired and the seatbelt is cutting into him when he leans one way or the other." She looked at Dave.

He didn't answer but took the next exit.

They pulled into a gas station and Dave announced, "If anyone needs to use the bathroom, now would be a good time."

Dave helped Earl tie his shoes, and they followed Delilah inside. She disappeared into the women's restroom, but the men's bathroom door was locked.

"Someone is in there," Dave whispered, and Earl nodded.

Dave strolled through the station's mini-mart and Earl followed. They spent a few minutes surveying an entire aisle of candy. Earl came to a standstill when his eyes fell upon the Snickers bars. Dave picked up two of them and took them to the front counter. While he paid for them, he noticed Earl looking at a row of magazine covers on a rack near the cash register.

A little Amish boy with suspenders and a broad-brimmed hat looked cute, though out of place, in a mini-mart. Dave looked to see what caught Earl's attention and drew in a quick breath. A scantily dressed woman adorned a magazine cover. She sat in a provocative position and her eyes flirted with whoever looked at the photo. Earl turned to Dave and their eyes met.

"What are you guys doing?" Delilah's voice surprised them both.

Dave swallowed hard and looked at Earl again. "The bathroom was occupied so we looked at the candy aisle for a few moments." He held up the candy bars to clear up any confusion.

Earl nodded his black hat.

She took Earl's hand. "I think the men's room is empty now."

They headed to the restroom and Dave gathered his candy bars and pushed open the glass door, taking in a breath of fresh air.

CHAPTER ELEVEN

Nap Time

Dave pulled his gym bag and pillow from the trunk. Within a few moments, his bag and a blanket had been shaped into a curved formation on the seat beside where Earl had been sitting. He tossed his pillow up front.

Earl came running out of the gas station first. He held onto his black hat and charged at Dave. He didn't slow his churning feet, gaining speed as he got closer. Dave didn't know what else to do but gather him up and swing him around. Earl chortled out a deep belly laugh.

As they came out of the spin, Dave muttered. "I'm surprised your dad was willing to send along his only son."

Earl's brown eyes grew wide and sincere as he spoke in English. "God sent His only Son."

Dave nodded and helped Earl into the backseat, arranging the blanket and duffle bag around the little boy like a nest.

Delilah appeared on the other side of the car and leaned in. "What are you doing?"

"We're gonna fix up a better spot for Earl," Dave said.

Earl smiled and nestled in like a lamb in a pile of straw.

"There, now that mean old seatbelt won't bite so hard," Dave said.

Delilah repeated what Dave said in Pennsylvania Dutch.

Earl chuckled and said, "Thank you, Dave."

"What's this for?" Delilah asked as Dave handed her a pillow.

"That's for you. I saw your head nodding. Take a little nap and you'll feel better when you wake up."

"Thank you, I am getting a little tired." Delilah carefully unpinned her crisp white head covering and put the straight pins back into the stiff, see-through material. She gently placed it in a round, plastic ice cream bucket.

Dave watched. "What are you doing?"

She glanced at Dave. "I washed this bucket thoroughly and brought it along as a safe place to store my covering and keep it from being smashed."

Delilah leaned over and set the bucket on the empty seat near Earl. After fluffing up Dave's pillow, she laid it against the window and tucked her legs up under her long blue dress. She straightened out her white apron to keep the pleats from getting wrinkled. In a short time, sounds of heavy breathing and deep sleep came from the backseat. Dave looked at Earl's chubby cheeks in his rearview mirror. With his bowl-cut hair and suspenders, the little Amish boy looked like a painting of Little Boy Blue fast asleep in the hay.

He let his eyes fall on Delilah, curled up beside him. He noticed a tiny mole on her neck where her long hair ended, and dainty, shorter strands curled. His gaze followed the line from her shoulder to her narrow waist. From there the line curved toward her hip, and he scolded himself silently. She sat up with a jerk, and he quickly averted his eyes. She took ahold of her seatbelt and wrestled with it as if trying to stretch it out.

"There's a lever on the far side that will lower the back of your seat," Dave said.

She leaned forward and reached below. The release bar let out a pop and her seat lurched back until it reached its limit and stopped with a bang, tossing her head back against the headrest. "Oh no—did I break something?"

"No!" Dave sputtered as he tried to hold back a laugh. "There's another lever down beyond your hip. Pull that, and the back of the seat will lay down."

She fumbled around for a moment until the back of her seat moved slightly.

Dave reached over with his right elbow, pushing against the seat. "Pull that lever again." He felt the seat give and he pushed until her seat leaned back fully. "There, now you'll be more comfortable."

Delilah turned on the seat until she faced Dave and placed the pillow between them. She tucked her legs back under her dress again and replayed the routine of smoothing out her apron. She nestled into Dave's pillow. He glanced at her.

Her dark eyes met his. "Thank you, Dave."

"No problem."

The Mustang raced smoothly along the highway. Dave focused on his driving and checked his rearview mirror occasionally. He tried to be polite and give her privacy while she rested, but he couldn't keep from occasionally stealing a glance at her.

He studied her dark brown hair wound into a bun. She lay on the seat beside him like a sleeping princess. He smiled as the sound of her breathing deepened and he noticed the curve of her outline again, then scolded himself. *How could anyone look at a girl like Delilah that way?* He tried to focus on the road and then caught himself still eyeing her curves.

Dave drove for quite a stretch, listening to the sound of Delilah and Earl's slumbering breaths. He glanced over at her frequently, and at one point he suddenly realized her eyes were open and she returned his gaze. He quickly averted his focus back to the road.

"What about you?" she asked.

"Me what?"

She didn't lift her head from the pillow, but said, "Tell me more about you."

Dave lifted his fingers without removing his thumbs from the steering wheel. "There's not much to tell. I just finished college up at Rapid City, and I've been trying to save up money to start a restaurant in my home area. I studied business in college. There's an awesome sub-sandwich shop up in Rapid City. It seems like it would be really nice to have my own business, and I want to start up my own sandwich shop."

"I . . . see . . . I'm sorry I messed up your chances to get that money," Delilah said and stared at Dave as if trying to read how he felt.

He shook his head. "It's okay. And, it's not too late if you change your mind."

She waved a hand. "There's no way I could do that even though we really do need the money."

"That's what my mom told me," he said.

"Your mom must know something about us Amish."

"Yeah, you remember me saying her grandparents were Amish and she still has a lot of relatives and friends that are Amish? But I told her that all of the girls I know, would be thrilled to be on a magazine cover."

Delilah bit her thumbnail for a moment, deep in thought. "Do those girls know that little boys will see those magazine covers?"

"Oh, like the one Earl saw in the gas station?"

She nodded with a sweet concern on her face.

"I doubt those girls thought about it at the time." He glanced at her and she nodded. He continued, "They get caught up in all the compliments the photographers are giving them, and all the money they'll make and forget about who will see the pictures."

"That's another reason I can't let them take my picture. It might make me vain." Her innocent eyes met his. "Maybe I'd fall into bad things too. If I made lots of money, I might get greedy."

"You're a long way off from that," he said. "You're the most humble girl I know."

"Do you have a girlfriend?" she asked.

"Something bad happened between me and a girl in high school, and I haven't dated much since."

She didn't respond. Dave glanced over to see if she was asleep. He could see her eyelashes moving.

He whispered, "How about you?"

"Do you mean boys?"

"Yeah, do you have your eyes on a certain guy?" Dave asked.

Delilah covered her face with one hand.

"You don't have to answer that," He said with a laugh.

She looked out her side window. "There was a boy I was interested in once. My parents didn't feel good about it, and they kept me from seeing him."

Dave felt a twinge of jealousy as he imagined a handsome young Amish man, strong as a bull and kind to boot.

She wrinkled up her nose with a smile. "Since then, I haven't had much time for boys."

"What do you mean?"

"Well, around the time I could start going to the young folks' gatherings, Dad had his accident. Mom stayed with him at the hospital, and I needed to take care of my younger sisters and Earl, so I didn't go to the singings and things. I didn't really feel like it anyway. Our whole family was sad and worried about Dad. That was about all we could think of. When I did start to go to singings, a lot of couples had paired off already and nobody really ever asked me to date."

"What?" Dave said loudly, and then looked into the rearview mirror to see if he'd disturbed Earl. He started his sentence over with a softer voice. "What? Isn't that ridiculous. Here you are, famous all over America, and boys in your own backyard aren't smart enough to ask you on a date."

"I'm not famous. That's the Delilah in the book, not the real person," she said as though she really believed what she was saying.

"Nope, it *is* you," Dave argued. "I've read that book, and I've been around you for a couple of days. The book describes you perfectly. It's you they all adore. I haven't had anyone offer me money to find Samson. Nobody is looking for him. Everyone wants to meet Delilah." He looked to see her reaction.

She covered her face with both hands. "Stop," she said, "you're embarrassing me."

"You remind me of Princess Di," Dave said.

"Princess who?"

"Princess Diana, of England. Everyone in the whole world loved her and thought she was about the nicest, prettiest girl ever. The only one that didn't love her was her own husband, Prince Charles."

"Maybe he knew the real Di. Maybe she wasn't as nice in real life?"

"No, I don't believe that," Dave argued. "She was in the media spotlight for years. If she wasn't a really nice woman, everyone would have figured it out. Plus, you could see how kind she was in her eyes, just like you. And you are just like that. Boys all over the whole country would love to take you on a date, and the boys who live near you don't have enough sense to see it."

She held up a hand toward him. "Stop, please don't keep on complimenting me. The way I grew up, we don't go around giving compliments. We don't believe in it. It makes people vain."

"Well, maybe that is why you are so nice?" He bit his lip for a moment. "Oops—sorry—I didn't mean to give you another compliment. I'm just saying—growing up like you did is probably why you are like you are. I hope this book thing doesn't change you."

She played with her fingers on her lap. "I did think about giving up on myself for my family's sake."

"What do you mean by that?"

"Maybe I should let you tell your boss where I am, even if it ruins my life. Then at least my parents would have the money they need. Do you think I should do that?" She looked at Dave and raised her eyebrows.

Dave glanced at her for a moment. "It wouldn't necessarily ruin your life. Why do you think that having a few pictures taken and talking to news people would be a problem? Maybe it wouldn't be that bad?"

She shook her head. "You need to learn to understand Amish people. Before you came to Falls, I had heard of this Delilah and thought she must be some fancy Amish girl who fought all the rules and wanted attention."

Dave leaned over to make eye contact. "But that wasn't true at all."

She made a coy face. "I know, but that is what it would seem like to other Amish people. I'm afraid that it is already too late for me. Everywhere I go among the Amish, people will say, 'There is that Delilah.' If I let people take my picture and put it on magazines, they will think that I wanted all the attention. That is not okay with us. We believe that it's important to avoid giving ourselves to pride."

He scratched his scruffy chin. "I hope I didn't mess up your life by bringing the media to you."

Delilah examined her fingernails and let out a sigh. "I had troubles before you came around."

Dave cocked his head and tried to get her to meet his eyes. She continued looking at her fingers while Dave alternated between watching the road and trying to read her expression.

She didn't look up at him as she quoted Proverbs 16:18–19: "Pride goeth before destruction, and an haughty spirit before a fall. Better it is to be of an humble spirit with the lowly, than to divide the spoil with the proud."

Dave didn't reply. He wasn't sure what to say.

CHAPTER TWELVE

The Phone

"What happened to Princess Di?" Delilah asked.
"I hate to tell you." Dave winced. "Her driver was trying to outrun the paparazzi, and he was going over a hundred miles per hour when they crashed."

Delilah started biting her fingernails again. She returned his gaze with a troubled look and said, "Please don't drive that fast if they catch up with us."

"I won't." He assured her.

"Could I look at your phone?" Delilah asked.

"Sure, have you looked at a cell phone before?"

She nodded. "Yes, but only once."

"You have to type in my password, it's just 5555," Dave explained and watched her try it.

"Oops, I think I made a mistake." A moment later she said, "Hello."

He wondered if she called someone she knew.

She shook her head and looked at the phone. "No, this is Delilah." Dave looked at her to see what was going on. She listened to a person talking on the other end and then wrinkled her forehead. "Where are we, Dave?" she asked.

"Why, who wants to know?"

"Some guy named Charlie Rose." She passed the phone to Dave.

Dave winced. "Hello, Charlie?"

"You found the girl, huh?" Charlie shouted.

"Um, yeah, I guess."

"Thanks for letting me know right away like you promised," he yelled. Dave held the phone away from his ear and mouthed the word, "Ouch."

"When were you planning to call?" Charlie asked.

Dave shrugged. "At least I got her away from all your competition."

"You haven't answered my question. Why didn't you call me when you found her?"

"Well—Delilah isn't sure about letting everyone know who she is. You need to understand that she is Amish. They have a different view on life than most people."

"Offer her some money!"

Dave eyed Delilah. "We will talk about it and get back with you."

Charlie hung up.

Delilah shrugged her own shoulders as if mimicking him and looked at Dave out of the corner of her eye. "Sorry about that."

"It's not your fault, Delilah, He's been trying to call me all day and you just happened to touch the phone when it was ringing."

"I . . . see . . . I never even heard your phone ring," Delilah said.

"I turned off the sound when I got to your parents' house. I don't need to talk to anyone anyway." He tried to make eye contact with her. "You think about the money. I can still call Charlie and set up a time and place to meet if you decide that's what you want to do."

"It's doing that vibrate thing again," Delilah said.

"What does the screen say?" Dave asked, "Is it Charlie again?"

"It says Mom," Delilah answered slowly.

"Oh, it's just my mother. I'm not talking to her right now."

"What? If it's your mother you should answer right away," Delilah said. She tapped the screen. "Hello, this is Delilah." She listened for a moment and then looked over. "Dave is busy driving. Do you want me to give him a message?"

Dave smirked at Delilah.

She giggled. "Okay—okay, I will." Delilah peeked over at Dave and wrinkled up her nose with a smile. "Yes, I've already seen that—yes, he is. Okay—I'll tell him. It was nice to talk to you too. Bye."

Dave scrunched up his brow. "What was all of that about?"

She smiled coyly. "Your mom was wondering if you are being nice to Earl and me."

"What did you tell her?'

"I just said, 'Okay.' "

Dave lifted his hands off the wheel. "What, why did you say that? Now she is going to get after me."

"Well, you should answer the phone when your mom calls," she retorted.

"You know how moms are. She worries too much." Dave looked at her and grimaced. "Besides, you don't even believe in phones. Why would you get after me for not answering?"

"I didn't say that I don't believe in phones. And, if I knew my mother was calling me, I'd answer the phone. Moms only worry because they love their children so much."

She fumbled through her old-looking black purse and pulled out a container. "Your mom asked me if I have any aloe vera."

"No—she did not!"

They rode in silence for a few moments. Delilah turned to Dave and asked, "Do you have any brothers or sisters?"

"Nope—it's just me."

"No wonder she worries about you. Mothers worry about their children by nature—and you're all she's got."

Dave glanced at Earl in the rearview mirror. The little boy's innocent eyes returned a questioning look. A pang swelled in Dave's heart. He didn't know why for sure. Maybe looking into those honest eyes brought truth to the surface. A truth that Dave had practiced ignoring and denying.

Earl let out a moan and spoke in Pennsylvania Dutch.

Dave turned to Delilah. "What'd Earl say?"

"He says that his tummy feels icky."

Earl's face seemed pale when Dave checked it in his mirror. "I'll stop at the next exit and let him get out for a minute. This has been a long drive for such a little guy."

She nodded. "Amish children often get sick when riding in cars— they're just not used to it."

Earl moaned, "I need to cutz."

Delilah frantically sorted through her bag of things she kept near her feet.

"Does he have to go potty?" Dave asked.

Earl coughed and gagged.

Dave and Delilah bumped heads as they both turned to check on Earl. The little boy leaned forward as far as his seatbelt allowed and threw up into a small white bucket.

Dave relaxed and faced the road again. "Wow—that was lucky. Where did he get that little ice cream bucket?"

"It's the one with my coverings in it," Delilah moaned. "Remember that I took it off so I wouldn't smash it while I napped? I should have put it right back on when I woke up."

"Do you have a spare?" Dave looked to see her reaction.

She pulled her hand slowly across her forehead. "Yeah—but it was in that bucket too."

She reached back and handed Earl a napkin. Earl wiped his mouth and said a cute little, "I'm sorry," in English.

Dave watched Delilah as she bit her own lip. He asked, "What will you do?"

"I have a headscarf along, but I never wear that except for around the farm." She picked up her black bonnet. "I can wear this if we get out of the car."

She started fidgeting with the pleats on her apron. Delilah turned to face Dave when she realized he was watching her. "I'm worried about what my aunt will think when I tell her that I took my covering off."

Dave didn't have any suggestions to give her about that. He lifted his water bottle from the cup holder. "Maybe Earl would like a drink?"

Earl and Delilah had a short conversation in their native language as she passed the water to him and brought the empty bottle back up front.

Dave glanced at Earl and then Delilah. "Is he gonna be okay?"

"He's fine. He is just saying that he's still feeling icky."

"I'm going to stop at the next exit so Earl can get out of the car for a bit," Dave said.

Delilah snapped a plastic lid on and lifted the little bucket. "I'd better try and rinse off these coverings."

When they stopped at a gas station, Dave unbuckled his seat belt and started to get out.

"Wait!" Delilah ordered. "Your mother asked me to give you this aloe vera for your sunburn."

Dave unbuttoned his top button. "Okay—this is a little embarrassing."

She handed him her container of aloe vera, and he tried spreading some on his back through the top of his shirt collar.

"Unbutton that shirt and I'll do it," Delilah said.

"No—I'm fine!"

She met his eyes and raised her brow. "Unbutton your shirt."

Dave slowly complied. He lowered his shirt with his back toward her.

"Oh my—your back is bright red!" She smoothed aloe vera over his shoulders and exclaimed, "It's so hot to the touch too!"

He didn't comment, but he couldn't help enjoying how nice it felt to have a cool gel smoothed over his sunburnt back by her soft hands.

"Thanks," he said.

"Thank your mother," she answered.

Dave buttoned up his shirt and helped Earl tie his shoes again. Delilah tied on a headscarf and placed her black bonnet on over that. She toted her little ice cream pale in with her and headed into the women's restroom. Dave helped Earl push open the door to the men's room and waited for them by the doors.

Delilah came out first and tilted the ice cream bucket, showing the coverings to Dave.

"I don't know, Delilah, they look kinda yellow to me," Dave said.

"I . . . see," she said. Her nose wrinkled with a smile. She placed the plastic bucket in a nearby trash can.

A teenage girl, who had been filling up a cup with pop, stopped short when Delilah said those words. "Are you Delilah?"

"Yes," Delilah nodded her black bonnet. "How do you know me?"

"From the book," she exclaimed.

Earl stepped out of the bathroom and Dave said, "We're over here, Earl."

"And this is Earl?" the girl's face broke into a huge smile. "He's so cute! Just how I imagined he'd be." Earl hid behind Dave's legs and peeked at the girl. She turned and scrutinized Dave. "But you're not Samson, are you?"

"Maybe I am," Dave teased.

The teenage girl shook her long hair. "No, you're too tall and thin to be a Samson."

Dave rolled his eyes and let his mouth fall into an offended frown. Delilah and the girl both laughed. He wondered if the girl realized that she had entered into the storyline and had fulfilled a scene from the book, *Samson and Delilah*.

"It was sure nice to meet you," the girl said to Delilah. She bent down and shook Earl's hand. "And it was nice to meet you too, Earl."

Earl noticed a toy section in the store as they passed through. He picked up a clear bag full of plastic horses and showed it to Delilah.

"Un fa shdendich—there are lots of horses in there," she said.

Earl chuckled and put the bag back where he found it. Dave retrieved it and took it to the counter. Delilah gave him a questioning look. Dave explained, "I like to buy something when I use the restrooms at a gas station."

"I'll pay for it," she said, opening her purse with frayed edges.

Dave watched as she withdrew a tiny coin purse and open it with a snap. He could see a few wrinkled bills and a couple coins. She looked at them carefully as if calculating.

"Please— Delilah— we're going to be at your aunt's house soon. I'd like to buy Earl a little something."

Delilah and Earl headed out while Dave paid the cashier. He noticed a rack with purses and handbags a few steps from the counter. "Eh—just a second," he said, and found a pretty black handbag about the size of Delilah's worn-out purse. He laid it on the counter and bought it along with the horses.

When he met them at the Mustang, Dave said, "I'm afraid you're not going to be able to go anywhere without people knowing who you are."

"Maybe you shouldn't call me by name when we're in public?"

He opened the passenger door for her and the rear door for Earl. "I guess you're right. I should've thought of that."

When they got situated, Delilah took off her black bonnet. Dave took a moment to admire how she looked in a headscarf. Her eyes sparkled chocolate brown. He wondered if the scarf made her more attractive, or if her simple beauty had merely grown on him.

She noticed him staring at her and asked, "What?"

"I just realized your eyes are coffee-colored like in the book."

Her mouth turned down in the corners. "I . . . see. You just now noticed my eyes?"

"I just noticed the color now," he said and winced. "Can I give this to Earl now?" Dave held up the plastic bag full of horses and Delilah nodded.

"Un fa shdendich!" popped out of Earl's mouth.

Dave and Delilah looked at each other and laughed.

"What do you say?" Delilah asked.

Earl held up his bag of horses. "Thank you!"

Dave drew out the little handbag and said, "And, I thought you might like this."

Delilah's eyes almost looked fearful. "I can't take that."

"Don't you like it?" Dave studied her face to see what the problem might be. "Is it not in line with your church rules for some reason?"

"I like it," she said. A tear appeared in the corner of her eye. "You should be more careful with your money."

"Please, take it. My dad once told me that the best use of money is to be giving."

She nodded, held the new purse in her hands for a long time, and ran her fingers over the smooth leather. She took everything out of her old purse and carefully placed it all inside her new one.

Earl talked in long Dutch phrases as his little herd of plastic horses romped across his legs and over the backseat of the Mustang. Whinnying noises rose along with snorts and clicking hoof sounds for miles and miles. Delilah continued reading from her book.

She set the book down at one point and looked at Dave with a slanted brow. "Does it seem funny to you how much this book is like the trip we are on?"

Dave laughed awkwardly. "Yeah—it is a little. But you'll be at your aunt's house soon, and that's where the comparison will end."

She nodded. "My aunt's house is only a few miles from here." Delilah turned her face slightly toward the back. "Earl, you need to put your horses back into their bag and get your shoes on. We are almost there."

Dave looked at Earl in the rearview mirror. He smiled as the little guy quickly gathered his herd of plastic horses.

"Tell me when to turn," Dave said.

"Turn here, quick!" Delilah shouted.

Dave braked and rounded the corner at the same time. As soon as the Mustang came out of its slide, he looked at Delilah and asked, "What happened? Did we almost miss our turn?"

"No, that's my aunt's house over there across the field," Delilah whispered. She pointed across an open field at a white farm house behind a road lined with news vehicles with large dish antennas. Delilah's face was as white as the house.

"Oh Delilah, I am so sorry about this. What are we going to do?"

"Just drive!" she shouted. "Here they come!"

CHAPTER THIRTEEN

Smokers

D ave stomped on the gas pedal, and the Mustang fishtailed on gravel until the tires met the road. Earl
laughed. Delilah held onto the sides of her seat. Dave
gripped the steering wheel with both hands, gritting his teeth
and pursing his lips.

The Mustang's tires squealed the moment they hit pavement
again. Delilah thrust one arm over the top of her seat, twisting
enough to see behind them. "They are catching up with us!"

"Hold on!" Dave yelled. He punched his throttle again, and the Mustang roared over a set of railroad tracks, bouncing all three occupants vigorously.

Earl's deep chuckle filled the car. He didn't stop laughing as he jabbered something in Pennsylvania Dutch. Delilah quickly interpreted, "Earl says, 'This horse car is fast!' "

Dave couldn't help laughing to himself as they rounded a curve and all three of them leaned left and then swung right. He revved the Mustang's powerful engine, throwing all three of them back against their seats. A van with a huge dish on top loomed in Dave's rearview mirror.

"They can't catch our horse car!" Dave shouted, "Hang on— I'm gonna have to lose this van that's following us."

Delilah gasped. "How are you gonna do that?"

Dave glanced at her for a split second and smirked. "Something I learned in high school. We called it a fox and hound loop. I'm gonna take four left turns."

Dave turned left onto the next gravel road they came to. The Mustang fishtailed furiously as Dave punched the accelerator to the floor, leaving the large van in a cloud of dust. Earl's chuckle rose from the backseat as they bounced over a small hill. Loose gravel rolled under the wheels, creating the same effect as a million marbles on a roadway. The Mustang swayed back and forth as Dave suddenly spotted a stop sign and an intersection coming up quickly. Glancing to his left, Dave realized a huge tractor filled the road, heading straight toward the intersection. He made a split-second decision to veer right, barely squeezing between the oncoming tractor and the stop sign on the right.

"Whew, that was close!" Delilah muttered, holding onto the dashboard and looking behind them. "I thought you were going to take four left turns?"

"That tractor changed my mind," Dave stated. "I think that camera crew will get stuck behind the tractor for a while, and we'll take another right and get back on the main road."

Unfortunately, there wasn't another right for several miles. Dave checked his rear-view mirror for any sign of the van. A cloud of dust billowed out behind the Mustang, limiting his vision. The next opportunity to turn right came up as they passed over a hill, revealing that they would have to cross a bridge just after the turn. Dave opted to speed past that intersection as well.

He glanced at Delilah. "I have another idea."

She met his eyes and shook her head, smirking. "I wonder why."

A short way ahead stood a field entrance with a few trees. Dave swung the Mustang between the gates and pulled right sharply, coming to a stop under one of the trees.

He nodded with a smile. "We'll sit still here for a while and those camera guys won't be sure where we went."

Dave shut down his engine and they sat quietly as if they might give away their location if they spoke. Dust stirred up by the Mustang settled, and the road seemed empty. Sunlight flittered across the windshield as a slight breeze moved through the leafy branches above them.

Earl whispered in Dutch.

Delilah unbuckled her seatbelt. She turned and knelt on her seat, leaning over the armrest between her and Dave, and unbuckled Earl.

Dave asked, "What's going on?"

"Earl needs to step outside for a moment."

"Oh, okay. I get it," Dave said.

Earl gathered his hat from the back window and popped it on his head.

Delilah suddenly untwisted, clipping Dave's chin with her elbow.

His head flung back. "Ouch!"

She reached over and touched Dave's hand as he rubbed his chin. "I'm so sorry!"

"It's okay, really. It just surprised me."

Delilah took her hand back and rubbed her elbow. "If it makes you feel any better, your chin got me in the funny bone."

Dave felt his stomach shake before he allowed the laughter to escape his lips. She began giggling as she held her elbow and continued rubbing it. Earl managed the car door by himself. His little hat passed by the car hood, and he pushed through some tall grasses toward the trees.

Dave let his face become sober. "I'm so sorry we had to race away from your aunt's house."

"It's not your fault," she said.

He tilted his head in the direction where Earl had disappeared. "I feel so bad for Earl. There's no way he can understand what's going on with those camera men."

She shook her head. "He gets it. He knows they want to take my picture and understands that we left home to keep them from doing it. It's part of our faith, and he understands that."

Earl reemerged from behind the tree. He ran toward the car and knocked on Dave's window. "Those men!" He pointed through the trees.

"Quick, get in the car," Dave ordered.

Earl struggled to open the door. Dave jumped out and flung the door open, hoisting Earl inside. Delilah and Earl rattled back and forth in Pennsylvania Dutch words while Dave shoved his keys into the ignition.

Delilah grabbed Dave's arm. "Wait—don't start it yet."

He kept his key in place and questioned Delilah. "What? Why?"

"Earl says their van is broke down and they are trying to fix it."

Dave let his lips curl into a sinister grin. "Perfect. Let's get outta here while they are stuck."

She cocked her head to one side. "Maybe we should help them?"

"Are you serious?" Dave searched her face. "After all the trouble they've caused us, you want to help them?"

Her eyebrows raised sympathetically. "They're stuck way out here in the middle of nowhere and you're just gonna drive off without helping?"

"They have cell phones. Let them call their friends."

Delilah sat and stared at him until he felt ashamed.

Dave drew in a deep breath. "Okay, I'll take a look."

He slipped out of his car door and snuck to the place where Earl had been a few moments ago. Peering around a tree, he could see the big van with a dish on top sat near the bridge. A heavyset guy with a beard yelled at a skinny little man while he tried to get a tire from under his vehicle.

"What's the matter with you Joe? Don't you know how to change a flat tire?"

"I've never done it!" the littler man growled back. "Why don't you do it, if you're so smart?"

" 'Cause, I've got a bad back!" he shouted, "You know that!"

Dave watched with amusement. He couldn't help letting out a chuckle. Just then he felt someone touch his back, causing him to jump.

"Sorry. I didn't mean to scare you," Delilah said. "C'mon, let's go help them."

"Okay, *I'll* go help them—only if you and Earl stay here."

She wrinkled her brow. "Why?"

He shook his head. "Because, they'll take our help and our pictures."

"They wouldn't do that if we helped them."

Dave took a deep breath and scratched his head. "Delilah, you trust people way too much. I'll go and see if they need help—only if you promise to stay here with Earl."

"Okay, we'll stay here." She smiled and pointed to the Mustang.

Dave headed around the trees and through the gate. Gravel poked through dirt on the road and pressed into the bottoms of his shoes. A puff of dust rose from every footstep as He jogged toward the truck. Curse words grew louder as Dave drew near the van.

The heavyset guy with a beard shouted, "What's wrong with you, Joe? It's simple, just put that jack under there and turn the handle!"

"I'm trying," Joe whined.

The bigger man hunched over and wiped sweat from his forehead. "No! Move that jack further back!"

Joe sat up and hit his head on the bumper. "Ouch! If you're so good at it, get down here and do it yourself!"

The heavy man put his hand on his lower back and winced. "I would but my back is killing me!"

Dave trotted up and asked, "Do you guys need help?"

The big man twisted in surprise and shouted, "Ouch!"

Joe, the skinny man, sat up and hit his head on the bumper again. "Oh—crap that hurt!"

"Sorry guys." Dave raised both hands. "I didn't mean to startle ya. Can I give ya a hand with that flat tire?"

Joe shook his head. "I don't need any help. I've got this!"

The big guy wiped his hand on his pants and held it out for a handshake. "Hello, my name is Moe, and this is Joe." He pointed to the man on the ground. "Joe definitely needs your help."

"No, I don't!" Joe insisted with his whiney voice as he wiggled under the van on his back.

Dave shook hands with Moe. "Your friend has the jack upside down."

Moe kicked Joe in the seat of his pants. "Quit rolling around on the ground and get outta the way."

Joe rolled onto his stomach, rose up onto his knees, and brushed himself off. Dust billowed in a cloud.

Moe coughed and swung his hat to fan away the dust. "Get away from me if you're gonna brush yourself off!"

Dave flipped the jack upright and slid it under the van. He picked up the tire iron Joe left lieing in the dust and popped off the hubcap from a completely flat tire. "You have to loosen the nuts before jacking up the van."

"I knew that," Joe wailed.

Dave loosened the nuts and asked without looking up, "Where is your spare tire?"

Joe patted Moe's stomach. "We keep it around Moe's waist." He laughed at his own joke.

Moe slapped Joe's hands away and shouted, "Go get him the spare tire and quit messing around!"

Dave spun the jack handle after he loosened all five nuts. He pulled the flat tire loose and took the donut tire from Joe and pushed it onto the lugs. "You won't be able to drive as fast with this donut on your van."

"You're just saying that because you don't want us to catch up with ya," Moe said. "I know who you are."

Dave shrugged. "You can try to catch up with me if you want, but I'm telling you, you'll kill yourself if you go more than fifty with this donut on that big van." Dave looked at them. "Which one of you guys just finished smoking a cigarette?"

"We don't either of us smoke," Moe said.

Dave wrinkled his nose. "Don't you guys smell it?"

They both shook their heads and Joe sniffed his own shirt. "It's probably in my clothes, my wife smokes like a chimney."

"Really?" Moe asked, with a belly laugh, "My wife does too!"

Joe still worked at brushing off his pants, but he stopped long enough to ask, "Where are you hiding that Delilah, anyway?"

"Look guys," Dave pleaded as he stood up, "leave that poor girl alone. She is so nice she made me come and help you with your tire. The least you can do is leave her alone!"

Moe took the flat tire from Dave's hands. "We'll leave her alone alright—as soon as we get a few good pictures!"

Dave took off running and jumped the fence instead of taking the road. As he ran through the field he could hear Moe yelling at Joe.

"Don't try chasing him, Joe! C'mon get in the van. Let's get turned around before he gets to his Mustang!"

Soybeans slowed Dave's progress a little until he found he could run between rows. He headed for the clump of trees where he had left Delilah and Earl in the Mustang. He puffed as he ran but still heard the van start up over his heavy panting. Just as he got near the trees, he saw Delilah stand up and run to the car.

"Quick, get ready," Dave shouted, "Those guys are heading this way!"

Both Delilah and Earl had their seatbelts on when Dave jumped in and started his engine with a roar. He threw the shifter in reverse and they all rocked in their seats. A moment later, Dave had the Mustang charging away from the media van on gravel roads again.

Dave glanced at Delilah for a split second. "What were you doing?"

She eyed him. "Do you mean out by the tree?"

"Oh, never mind," Dave said.

Delilah held onto the dashboard as Dave fishtailed the Mustang. "I didn't know you would come back through the field," She said under her breath.

He glanced at her as he took the next right. "Sorry about that." Her face flushed.

They bounced over a hump as the Mustang surged onto pavement, leaving the gravel road and the van behind.

"Why do I smell cigarette smoke?" Delilah asked.

Dave sniffed his hand. "It's from those media guys!" He held his hand to Delilah and she put her nose to it and turned her face away in disgust. "Neither of those guys smoke but their clothes stink like crazy."

"Why would that be?" she asked.

Dave laughed for a moment before he could explain. "Both of their wives are heavy smokers and they both reek like it. Neither one of them knew it because they are both so used to the stink!"

Dave and Delilah looked at each other and shared a good laugh. Earl chuckled in the backseat, obviously wanting to share in the laugh even if he didn't know what was so funny.

Delilah opened one of her bags and pulled out a wet wipe, handing it to Dave. "Would you like to wash off your hands?"

"Yes. Thank you." Dave took it and tried cleaning his hands while holding the steering wheel. When he finally managed to get them somewhat clean, he wadded up the wet wipe and tossed it on the hump between his and Delilah's feet. She retrieved it and opened it up carefully. She wiped her hands and then passed it back to Earl, who did the same.

"I'm sorry," Dave said, "I didn't know that was your last wet wipe."

She shook her head. "It's not the last one. We just don't like to be wasteful."

Earl spoke, and Delilah smiled as she repeated his words in English: "I like the horse car!"

CHAPTER FOURTEEN

A Fun Drive

D ave fumbled with his cell phone and tried speaking "Home" into it.

"What are you doing?" she asked.

He handed the phone to her. "Could you type the word *home* into Google Maps?"

"What kind of maps?"

He took her wrist and pulled her hand closer. "Tap this app here. That's Google Maps."

She touched it and the map popped up.

"Now type the word *home*."

"Dave!" she shouted. "Please watch the road!"

He yanked his wheel and veered back into his own lane as a car swooshed past.

She held the phone close to her face for a moment, peering into the screen. "It says that it's an eight-hour drive. It's already three, and with the time change we wouldn't get there until midnight."

He shrugged. "What else can we do?"

"There's another Amish community not too many miles from here. We have some family friends in that community. Maybe we should go there tonight?" She suggested.

"What is the name of that town?"

"Kalona."

Dave touched the phone in her hands. "Type that into Google Maps—unless you know the way there?"

"Un fa shdendich—I don't have any idea where it is. I just know it's not far from Hazelton."

She tapped and typed on his phone.

"There," he said, and pointed. "Tap that place where it says, 'Get directions.' "

She pushed his hand away. "You just watch the road. I'll do this."

He laughed and let her figure it out.

A woman's voice said, "Take the next left onto Interstate two-eighteen." After they turned, the woman said, "Stay on Interstate two-eighteen for forty-nine miles, then take the exit nine-one for IA-one toward Iowa City/Kalona/Village Museum."

Earl asked Delilah a question in Pennsylvania Dutch.

She looked at Dave. "Earl wants to know who that lady is."

"Oh—she's just a computer-generated voice."

Delilah wrinkled up her nose and said something to Earl in Dutch.

"Could you call my mom's number?" Dave asked Delilah. "I should let her know what's going on or she'll be worried about you and Earl."

She tapped the phone screen and watched it. Dave heard his mother's voice.

Delilah put her ear to the phone. "Hello, this is Delilah. Dave wanted me to call you and tell you that we're gonna stay with our family friends in Kalona, Iowa."

Muffled sounds came from the phone at Delilah's ear.

"Well—we saw camera people at my aunt's house in Hazelton, so we got away from there," Delilah said. She listened for a moment, nodding the whole time.

"Okay," she said, "here's Dave."

Delilah watched him closely as he talked. "Mom, I just wanted to tell you that we had a change of plans. I'll spend the night at Delilah's friend's house in Kalona."

"That's a nice idea. How are things going?"

"It wasn't going bad at all until, like Delilah said, we got to her aunt's house and found the media waiting for us there."

"Did they take pictures of Delilah?"

"No," Dave answered, "We saw them before they saw us. Hopefully, they didn't see which way we went. We'll head out to Indiana tomorrow."

"Oh, poor Delilah and Earl," She said.

"I know, Mom. Please pray for them. It's a long ride and they look pretty tired."

"I will pray for them. Tell Delilah and Earl that I am praying."

"Thanks, Mom. Bye for now."

"I love you, David, good-bye."

Dave looked at Delilah and said, "My mom wants you to know that she is praying for you."

"Your mom seems really nice," Delilah answered.

"Yes, nice," Earl echoed.

Delilah cocked her head. "Does your mom call you David?"

"Yeah, I guess she does."

"I like that. Earl's middle name is David," she said.

"Earl David," the little guy piped up from the backseat.

Delilah pulled open a bag and took out an apple. She carefully laid a napkin on her lap and produced a paring knife from somewhere and quickly cut several narrow slices. Next, she cut thin sections of cheese and put the two together like an open-faced sandwich. She passed the first one to Dave.

"Here's a little snack," Delilah said. She passed a set to Earl and then made one for herself.

Dave wiped his mouth with his shirt sleeve. "Mmm, that's good."

She smiled and held out her hand. "Here's another."

Delilah brought out her mason jar with goat milk. She carefully unscrewed the lid and took a sip before passing it to Dave.

"Here you go, Earl," Dave said as he handed the jar to him in the backseat.

Delilah continued cutting up apples and cheese.

"Hey—I almost forgot," Dave said. "Can you get those Snickers bars out of the glovebox?"

Delilah pulled them out and handed them over.

"Those are for you and Earl," he said. "I wanted you two to have something sweet while I'm eating my other cinnamon roll."

Delilah giggled and opened her bag and passed Dave his roll. She passed Earl his candy bar and opened hers. They all ate their sweets and finished off the goat milk together.

Dave wiped his mouth with his shirtsleeve again. "This reminds me of road trips my dad, mom, and I took when I was a boy around Earl's age."

Delilah put her knife back into the container and brushed the crumbs onto her hand. "I never hear you say anything about your dad."

"He died about a year ago."

Her eyes seemed to sag with sympathy. "I'm so sorry—I didn't know." She held the crumbs in her palm and stared at him.

He pressed the button, winding down her window. She jerked her head to see what was happening. "You can toss those crumbs out," Dave said.

She tossed them, and Dave powered her window back up.

"No wonder your mother focuses on you and your life so much. You should be more patient with her."

"I try," Dave said.

Delilah opened the book again and began reading. Soon her foot found its way to the dashboard and her toes began to move again. At times she fanned out all her toes, which were cute and even. Sometimes only her little toe stretched out and wiggled by itself. Dave smiled and stole glances at her while she focused on the book. He found himself looking at the little mole, hidden in the soft curls of her hairline at the base of her neck. Earl played with his tiny plastic horses. Whinny sounds and snorts came from the backseat.

Suddenly, Delilah looked up and caught Dave eyeing her. She smiled and said, "This book is about a road trip like ours."

Dave flipped his blinker switch and passed a slow-moving tractor. As soon as he maneuvered back into his lane, he glanced at her with a smirk. "Since you're Delilah, I guess that makes me Samson."

She laughed. In her high-pitched English she teased, "You don't seem like a Samson."

He feigned a stab in his heart, grabbing his chest. "Thanks a lot! Maybe I am, and you need to trick me into telling you the secret of my superhuman strength, like how Delilah tricked Samson in the Bible."

She laughed again. "I'm gonna try to trick you into telling me the secret of what happened between you and that girl in high school."

Dave felt himself tense up. "You won't get that out of me. I'd never want you to know the whole story, or you wouldn't think much of me."

She pursed her lips and looked puzzled. "Could we roll the windows down for a bit? I think some fresh air would feel good."

They powered down the windows, including those in the back. Wind poured in, making the pages of Delilah's book flap.

Earl shouted, "My hat!"

Dave pressed the brakes, and Delilah twisted at her waist to see where his hat went. "Don't worry—your hat didn't blow away. It's on the floor here."

She unbuckled her seatbelt and knelt as she reached deeper to try and situate the hat better. Her body twisted close enough to Dave that he could feel her warmth. He glanced at her legs and had to swerve a little when he realized the Mustang had veered right. When he adjusted quickly, she momentarily lost her balance and her hip slammed against his arm.

She braced herself by grasping Dave's shoulder. "Whew—what happened?"

"I'm sorry. I should focus on the road and not what's going on in here."

With the hat issue under control, Delilah settled back into her seat and put her seatbelt back on. A beautiful scent of mown hay flooded the car. Dave stretched his left arm out of the open window and cupped his hand. She watched his hand with a girlish smile.

"Have you ever tried this?"

She shook her head.

"Go ahead—stick your hand out the window and try it!"

Her cupped hand went straight up in the air and she squealed, pulling it back inside.

"Make it flat like this, first." He showed her what he meant. "Then, pretend it's a wing and you're flying."

She flattened her hand and gave it another try. Her face gave way to a cute girlish smile again and she crooned, "Can we move Earl over so he's near the window? He should try this too!"

Dave pulled over onto the shoulder of the road and moved Earl toward Delilah's side. Earl stuck his hand out the window and chuckled.

"Just watch out for bugs," Dave said, "it hurts when they hit your hand."

"Un fa shdendich!" Delilah shouted and pulled her hand back inside. A bright red welt appeared on her palm. "You're right those bugs do sting." She popped her hand back out through the window and they all enjoyed waving their hands in the wind.

Delilah said, "You need to turn here."

A train appeared, coming up alongside them.

"Should I try to beat this train?" Dave questioned her.

"No!"

Dave made his turn slowly and pulled to a stop as the crossing bars lowered right in front of them. A loud whistle blasted, and the roar of the engine grew. Dave wished that he had rolled the window up, but his hands froze, grasping the wheel. Deep rumblings shook the car and vibrations grew in the seats. The horn made an incredible roar as the engine zoomed past right in front of them. The rumbling and vibrations continued with each car, and Dave's eyes automatically followed every one as it passed by. Each passing car brought back part of a memory from his high school years. He attempted to pull himself out of it. However, he felt powerless until the caboose rumbled away, and everything became quiet.

Dave turned to Delilah. Beads of sweat appeared on her forehead, creating tiny curls in her hairline and around her ears. She slumped back in her seat breathing heavily.

He leaned toward her. "Did that train scare you?"

She swallowed hard and spoke with a breathy voice, "Yeah—a little."

"I like trains," Earl said.

Amish farms came into view and Dave felt a wave of relief sweep over him. Delilah said, "I think our friends live a couple of miles north of town."

"You're not sure?"

"I can find it if you can find the sale barn," She answered.

Dave picked up his phone and said, "Siri, how do I get to the sale barn in Kalona."

The phone answered, "I'm searching for directions."

"She sounds nice," Earl said.

"Turn left onto East Avenue in point seven miles turn right onto Ninth Street." the phone said. They turned right, and a sale barn came into view.

"That's it," Delilah said, "now turn back and go the way we came."

Dave scrunched up his face. "Turn back?"

"I don't know the address. I just know how to get there from the sale barn."

Dave laughed and turned back the way they had come in. Delilah directed him from there.

"What time is it?" she asked.

He winced. "It's almost five. Is it bad to show up at suppertime?"

She tilted her head as if confused by his question. "Why would that matter?"

"Someone might think it's rude to show up uninvited at mealtime."

Delilah gave a quick shake of her head and wave of her hand. "Not Amish people."

They pulled up in front of a large white farmhouse.

Delilah pulled her black bonnet over her headscarf. "Earl, put your hat on," she instructed.

CHAPTER FIFTEEN

Another Amish Farm

D ave sat in the car while Delilah and Earl went up to the house and talked with a young-looking Amish woman on the porch. He took in the familiar sight of an Amish farm. A large, boxy farmhouse painted bright white. Clean sidewalks cut through their nicely mowed grass. Red and yellow flowers lined the sidewalks and edged the huge garden. A windmill towered over the house, spinning peacefully in a gentle breeze. A clothesline, between the house and barn flapped in the breeze with diapers and brightly colored Amish dresses.

Earl returned, running to the car. "David, come!"

Dave reluctantly followed Earl and climbed the steps. A young Amish couple studied him as though sizing up whether he could be trusted or not. Finally, the man said. "We should hide that car down the road a ways, just in case news people come looking for you."

"Okay, that sounds like a good idea. Should we take it now?"

"Sure," the Amish man said, "I'll come along with you and show you where. Let's get everything you need out of the car first because it is a little walk from here."

They took a few things out of the trunk and set it all on the porch.

"My name is Jacob." the man held out his hand. Jacob had a friendly face. His bushy black hair popped out from under his straw hat and his wiry eyebrows over the tops of his glasses. His dark black beard was thin in places. Dave guessed him to be around twenty-five.

"I'm Dave, it's nice to meet you."

They got into the Mustang, and Jacob pointed for him to drive up a gravel road bordering Jacob's farm.

"Delilah told us that you're from the Goshen Hershburger family," Jacob said.

"Yeah, my grandpa was Menno."

Jacob pointed for Dave to pull in through an open gate. "Follow this lane," he instructed and then added, "I knew your grandpa, Menno. He was a carpenter, wasn't he?"

Dave nodded. "Grandpa built custom cabinets."

"Yes, that's the Menno Hershburger I'm thinking of. My uncle worked for him before he got married and really liked Menno. He said that he was a nice man, and he took his Christianity seriously." Jacob pointed at an old barn. "We'll park your car in here.

This is the backside of my farm. We don't have to worry about anyone seeing your car here."

Jacob slid open a large door and Dave backed his car in to make it easier to get out in the morning. Dave followed Jacob over a fence, and they walked along a dirt lane that curved through Jacob's pasture and along a fence. "Are you a carpenter like your grandpa?" Jacob asked.

"I've always liked working with wood. My grandpa used to let me build birdhouses with his wood scraps. I never really learned enough to do it for a living though. My dad worked for him when my parents first got married, but he found he could make more money working at a trailer factory. Grandpa died when I was in eighth grade."

Jacob stopped walking and took off his hat and scratched his head. "Delilah lost her grandpa, too. They are such a nice family—and then all those bad things happened at the same time."

"Her dad's accident, her grandpa died, and what else?" Dave asked.

Jacob put his hat back on and walked ahead. "Around the time of her grandpa Earl's death, Delilah got ill. She had taken on the responsibility of keeping up the household while her mother stayed at the healthcare facility with Virgil. By the time her dad was able to come back home, it was clear that Delilah had worn herself down. The stress of her dad's accident, caring for her siblings, and everything else almost did her in. They've had enough trouble to last most people a lifetime."

Dave wanted to ask more about Delilah's illness, but he thought it might seem questionable to an Amish man if he seemed too interested. As they passed through a wooded area, they came to a creek spanned by a heavy plank that rested on either bank. Jacob walked on while Dave stood looking into the chasm below.

"Come on over," Jacob called.

Dave drew in a deep breath and held it in his chest as he slowly balanced across the plank with arms outstretched.

Jacob stared with eyes wide. "What's the matter?"

Dave exhaled as he took his final step. "I'm a little nervous about bridges."

A chuckle rose out of Jacob and echoed along the creek and through the trees that hung over both banks. A large barn met them when they walked out of the trees. Jacob led the way through the belly of his barn. Massive work horses filled the stalls on both sides. Dave stopped walking and admired the huge horses, which had their rumps toward the aisle. Jacob walked close to one row, right behind their huge legs. There only seemed to be a very narrow path of safety between the two rows of heavy-boned legs.

Thick blond tails flicked at flies and swished past Dave's nose. "I need to bring Earl out here. He is quite the little horseman. He looked for horses all the way from Wisconsin, and there weren't too many for him to see."

"We have horses, if Earl likes horses." He pointed to a team with a harness on. "We could hitch this team to a wagon after supper and you could take Earl for a ride."

Dave followed Jacob past a windmill and hand pump toward the large farmhouse. The thick foliage of nearby fruit trees hung in rich green clusters, contrasting with the home's pure white siding.

Jacob stopped at his cellar door and faced Dave. "I need to run down to our basement for a moment. You can head around to the back porch. I hear the women talking, so they must be sitting there."

Dave followed the sound of women's voices until he spotted them through a latticework on the edge of the porch. Vines climbed the lattice, covering the white interweaving boards with leaves and dainty purple flowers. He intended to step around the corner and join the women on the porch. Instead, he paused and admired Delilah's smile. Jacob's wife, a handsome woman with blond hair and blue eyes, held a baby and crooned over it. Dave carefully stepped over a calico cat that had flopped herself comfortably across the narrow sidewalk. Delilah laughed as she talked to the kind-looking woman. He could see her face clearly between the leaves and lattice and felt certain she didn't know he was there.

Jacob's wife questioned Delilah. "Aren't you a little nervous? I'm surprised your parents sent you off with a strange man."

She waved a hand. "No, I trust him completely. He's such a nice man, he wouldn't hurt anyone. And he's not that strange—he's related to us."

Jacobs wife said, "Be careful you don't get interested in him. He's very handsome."

Dave decided to take a step closer, hoping to hear Delilah's response or at least see her expression. Unfortunately, he stepped on the cat's tail and she yowled in full force.

The women instantly leaned over the porch railing. They both eyed Dave and the cat. The calico slunk off through lush green foliage. Dave wished he could follow it and slink off himself. Jacob reappeared and they all headed inside for supper.

Delilah and Martha, set the table with bacon, lettuce, and tomato slices for sandwiches on homemade bread. Jacob and Dave sat at one end and the women across from them. Earl took a place on a bench near Delilah. Martha placed her toddler daughter between her and Delilah. She set a little boy barely big enough to sit in a highchair at her other side.

Jacob said, "Let's pray."

They all bowed their heads in silent prayer.

During the meal, Jacob announced. "Dave told me about how much Earl likes draft horses. After supper we'll hitch up a big team and let Dave take Earl for a wagon ride."

"Do you know how to drive a team?" Martha asked.

"Er—not really."

Delilah set down her sandwich. "That's not true. You drove a team at Martha's parents' house in Wisconsin."

Dave couldn't help letting his eyebrows show his surprise. "Martha's parents?"

Delilah nodded enthusiastically. "Yes— that's how I know Jacob and Martha. She's R. Duane's oldest daughter."

He wasn't sure which surprised him more—that Martha was R. Duane's daughter, or that Delilah knew he had driven horses at R. Duane's farm.

Dave shook his head. "I can't believe that you're R. Duane's daughter. You have such a nice family."

Jacob's face broke into a wide smile and he asked, "How do you know Martha's family?"

"I drove my car into a ditch in front of their house and they pulled me out with a team of horses," Dave explained.

Earl said something in Pennsylvania Dutch, and they all roared with laughter.

"What did Earl say?" Dave asked.

Delilah interpreted. "He told them that you left the brakes on your horse car locked."

Dave explained, "My car is a Mustang, and Earl likes the horse emblem on the trunk." He hesitated for a moment as they all laughed again. A wave of heat rose up his sunburned back and flooded his face as he muttered, "I forgot about the emergency brake being on until it was too late. The horses didn't seem to notice."

Jacob and Martha both covered their mouths, trying to contain themselves. Martha finally brought her laughter under control and gave Dave a kind look as if trying to console him. "That curve in front of Dad and Mom's house is a bad one!"

Delilah kindly changed the subject. "Dave also drove a buggy once, in Falls."

Dave shrugged. "Maybe I'd better try driving horses since I can't keep my car on the road."

They all laughed at his joke.

Martha took the baby out of the highchair and passed him to Delilah, "Could you hold Merle while I slice a pie?"

Delilah gathered the baby in so naturally, and Merle nestled in as though accustomed to her arms. It seemed clear that her maternal instincts were ripe.

When everyone finished eating all the BLTs and apple pie they could hold, Jacob said, "Dave—let's go take Earl on a wagon ride."

CHAPTER SIXTEEN

Wagon Ride

Jacob and his toddler daughter, Laura, led the way out to the barn. Little Laura teetered along in her tiny Amish dress. Her blond hair peeked out from under a small headscarf, and her bare feet pitter-pattered on the sidewalk in a quick rhythm. Earl followed, his little feet keeping time with hers. Dave couldn't help but imagine how cute Delilah must have looked in her Amish clothes at that age.

Jacob untied his big sorrel team and led them out of the barn, each footfall clunking heavily. They towered over Dave, and his heartbeat began to race, wondering if he could drive such huge horses.

"Don't worry," Jacob said, "this is a quiet team. You can't make a mistake with them. If you know how to say giddyup and whoa, you'll be fine."

Jacob hooked the heel chains of his horses to the wagon while Dave and Earl watched. Laura climbed into the wagon by herself. She stood at the front of the wagon waiting for a "horsey ride."

"You can take them anywhere you want in this hayfield," Jacob said. "Just watch for a ditch in that far corner. There's a washout that's pretty steep, and you wouldn't want to drive through there on purpose."

Earl climbed the wagon wheel and stood beside Laura at the front.

Jacob passed a hay bale to Dave. "Set this a few feet behind the children, and you can use it like a chair."

Dave set the haybale on its narrow edge, instead of on its broader side. He looked at Jacob and asked, "Are you sure you don't want to come along?"

Jacob's friendly eyes encouraged Dave. "You'll be fine. Just tell them 'whoa' if there's a problem and they will stand like a rock until told otherwise."

Dave sat down on his haybale and clucked. The horses set off at a good clip and Earl chuckled. Little Laura giggled with him. Dave gave the horses all his attention until he heard a woman's voice.

"Wait! I'm coming along!"

Dave turned to see who yelled at him and realized Delilah was running beside the wagon. He stood to pull the horses up with a "whoa," but before he could get out the word, she jumped onto the stepping board on the wagon's side and rolled onboard.

"I could've stopped the horses," Dave said with a laugh.

"No problem. I got here." She smiled and grasped Dave's shoulder as she climbed over the bale and took a seat beside him. "Why do you have the bale on edge like this?"

"It sets higher this way. and I want to see the horses better."

She laughed. "That's all good—except it's more likely to tip over."

Dave shrugged, and they headed across the open field. Delilah nudged Dave with her elbow and pointed to Earl and Laura. They looked like a miniature Amish couple standing in the front of the wagon together. Delilah and Dave met eyes and shared a smile about how cute they looked.

"Maybe I should let you drive?" Dave asked.

"You're doing fine," she said, and then added, "I'll take over if we cross a bridge."

He elbowed her, which drew out a giggle. "How did you know about me driving horses at R. Duane's farm? I never told you that."

She gave him a questioning look. "R. Duane is our neighbor." She said it as if that explained everything.

"What does that have to do with it?" Dave asked.

She shook her head and giggled again. "Why wouldn't our neighbors tell us about a city guy that drove his car into their ditch, left his emergency brake on while the horses pulled him out, and then got excited about driving a team of horses?"

Dave eyed her with a smiling frown.

Earl ducked under the driving lines, stood between them, and grasped both leather straps, one in each hand.

"We let Earl practice driving buggy horses like this," Delilah explained.

"Good job, Earl," Dave said. "I probably need your help anyway."

Earl clucked to the horses, encouraging them to speed up and the wagon lurched up a small hill. Dave and Delilah slowly leaned back and neither of them could stop their momentum.

Their feet went straight up as the bale tilted and dumped them on their backs in the wagon-box. Dave looked to be sure Earl had the driving lines. Earl stood like a little farmer, holding the lines. His look-a-like Amish wife stood beside him. Dave and Delilah let themselves lay back and enjoy the sight of Earl and his little woman driving a team of horses. Suddenly Earl call, "Whoa!"

Dave sat up and looked beyond Earl and Laura. He couldn't see the massive horses that had been towering above the wagon. "Where are the horses?"

"Down there," Earl said.

Dave struggled to get to his feet as quickly as possible. The horses were over the edge of a sharp embankment looking down into a ravine. Dave pulled Delilah's hand, helping her to her feet.

He faced Delilah. "Should we try and back the horses out of there?"

Delilah shook her head and took the lines from Earl. "No—we'd better drive them on down and find a way to turn around."

Dave pulled little Earl and Laura by their hands and said, "You two better sit here on the floor while Delilah drives the horses down that slope."

Earl looked at Dave with big eyes. "I'm sorry."

"No—it's my fault," Dave said. "Jacob warned me about this ravine, and I wasn't paying attention."

Delilah knelt at the front of the wagon and took a firm grip on the lines as she studied the ditch. "You'd better kneel down here beside me Dave, or you may topple out of here."

The wagon lurched as Delilah spoke to the horses calmly. Both horses moved forward slowly drawing the wagon down behind them. Earl and Laura slid on the hay covered wagon floor until they and the bale of hay were pressing against Dave and Delilah's legs. Delilah continued speaking soothing words to the horses as they picked their footing down the slope. The wagon jostled and creaked as it followed, shaking the occupants until they jiggled together into a heap at the front of the wagon.

"Sorry about that," Dave said as he tried to keep from crushing Delilah.

As soon as the wagon leveled out, Delilah began to laugh. Earl's chuckle followed, and then Laura giggled with a cute little sound.

Dave didn't laugh. "I'm so embarrassed. Jacob told me to look out for this ravine. Now what'll he think of me?"

Delilah laughed all the harder. "Don't worry," she said, "Jacob and Martha are super nice people. They'll think it's as funny as I do."

Dave still didn't laugh even though the other three continued to giggle as Delilah turned the horses carefully at the base of the ravine.

Dave moved the haybale to the very back. "Earl and Laura, you'd better sit back here and lean against this bale while we drive back up."

They both scampered obediently to the back and sat side by side as if anticipating a fun ride. Dave joined Delilah at the front and braced himself nervously. He held onto the front of the wagon with one hand and passed an arm behind Delilah and held onto the wagon side behind her, to hold her in place while she drove. She let her elbows hang over the front of the wagon to help brace herself as she clucked to the horses.

The horses didn't pick their way slowly uphill as they had down. Instead, they both surged ahead, digging and lunging forward, yanking the wagon behind them. Dave held on for all he was worth, bracing his feet against the sides to keep from sliding back onto the children. He glanced at them and they both had smiles on their faces. He felt the weight of Delilah pressing against his arm that passed behind her as he clung to the wagon. His fingers started to slip from their grip just as the horses rounded the top and the wagon leveled out. She called "whoa," and the horses stopped on the flat field.

Earl and Laura jumped to their feet and scurried to the front of the wagon again. Dave recovered the haybale and set it a short way behind the children. This time he laid it flat as he should have in the first place.

Delilah passed the lines back over. "Here you go."

"I should probably let you drive," he said.

"Why?"

Dave shrugged, took the lines, and sat down.

She sat beside him and nudged him with her shoulder. "Don't be so hard on yourself. It was partly my fault."

He let himself smile a little. "No—it was all my fault. I would have been in big trouble if you hadn't come along?"

She giggled. "If I wasn't along, you would've been paying better attention to the horses and where you were going."

"Yeah—you're right! It's all your fault for distracting me," he said and they both laughed.

The horses trotted along a wagon path around the edge of the field. Their soft hoofbeats on the soil and the jingle of their harnesses made a nice sound, and Dave started to enjoy himself again. Earl and Laura spoke to each other in Pennsylvania Dutch and birds sang sweetly along the field's edge.

Dave turned to Delilah. "Was it awkward about you not having a covering?"

She giggled. "No—not nearly as bad as if we'd gone to my aunt's house. Martha and Jacob are young, and they didn't judge me for it. My aunt might have scolded me." She glanced at Dave before adding. "I didn't do anything wrong, but aunts worry like moms do."

Dave nodded. "Did you get another covering?"

"Yeah— Martha gave me one of hers." Delilah touched her headscarf. "I'm wearing this now because I already had it on and we're out on the farm. I'll put the covering on in the morning."

As soon as they pulled up near the barn, Jacob came out and asked, "How'd it go?"

Before Dave could answer, Earl and Laura spoke excitedly with words Dave couldn't understand. Dave could see Jacob's eyes light up as he listened to the children and began to laugh.

When everyone went to bed, Dave sat alone in a quiet room. His phone vibrated, and he saw his best friend was calling.

He tapped the screen and whispered, "Hello Nate."

"Why the whispering?" Nate asked. "Are you hiding from the cops?"

Dave shook his head. "No, I'm in Kalona, Iowa, staying with Jacob and Martha Yoder. They're some of Delilah's family friends."

"It's only 8:30! Don't tell me those Amish people are in bed already?"

Without thinking it through, Dave held a finger to his lips with a "be quiet" sign. "It's 9:30 in Iowa, and they get up at the crack of dawn to do chores."

Nate laughed. "Did you talk this Delilah into some pictures yet?"

"I'm working on it," he said in hushed tones. "She has strong convictions about her faith."

"It must not be the same girl you had a crush on in high school. That girl was a little more on the wild side." He whistled through the phone. Dave covered it with one hand until Nate's whistle ended. Dave listened as his friend continued. "I remember that Delilah! She wore tight jeans and tan swimsuits. And hung out with guys like you at parties."

"Shhh," Dave ordered through the phone and then whispered, "Yeah, you're right. That Delilah sure looked great in a pair of jeans. Keep it down though, I don't want them hearing me on the phone. And— I don't want *this* Delilah to know about *that* one."

"Ooh, you *are* falling for another Amish girl!" Nate shouted into his end of the phone line.

Dave returned with a loud whisper, "Shhh! It's just that this one is super innocent, and she'd hate me if she knew what happened between me and that other Amish girl."

A loud humming came through the phone. "So, you *are* falling for her?"

"I think a lot of her," Dave whispered loudly. "I'm not completely over that other Delilah, and I don't want this one to hate me."

"You're in love," Nate teased. "I can see that right through the phone."

"You just mind your own business," Dave said through a smile. "I'll be home tomorrow night. I'm gonna take Delilah to Indiana tomorrow?"

"Where in Indiana? To your house?"

Dave looked at his phone as if he could see Nate through it. "Why? Are you gonna try to take her picture and sell it?"

A sound came through the phone that Dave didn't recognize. It almost sounded as if Nate choked on something. "Eh—I was just teasing ya," he said. "I gotta get going. Take good care of your little Amish girlfriend."

"Nate!" Dave shouted in a whisper and hung up.

CHAPTER SEVENTEEN

Teenage Delilah and the Train (flashback)

The first Delilah Dave met back during his high school years, had an aura of electricity around her. Dave wasn't sure if it only affected him or everyone that met her. She was the type of girl who stopped traffic with her sheer beauty alone. She seemed surprised by his swooning, which mystified Dave. How could any girl be so stunningly gorgeous and still be surprised when a guy was crazy about her? She appeared unaware of the power of her sensuality as well.

There were three times Dave saw that Delilah. All three times were during one short week between his junior and senior years of high school, almost six years ago. The first time he saw her, she was at the pool in her tan swimsuit. That interaction was brief. The second time they met up, it was late on Friday evening when she came to play volleyball and he raced a train to get her a pizza. Their final meeting occurred the next evening. Both occasions were after the sun went down. He wished he would have had the chance to see her face in the daylight so he'd recognize her if he did see her again.

On the Saturday evening after the volleyball game, Dave sat on a picnic table watching the footpath like a hawk. Finally, he spied a couple of girls heading toward him. Katie wore a pair of jeans and a T-shirt. Delilah was dressed in a long skirt and a button-up sleeveless blouse, which clinched Dave's theory that she was European. No ordinary girl from Indiana put together an outfit like that, yet it took his breath away. He guessed that she grew up in Ireland or Greece or on some exotic island. He meant to ask her about it when they were together, but every time he got near her, that electricity sparked, and he forgot everything but the moment, and her.

Nate shoved Dave to get his attention. "Let's ask Katie and Delilah if they want a beer. Me and the guys brought a cooler full."

Dave didn't take his eyes off Delilah as she made her way down the footpath. He answered Nate, "Go ahead and offer Katie a beer. Delilah is too classy to drink that cheap beer you guys buy. I brought a couple of bottles of wine. European girls want wine."

"Dude—you are pathetic!"

Dave pushed his buddy teasingly and grabbed his own head with both hands as if trying to hold it together. He tried to cough and clear his voice, which remained hoarse due to a lingering cold. "Have you seen her? That girl is drop-dead gorgeous and so much fun to be around. I'm crazy about her, and if she'd have me, I'd marry her!"

"Dude—she's cute but a little different." Nate shoved Dave again. "I think you're crazy—period! All the hot girls from our school that you've turned away, and then you go stark raving mad about this one? I don't understand you at all!"

Dave shook his head. "You're just too much of a redneck to understand a classy, beautiful woman when you meet one."

Nate wagged his head mockingly.

"Does my voice still sound dumb?" Dave asked his buddy.

"Don't worry about that," Nate replied. "She probably thinks that's your normal voice."

When Delilah walked around the swings in her long flowing skirt and button-up sleeveless shirt, Nate muttered under his breath, "Wake up Dude, this girl is not that hot."

Dave's eyes almost rolled back in his head at the sight of her. He turned to Nate and whispered, "You just keep impressing her cousin with stories about how amazing you are and stay away from Delilah."

Katie jumped out of the way as Dave and rushed over, grabbed Delilah by the waist and swung her around. Delilah squealed with delight, he assumed. Her long silky hair spun with her and brushed against his face. He set her down and she stood looking up at him like a little princess from a Disney movie. Without thinking about what she thought, or about what anyone thought, he reached out and ran his fingers over her hair. She shrugged her little shoulders and raised her eyebrows into an arch. "What?"

"What?" Dave repeated with a raspy voice, "I'll tell you what—I've never seen such beautiful hair in all of my life!"

She covered her face with both hands. "Stop—you're embarrassing me."

"I'm sorry, Delilah, I'm not trying to embarrass you. I'm just so glad I met you before some other guy put a ring on your finger."

"What's that mean?"

"Really—you don't know what that means?" he poked her side. "In America, that means, 'Ask a girl to marry him.' "

"Oh—yeah—I knew that."

"Anyway, let's take a walk alone. The last time we were together, I hardly got a chance to talk to you."

"We talked while we ate pizza."

Dave felt his face flush and awkwardly ran a hand over his buzzed cut hair. "I was hoping to get to know you a little better. I don't even know where you're from."

She eyed him sideways. "Where are we gonna walk?"

"I don't care—anywhere—just so we are alone. I don't care about all these guys. I can see them anytime. I know you have to go back home, and I'm afraid I'll never see you again."

She smiled and kicked at him with her bare toes. "We could play HORSE again!"

"I don't think you could sit on my shoulders with that skirt on." He winked.

He hoisted her up and spun her around once more, bringing out another adorable squeal. Her skirt caught the air and floated up as he lowered her to her feet. He couldn't help but notice her pretty legs by the light of the park lamps. She ran away from him teasingly, darting from side to side as he tried to catch her. She outran him and made it to the swings. She plopped herself on one of the swings and said, "Give me a push."

"I'll give you an underdog!" he said and ran behind her.

"What's an underdog?"

"This!" He pulled her swing back and then ran under her, pushing her high into the air.

She laughed and crooned, "Do it again!"

After he had her swinging high, he stood in front of her until her swing, swung back at him. He darted out of the way at the last second, giving the thrill of a near collision.

She covered her eyes and shrieked. "I almost hit you!"

The next time he stood with his back to her and waited until her momentum brought her close, all the while saying, "Where did that Delilah go?"

She giggled and tried to kick him with her bare toes as he dashed out of her reach. He gave her one more mighty underdog and then stood a short way out in front of her. "When you're ready—jump and I'll catch you!"

Delilah gasped as she braced herself to jump. "Don't drop me!"

"I promise I won't drop you—just jump!"

She squealed as she leapt into his arms. He caught her and then lost his balance. He slowly toppled to the sandy area beneath the swings with her in his arms. They let out a "humph" as they landed. And then laughter erupted from both of them as they rolled in the sand together.

"I brought us something good to drink," Dave said hoarsely. "I know you wouldn't like the cheap beer my buddies bring."

She smiled at him. Dave scrounged around under some bushes and pulled out a pair of wine bottles and a corkscrew.

He added, "My parents don't drink alcohol, but they had these bottles of plum wine in the basement someone gave them. I thought you might like it."

He struggled with the corkscrew and bottle while she watched and giggled. He finally pulled the cork and took a sip. "Mmm—this is good. Try it!"

Delilah took the bottle to her lips while Dave watched. "A trickle ran down her chin and he brushed it off. "It's so good!" she said.

They walked down to the railroad tracks while the other teens clumped together in their usual place at the picnic area. Dave carried the unopened bottle and Delilah the one they just took a sip out of.

"What is your real name?" she asked.

"You don't believe that I'm Samson?"

She stood as if she wouldn't go any further until he revealed his true name.

"My name is David."

Delilah eyed him seductively. "If you are David, then I am Bathsheba."

"Bathsheba with the tan swimsuit?" he asked with a wink. "C'mon—let's take a walk on this railroad track. He took her hand and she followed.

Within a few minutes they had made their way to a place where the tracks crossed a small stream. Delilah headed out onto the train trestle as though planning to walk across.

"Let's go down and wade in that water," Dave suggested.

Delilah stopped to tip the bottle of wine. He watched her in the moonlight. Never had he seen such beauty. Her long flowing hair waved behind her as her head tilted back to sip the wine. He took it from her hands. He tipped the mouth of the bottle to his. It was slick and smooth, still wet from her lips. He gladly tasted what remained from her mouth.

"Isn't that wine delicious?" she asked.

He nodded but didn't tell her that the fact that her lips had been on the bottle before he drank it made it twice as intoxicating.

They walked down to the water. Moonlight glowed on everything. The surface of the stream shown bright, like a silver road. The moon caused a slice of light to glint off the bottle of wine in Delilah's hands. She tilted her head back to take another draw.

"Easy there, Bathsheba, I don't want to have to carry you out of here."

Her giggle echoed along the banks of the creek. "I love this plum wine! I've never tasted anything like it before."

Dave took the bottle after her and drank a sip. "I like drinking after you. It's almost like I'm kissing you."

She stopped and turned her face to him. He reached to her chin and lifted it. He laid his lips on hers. They were softer than the mouth of the wine bottle and twice as sweet. She took the bottle and headed for the creek. Dave followed like a puppy. She took the hem of her skirt in her hand and tiptoed into the gurgling water. Her silhouette might have been more distinct by the light of the moon than she realized. Her skirt became see-through against the silver water of the creek. He watched her pretty legs as she carefully balanced her way along the rocks and water.

She stopped and tipped the bottle again. "I can't stop drinking this wine—it's delicious."

He lowered his voice, "I can't stop watching you—*you* look delicious."

She waved a hand at him as though pushing away his compliment. "Don't try to flatter me."

"I'm not kidding, Delilah, you are the most beautiful thing I've ever seen in all of my life."

She tossed her hair in the moonlight and hoisted her skirt up a little further as she stepped into deeper water. She stopped midstream and tilted the bottle again. He watched her silhouette. All of her female qualities visible. He wondered if she had any idea how intoxicating she was to a man. Something about her seemed so innocent and trusting. It was obvious that she had been a little girl only a short while ago and her maturity had burst upon her before she understood it.

He took off his shoes and waded into the cool, silver water to be near her. Moss grew on rocks, giving them a silky-smooth fur. In other places, mud as soft as satin squished between his toes.

He took her free hand in his and pulled her closer. "I need another drink."

She held the bottle and tipped it to his mouth, giggling.

"I like tasting your lips on the bottle. But, I'd rather taste them firsthand," he said in a teasing way, but he meant it.

She leaned into him and he wrapped an arm around her slim waist, drawing her close. Her lips were wet with wine and plum-flavored. He had never kissed a girl in his life. He had often imagined what it would be like and wondered if he'd know how to do it right. With Delilah, it came naturally. He didn't even need think about how. His fingers reached into her mass of hair that fell around her shoulders and instinctively cradled the nape of her neck as they kissed. Tiny delicate hairs curled where her hairline ended, and her soft skin began.

"I need to sit down," she whispered, her lips so close to his face he felt her warm breath. "I'm feeling a little lightheaded."

"Me too," Dave said.

He took her hand and interlocked her slim fingers with his as he led her under the trestle. Concrete, poured into a foundation for the railroad bridge, also made a nice seat for a couple to sit on and gaze at the silver water that flowed off into the woods. The moonlight silhouetted the railroad ties overhead, the light passing through the gaps between them.

"Are you okay, little Bathsheba?"

Moonlight glinted off her chocolate eyes as she nodded. "I'm fine, King David."

Her humor brought a smile to his face. *This girl*, he thought, *is too good to be true*. A low rumble signaled that a train would soon reach the bridge they were sitting under.

"I better warn you, Delilah, a train is coming and it's going to pass right over our heads. Should we get out of here before it does?"

Her dark hair shook, and moonlight glowed in her eyes as she answered, "Nope, I have my Samson here to protect me."

"Okay, but don't say I didn't warn you. It's gonna be loud."

He got to his feet and pulled her hand as the sound deepened. "Let's get up under the bridge a little further. There is an area where we can lay to watch without debris falling on us as the train passes."

"Oh, so you've brought other girls under this bridge before?"

"No—me and my friends used to come down here all the time as kids. We liked to lay back on this concrete slab and watch as a train passed right over our heads. It's quite a thrill." He paused and touched her cheek. "You're the first girl I've ever brought here. And, the first girl I've ever kissed."

They each took a long drink from the second bottle of wine and then stretched out on the concrete to watch the train fly over them. She leaned in and kissed him again while the rumble grew into a deafening roar. They rolled into an embrace, igniting a flame he couldn't put out. Her senses were too drenched in wine to resist him. The weight and power of a locomotive reverberated within the concrete under them. Those vibrations shook both wine bottles and they tipped over, spilling everything they had left in them.

Another Bridge to Cross

S unlight gleamed through the curtains and danced on Dave's face. His eyes trembled open, and he studied his surroundings. A dark blue quilt with black edges covered his feet. The rest of it had been pushed off during the night when he got too warm. Gentle birdsong floated in through the screen with the breeze that stirred the sheer curtains. He could smell cinnamon and something baking and remembered that he had spent the night in Jacob and Martha's Amish farmhouse.

Dave pulled on his jeans and buttoned up a clean shirt he had set aside for the day.

Women's voices echoed in the stairwell as Dave tiptoed down the wooden steps toward the kitchen.

"Good morning, Dave," Delilah said with a wrinkled nose.

Dave returned her smile. "Morning." He looked toward Martha. "I hope I didn't wake up your children?"

She smirked at him. "Earl and Laura are out helping Jacob with the chores. You can go join them if you want."

Dave hurried for the door. "You should have woken me up. Earl and I wanted to help with horse chores."

"Don't worry," Delilah said, "Jacob is saving horse chores for after breakfast so you and Earl can help."

"Oh good!" Dave headed on out the door and down the porch steps.

Jacob's farm basked in golden morning light. Birdsong sounded from every tree. Bawling calves made their plea for breakfast behind the steel gate near the barn. Chickens clucked and scratched the path. They ran ahead of Dave and flapped their wings when he got close. A cry from within the barn drew Dave through the large doors. He searched for what made the sound and found the calico cat nursing a litter of kittens. She had a kitten of each color common to cats. Black and white, tiger-striped, dark gray, and light gray. Earl and Laura ran into the room and each chose a kitten to hold.

"Where's your dad?" he asked Laura.

She pointed, and Dave headed down a straw-covered hall. He found Jacob tying up a goat.

"Have you ever milked a goat?" Jacob asked.

"No," Dave said.

Delilah came into the barn and walked past Dave, swinging a metal bucket. She crouched down politely in her long Amish dress and immediately milk sang out a tune as it squirted into the metal bucket. Her bare toes wiggled in a layer of straw. Earl hurried and sat near her waiting for a turn to milk the goat. When he got his turn, he also made the job look easy, sending a stream of milk into the pail.

Jacob placed a hand on Dave's shoulder. "I guess you ought to try your hand at it."

When Dave squatted down and gave it a go, nothing came out of the goat. "She must be all milked out," he said.

Delilah giggled. She reached over and showed Dave how to milk a goat. A stream shot into the bucket.

Dave tried it again to no avail.

"Hold out your thumb," she said.

He held it up. Delilah turned his thumb facing down and showed him, by squeezing his thumb and teaching him by feel, how to make the pressure start at the top and work down.

"Oh—I get it now!" Dave tried it on the goat again and a little trickle of milk came out. "Well, that's a little better, but maybe Earl better do it."

Earl nodded with a smile and took over.

As soon as the stream of milk stopped ringing in the pail, Delilah said, "Good job, Earl." She took the bucket of creamy white milk back inside. Earl and Laura ran off to play with their kittens. Jacob headed out behind the barn to check on his other livestock and Dave followed. They passed through an open door and witnessed a stallion and a mare interacting.

Jacob turned to Dave. "I'm glad to see this. It's good to know my mare will have a colt next spring."

Jacob headed off to check on other things while Dave stayed at the gate, amazed by the sight. The male snorted and arched his neck, reaching toward the mare's mane, he bit her gently.

"Why's he doing that?"

Dave jumped at the sound of Earl's voice. He wasn't sure he understood his words, so he crouched down and asked, "What was that, Earl?"

Earl opened his mouth and imitated the bite.

"It's not a mean bite. It's almost a kiss," Dave said.

Earl nodded as if he understood and took Dave's hand as they headed toward the house for breakfast.

Jacob and Martha asked Delilah questions about her family while they ate pancakes. Dave had several large stacks and three big pieces of a delicious crumb-topped coffeecake. Creamy goat milk washed it all down perfectly.

Between bites, Dave asked, "Jacob, how did you meet Martha?"

Martha answered, "I came to Iowa to teach school a few years back. Jacob and I met during that time."

Jacob and Martha shared a smile across the table.

Dave let out a moan as he finished his last bite of coffeecake. "Martha, your coffeecake is amazing!"

She smiled and said, "Thanks—but you'll have to give the credit to Delilah. She made it."

Delilah waved a hand toward Dave as if pushing away any complement before he spoke.

After breakfast, Delilah put everything she and Earl had brought along into a cloth bag and told Dave, "Jacob says that we should take our things with us when we go to do the horse chores. We will be closer to where your car is parked, and we can leave from there."

Dave draped yesterday's shirt over his arm and held his bathroom kit in his hand.

Delilah opened her bag. "You can put your things in here until we get to your car."

"Okay, thanks," Dave said. "I'll carry that bag then."

"No—I've got it," Delilah answered. "You and Earl can help Jacob with his horse chores and I'll watch."

They said good-byes to Martha and baby Merle and thanked her for putting them up overnight. Laura teetered along beside her daddy as Jacob headed to the horse barn. Jacob whistled and a herd of horses charged into the stalls. Their feet clomped heavily on the concrete floor as they all found their own place. Laura poured a scoop of feed into the bunk by every horse as Jacob put a halter over each horses' ears and buckled the throat-latch, tying the horses at their bunk.

"What can we do to help?" Dave asked.

"I thought you and Earl might enjoy brushing the horses," Jacob said. He handed Dave a currycomb and a smaller brush to Earl. Earl stepped right in and began brushing a massive Belgian horse even though he could only reach partway up the huge horse's sides. Dave stepped in beside Earl and brushed the higher part that Earl couldn't reach. Delilah stood in the aisleway and watched them with a smile.

Partway through their brushing job, Jacob told Dave, "You could set Earl on that gray mare's back if you want. Laura likes to sit on that one. She's big but very gentle."

Dave hoisted him up and Earl sat smiling, his grin crooked because of the cute little cleft in his chin. His little legs stretched wide over the mare's broad back. Dave started brushing the next horse over.

"I smell cigarette smoke," Delilah said.

Earl pointed out through the double barn doors that hung open. He spoke to Delilah in Pennsylvania Dutch, and she quickly translated. "Here comes a man with a camera!"

Dave reached up and pulled Earl off the big horse and set him on his shoulders and huffed, "Delilah, follow me. We can cut through the woods and get to my car!"

Delilah put their clothing bag under one arm like a football and ran. She called, "Thank you, Jacob!"

Jacob's laugh echoed in the barn as Dave, Delilah, and Earl scrambled into the woods. Delilah outran them, and she turned and motioned to Dave. "Put Earl down! He's a fast runner!"

Dave lowered Earl to the ground.

Delilah shouted, "Earl, *schpring!*"

The little boy's legs churned. They all three swept through a wooded area down around some shrubs and through a ravine.

A heavyset bearded man with a camera followed about twenty yards behind. His skinny counterpart tried to keep up with a movie camera gripped firmly in both hands. Dave raced ahead of Earl and Delilah, trying to lead the way to the plank bridge. When he got there, he stopped and looked into the water flowing below. Earl ran on across.

Delilah started to scamper over before turning to check on her driver. "Come on, David, we've got to hurry!" She ran back and grabbed his hand and pulled. "Come on, I'll help you!"

Dave focused on the hand that held his to keep from looking down. As soon as his feet were on solid ground, he pointed up ahead and shouted. "My car is in that barn!"

He turned to see how far behind Joe and Moe were. He happened to see Moe tumble to the ground and Joe trip over him, tossing his camera in the process. Delilah and Earl beat Dave to the barn, and she slid open the large door. Dave pulled his keys from his pocket and clicked the unlock button with a beep. Earl and Delilah jumped in and Dave fired up the engine. "Fasten your seatbelts!" He punched his accelerator and the Mustang roared out of the barn, tires spinning, sending the car into a fishtail.

Delilah giggled. "Those camera people don't look very happy!"

"Yeah," Dave agreed, "we wouldn't want Earl to hear the words they're using right now."

CHAPTER NINETEEN

Kind Man

As Dave entered Goshen, Indiana, on his phone to find the best backroad to take, it occurred to him that maybe they were being tracked. He wrote down the directions to Goshen, powered down his phone, and threw it out the window.

"Why did you do that?" Delilah asked, dumbfounded.

"Because, I think they are tracking me by my phone somehow."

"Why don't we take your phone and send it to your house. I don't want you to just throw it away."

"That's not a bad idea, Delilah, I never thought of that."

"And maybe they will follow the mail truck hauling your phone instead of us." Delilah smiled at her own idea.

"You are ingenious!" Dave shouted.

"I'm not that smart. While you were looking up Goshen on your phone, I was praying. Maybe the Lord gave me that idea."

Dave jumped out of the car and ran to his phone. He called his mom as quick as he could. As he sat behind the wheel, he heard his mother say, "Hello?"

"Mom, hello, it's Dave. We made it to Delilah's friends' house in Iowa, but camera men snuck onto their farm this morning trying to take our pictures. We outran them and got away. Now we're getting ready to head to Indiana."

"Oh David, poor Delilah and Earl. They have to be worn out, and those paparazzi keep finding you!"

"I'm doing the best I can to hide. I don't know how they're finding us. Anyway, I think someone is tracking my phone. Delilah had a great idea, though. We are going to send my phone home. If they are tracking it, they will end up following the mail truck to our house. So, don't worry about me. Please pray for us though. I feel so bad for Delilah and little Earl. They are getting really tired of riding around the country in a car."

"Be careful with them in your car. I love you, David."

"Okay, thanks Mom."

After Dave set down his phone, Delilah said, "I don't understand why you struggle with your mom so much. She seems very kind."

"My mom babies me too much. It's a vicious cycle. The more I try to break free from her apron strings, the more she tries to mother me."

"Why don't you try turning everything upside down?"

Dave turned to study Delilah's face. "What do you mean?"

"I'm gonna guess that if you let her feel needed, she'd relax and back off."

Dave narrowed his eyes and nodded slowly. "That is so smart. I never would've thought of that."

She moved her hand toward him as if pushing away his compliment. Things got quiet for a few minutes.

He suddenly thought of something. "I should text my friend, Nate, and tell him what's going on. After we send the phone he'll be wondering why I don't answer his calls. Could you try texting him for me?"

"Okay," she said and looked at his phone, tapping in the passcode he'd given her earlier.

Dave reached over and tapped the text emblem. "Type Nate's name first and then you can write a note for me."

She pushed his hand away. "I can do it—you should watch the road." Her tongue stuck out a little as she typed Nate's name. She held the phone over so Dave could see without looking away from the road. "Is this right?"

He leaned in and glanced at the screen. "Yeah—now type this message: *The media is tracking us. I'm sending my phone home in the mail. We'll come back on Highway 6 so they can't find us.*"

Her tongue worked as she typed. She stared at the screen closely for a moment and then said, "Hey, your friend texted back already."

"What did he say?" Dave asked.

She kept the phone close to her face and read out loud, "Does she know that you are crushed on her?" Delilah wrinkled her forehead. "What's that about?"

"Oh—give me that phone. Nate is always messing around."

She didn't speak again for a long time. Instead, she sat staring out the passenger window. Dave feared that she might be upset that he had a crush on her.

Delilah finally cleared her voice and said in a matter-of-fact tone, "Don't worry, I know you're not interested in me like that." Her voice dropped lower. "No boys are."

"That's not true, Delilah! Boys all over America are crazy about you."

She shrugged. "I think mostly girls read *Samson and Delilah*. They are the ones who want to meet Delilah, not boys."

"Not true," Dave said and shook his head. "And besides, If I was an Amish boy, I'd be interested."

She waved a hand. "Don't try and make me feel better. I'm used to it."

There wasn't any way to tell her that he'd been interested since the moment he first looked into her eyes. She made it clear that she didn't want to leave the Amish lifestyle behind, and he knew that joining the Amish wouldn't be realistic. He glanced at her and she turned away. His eyes went to the mole on her neck. He studied the flyaway hairs for a moment and then realized she had two moles where there used to be one. And then, one of the moles seemed to move.

"Delilah, you've got a tick on your neck."

"A what?" she brushed her hand across the back of her neck. "A tick? Like one of those little spider things that suck blood?"

"Yeah—a little lower." He touched her neck near the spot.

She brushed her hand frantically over the area. "Get it off! Please get it off me!"

Earl's chuckle rose from the back seat. Delilah's panic escalated. Dave pulled the Mustang into a private driveway and parked.

"I don't know if I should just pull it out," Dave said. "Some ticks carry Lyme disease, and if you pull them off, their head can stay in your skin and get into your bloodstream."

She held both hands on her cheeks but kept her neck tilted toward Dave. "What—the head of it is in my skin? Get it off me—please!"

Earl's belly laugh deepened the more panicked Delilah got. Dave tried to grasp the tiny tick without pulling the delicate hairs on her neck. She squirmed as he gently tried to press aside those silky little curls. He reached his free hand around her neck to hold her in place as she writhed. Her voice grew even more shrill as he pinched the flat-bodied tick between his fingers. Suddenly, Dave realized a man stood just beyond Delilah's window yelling something.

"Take your hands off her, buddy!"

Delilah let out another scream. "Get it off!"

Dave struggled to grasp the tiny thing.

The man knocked on the car window and yelled. "Get your hands off of her and get out of the car, buddy, or I'm calling the cops!"

Dave retracted his hands holding the tick between his pinched fingers. Delilah wrapped both hands around her neck and shook.

Earl laughed all the louder.

The man pulled Delilah's door open and knelt on one knee beside her. "Do you want me to yank that guy out of the car and kick the crap out of him?"

All at once, Delilah regained her composure. She looked at the man and said, "I'm sorry—what did you say?"

"If this guy is roughing you up, just say the word, and I'll kick the living crap out of him!"

"No—I'm fine. He wasn't hurting me."

The man leaned in and looked her in the eyes. "Don't worry—be honest—you don't have to defend him. I won't let your husband do that again. Why don't you get out of the car and we'll call the police?"

"He's not my husband."

"Okay. Your loser boyfriend. You don't have to let him treat you like this."

Delilah giggled as she spoke. "I'm sorry. It probably looked like he was choking me but actually he was helping me. I had a tick stuck in my neck and he was pulling it out."

"Is that true?" the man looked her in the eyes to be certain.

Dave reached his hand over across Delilah and showed the man the tick he held pinched between is thumbnail and first finger. The tick's legs wiggled as it tried to escape Dave's fingers. Delilah squealed and leaned away from the tick.

The man laughed. "I seriously thought he was strangling you."

"I . . . see. No, he's nice. David wouldn't hurt a flea."

Just as the words left her lips, Dave worked his fingernails against each other and pinched the tick into two pieces.

"Okay—he might hurt a flea, or a tick, but he wouldn't hurt me," she said and giggled again.

The man laughed and stood back up. "I'm glad everything is okay here."

Delilah got out of the car and shook his hand. "You are such a kind man. Thank you ever so much for being willing to help. The world needs more men like you."

He accepted her handshake. "You're welcome. I've got to admit my heart is kinda pounding right now. I wasn't sure what to do when I saw his hands on your throat. I'm glad I didn't have to try and fight your boyfriend."

Dave stepped out of the car. He towered over the small man as they shook hands. Delilah didn't correct the man about Dave not being her boyfriend, so he didn't say anything either. After all, he liked the sound of it. They headed back on down the highway, all three of them smiling.

Delilah set down her book. "So, you want to buy a restaurant?"

Dave nodded.

"DJ has been trying to sell her diner. If you buy that one, I could work for you," Delilah said with a smile.

"Yeah, we could call it Samson and Delilah's." They both laughed. Dave added, "I'd need to put up a sign that says, 'No Pictures.'" They laughed again.

Little Earl echoed, "No pictures," and chuckled deeply.

Delilah toyed with her apron for a moment. "Maybe I could make a deal with Charlie Rose. He could just take one picture of me. Then we could give my dad some money and you could buy DJ's restaurant."

Dave studied her face for a moment. "I'm not gonna have you giving in to a picture just so I can get my restaurant."

She didn't say anything but stared at the road ahead.

He passed a slow car and when he got back into his lane again, he asked. "What do you want?"

Delilah cocked her head. "What do you mean?"

"I want a restaurant. What does Delilah want?"

She covered her face and looked away. "What every Amish girl wants."

"What's that?" Dave asked sincerely.

"A family, of course." She glanced at Dave for a moment, then covered her face bashfully.

"Oh—I get it," Dave said and raised his head in acknowledgement. "You want to get married and have a family."

She turned away and giggled as if the topic embarrassed her completely. She finally gained her composure and said, "I want you to buy DJ's. I'm worried about who will buy it, and I'd be happy to work for you."

"Maybe I will," Dave said, "maybe I will."

Dave pulled into a gas station and said, "Look, there's a post office right over there!" He got out and started pumping gas. Delilah got out and said, "Earl and I need to run in and use their bathroom while we are stopped."

"Good idea. I'll park right over there under that shade tree and walk to the post office after I'm done getting gas." He pointed to a shady area. Before she got too far, he called, "Just a minute,

Delilah. Can I have your parents' address? I want to send them a note about where we are and what happened."

Dave almost ran to the post office. He couldn't wait to get rid of his phone. In only a short time he came hurrying back to the car. Delilah and Earl were sitting at a picnic table nearby. "There, let them track me now!" he said and laughed out loud. Delilah didn't share his joy. She just sat looking at the ground with her head in her hands. "What's the matter, Delilah? Do you have a headache?"

"Go in the gas station and look at the magazine rack," she said.

It didn't take Dave long to understand why Delilah was so upset. He first saw a magazine cover with a picture of Princess Di and a caption that read, *Princess Di, the last days before her tragic accident.*

Right beside that magazine sat a copy of *Humans* magazine with a big bold picture of Delilah and himself on the cover. Above the photo the headline read, *Author Samuel VanRokel's Son Seen with the Real Delilah.* Below, in bold lettering: *Samson and Delilah caught leaving a hotel together.*

All at once, Dave recalled the man taking their picture as Delilah helped him get his things from the hotel in Falls, Wisconsin. At first, he got excited about seeing his own picture on the cover. Then, the realization of how bad this might be for Delilah and her family sank in. He put down the copy he planned to purchase and headed to the Mustang.

CHAPTER TWENTY

Sweet Song

Dave slumped in his driver's seat. He leaned on the steering wheel and couldn't bring himself to even look at Delilah. She sat like a statue. Earl also sat perfectly still in the backseat.

Finally, Delilah spoke—so low that Dave almost couldn't understand her words. "Why didn't you tell me the truth about who you are?"

"My name isn't Samson, it really is Dave." He glanced at Delilah and she looked away.

"You're the author's son? Why didn't you tell me that you're the son of the guy who wrote the book?"

"Because I was embarrassed."

Delilah folded her arms and her brow contorted. "Why would that embarrass you?"

"If you finish reading the book, you'll understand." Dave tried to make eye contact with her, but Delilah refolded her arms and stared out the window.

At first, the only sound in the car came from the air conditioner. Then a soft sniffling sound became audible. The sound grew, as did Dave's curiosity, but he didn't dare look at Delilah. Finally, she blurted out, "Call that man! Call him and tell him he can take pictures of me!"

"Delilah—what are you talking about?"

"I want the money!" her face turned blotchy shades of red. "My life is ruined. No Amish boy will ever ask me on a date. All of our friends and relatives will be ashamed of me." She pushed on Dave's arm as if trying to spur him to action. "Call him—now!"

Dave lowered his voice. "I'm so sorry about all of this, but I can't call Charlie because I sent my phone through the mail."

Delilah looked at the ceiling and moaned in frustration.

"Give this some time," he said. "I have this feeling that it's not as bad as it seems. I think your friends and family know you didn't run off with me."

She faced away from him, staring out her window. His eyes fell on the little mole hidden in her neck hair and the tiny red dot where he'd pulled out the tick.

She spoke very quietly again. "We'd better get going if we are ever going to get to my cousin's house."

Dave put the Mustang in gear and drove on down the highway. He glanced at Earl in the mirror. The little boy's face had grown completely sober. Dave took note of the interesting cleft in Earl's small chin. After a length of painful silence, except for the clicking sound of Delilah biting her nails, she picked up the book and started reading again. After a few pages, she looked at Dave and asked, "Have you read this book?"

"Just a few days ago."

"Your dad wrote this book, and you only read it a few days ago?"

"My dad wrote a lot of books about the Amish, and I'm not a big reader. Plus, I had a bad feeling it was going to be about me."

"I . . . see. Why did you read it a few days ago, then?"

"You know why." He looked at Delilah, and she squinted her eyes at him. Dave continued, "I read it because I was offered a lot of money to find you. I needed to read it to know what I was looking for, or I should say, who." She listened to him with a sad expression on her face. Dave felt like his heart was about to burst. He wished he had listened to his mother's advice. He wasn't sure what to say to Delilah. Everything he could think of sounded cheap and phony. He kept his eyes on the road and Delilah went back to reading. Dave couldn't bring himself to look at Earl in the rearview mirror. He was afraid that if he saw the little boy's kind eyes, his own heart would break.

After another fifty miles, Delilah set down the book and said, "Could we listen to some Christian music on the radio?"

"Sure," Dave answered. He searched for a good radio station and found one with contemporary Christian music. Drumbeats and rock guitar thumped out. Delilah looked at the radio with surprise. "Is that Christian music?" she asked.

"Yeah, didn't you hear the lyrics?"

"It doesn't sound Christian to me," she said. Dave shut it back off. They rode along in silence again for a while, until Delilah spoke to Earl in Pennsylvania Dutch. Then she began to sing, and little Earl joined in. They sang the words to "Gott ist die Liebe" in German. Their voices blended perfectly. Then they sang it in English.

For God so loved us, he sent the Savior.
For God so loved us, loves even me.
Love so unending; for God so loves us,
For God so loves us, loves even me.

Dave felt hot tears stinging in his eyes. He could feel Delilah staring at him. After a few moments, she asked, "What's the matter?"

Dave choked out, "'God is Love' was my dad's favorite song. He put it in a lot of his Amish books, and we sang it at his funeral."

"I'm sorry. I didn't know it would make you sad to hear that," she answered.

"That's not it. I was just thinking how sad my dad would be about all the trouble we brought on you and your family." Dave's throat squeezed in on itself as he tried talking and another tear spilled down his cheek. "Please forgive me, Delilah. I'm so sorry that my greediness brought all of this trouble onto you and Earl." He used his sleeve to dry off his face.

She whispered, "I forgive you."

Dave heard Earl's little voice rising from the backseat, "I forgive you too."

Dave pulled over on the shoulder of the road. He leaned on his steering wheel and hid his face in his shirt sleeve. Finally, Dave regained his composure and pulled back onto the highway.

A few miles later, Dave forced out the words, "My dad would want you to forgive him, too."

"I can't," Delilah responded.

Dave glanced over. "You don't feel you can forgive him?"

"No—he doesn't need my forgiveness, because he didn't do anything wrong. I believe he meant well. He can't help what other people did with it."

"Oh good, I'm so happy you feel like that. My dad thought so much of you. He would hate it if you were hurt by what he did. But I have to say, he sure would be happy to know that you and

I became friends." He looked at Delilah and she was smiling. He thought about how innocent her eyes were. He knew the first Delilah couldn't have such an innocent look. He had stolen at least a part of her innocence himself.

She spoke and drew him away from his thoughts. "I'm sorry you've had to drive Earl and me all over the country."

Dave glanced at Delilah. "I've enjoyed it. This trip has been reminding me of trips my dad, mom, and I used to take when I was a boy. I was an only child, and we three took road trips like this one."

In only a few miles, Earl spoke to Delilah in Pennsylvania Dutch.

Delilah looked exasperated. "Earl needs to learn English or David should learn Pennsylvania Dutch."

"Why?" Dave asked. "What did he say?"

"Earl wants me to tell the sheep story again," Delilah said with a smile. She sat without speaking.

Dave asked, "Well, aren't you going to tell it?"

"I told Earl that you didn't want to hear that story again."

Dave shook his head and raised a hand from the steering wheel. "That's not true. Earl and I both want to hear that story again." He looked in the rearview mirror for the first time since they left the gas station. Earl returned the look with a big grin, and one crooked tooth.

"I . . . see," Delilah shook her head and smiled. "If you two insist. A few years ago, before our dad had his accident, we used to have a lot of sheep." Earl let out a low, "Baa." Delilah's cheeks balled up with a smile. She continued, "One time we bought a couple hundred lambs at the sale barn. Our dad planned to fatten them up and resell them. The only place we had to keep that many sheep, was in a lot right beside the house. Mom had invited our Bishop and his family over for supper that night." Earl bleated again, and this time Dave joined him. Delilah's teeth all showed, her smile was so big. However, she continued, "while we were eating, we had trouble hearing each other because the sheep were so loud."

"Baa!" Earl called, and Dave answered him, "Baa!" The two of them kept up as many bleating noises as they could make. High-pitched baa sounds and deeper-sounding baa noises. Delilah's face turned red, and she laughed as she finished telling her story, almost yelling. Little beads of sweat broke out among the tiny curls in her hairline. "We were going to play Dutch Blitz after supper, but we had to give it up because we couldn't hear a thing. Our Bishop finally said, 'We might as well go, since we can't hear a word you are saying.'"

Delilah joined in bleating, and they all kept it up for at least ten miles. Dave and Delilah looked at each other, laughing.

Finally, the sheep quieted down, and Delilah picked up her book and started reading again.

After a few pages, she covered her face and giggled.

Dave turned to look at her, "What's the matter?"

"I get it now. Samson is really *Sam's son.*" She covered her face in an obvious effort to hide her blushing cheeks. She read on for a little while longer and then set the book down and covered her face again. Dave glanced over and could see one of her eyes peeking between her fingers. "It's us! it's about us, isn't it?" she asked.

"Yep," Dave answered.

Earl called from the backseat in English, "It's about us?"

Delilah turned and looked over her shoulder. "Yes, you're in the story too, Earl," she said. "You and me telling the sheep story."

Dave could see Earl beaming in his rearview mirror. His tongue pushing his loose tooth in a semicircle.

"That's what I don't understand," Dave said as he wrinkled his brow. "How did my dad know about Earl and the sheep story?"

Delilah shrugged her slight shoulders. "Your dad—Sam, we called him—knew my whole family. He wanted to buy eggs, and I told him that we sold eggs at our farm. Your dad used to come to our house whenever he was in Falls. He heard me and Earl tell the sheep story more than once. We only knew him as Sam, so I didn't make the connection with Samuel VanRokel. If my parents would have known that you were Sam's son, they would have trusted you even more.

"Now do you see why I was embarrassed to tell you who I was?" Dave asked.

Her eyes met his and she blushed again. "I didn't know it was a story about us."

Dave swallowed hard. "Well—just up to this part. I don't think the rest of the story will compare with us at all."

She looked him in the eyes, and he felt a sting in his heart. "Up to this part, it is *a lot* like us and our trip—don't you think?"

"To tell the truth, it's kinda scaring me a little."

She let her fingers wrestle on her lap again, and then whispered, "Why would your dad write a book about you and an Amish girl?"

Dave felt heat rise up his back and flood his face. "He told me that he always used real people as mental images when he wrote books. That gave him something to build his characters around. He told me that he used me as a character because I reminded him of a younger version of himself."

She gave him a quizzical look. "Why would he put us together in a book?"

He coughed nervously. "My dad thought you were about the nicest girl he ever met, and he wanted me to meet you. He actually brought me to DJ's Diner one time to introduce us. I didn't take it seriously. That's how I knew where to find you when the magazine offered me money."

She gave him a coy smile. "I remember it now." She paused and then added, "You seemed so sad that you wouldn't even look me in the eyes."

"Yeah—it was a bad day." Dave scratched his chin hair. "That afternoon we thought we found the girl I liked in high school, and when I realized it wasn't her, I got really depressed. The last thing I wanted was to meet another girl."

"I prayed for you that day," she said.

He turned to face her with a smile. "You prayed for me?"

"Yes. Your dad was always such a kind man and usually happy. I didn't know what happened, but I figured something really sad was going on in your life."

"I feel really bad that I wasn't nicer to you." He glanced at her, giving her a frowning smile, and continued, "My dad thought so much of you. And now, the very least I can do is help you get away, if you didn't want the publicity. Your boss, DJ, thinks that I took you away from Falls so I could keep the others from finding you and get the money."

"I know, Earl told me."

"Earl told you that?" Dave asked in surprise. "When did he tell you?"

"After you two came back from taking the rolls to town."

"Oh, I guess DJ *did* say that right in front of Earl. I didn't know he understood her, much less that he would pass that on to you."

"Yeah, Earl is pretty smart. You can't get much past him."

"Well, I didn't take you away from Falls only to get all the money. I should admit that I was still hoping for a chance at the money." He stopped to check the look in her eyes. "After I met your family and saw how upset they were, I also wanted to help you."

"I . . . see. I told Earl that I trusted you."

"What did Earl say?"

"He said, 'Me too.'"

Dave shrugged. "Maybe you two trust me more than I deserve."

She didn't say anything but sat staring at him while he focused on the road.

He tried to change the subject. "I still don't get how the paparazzi always figures out where we are."

She put a finger to her chin. "Is there a chance that your friend, Nate, is telling them?"

His jaw dropped for a moment. "Oh—that's it!" Dave pursed his lips and clenched a fist. "Why didn't I think of that? That punk is telling them where we are!"

She shrugged. "We don't know that for sure."

"No—I think we do!" He shook his fist. "I'm gonna punch that guy the next time I see him!"

She lowered her voice. "Calm down. Why would you hit him?"

"Because he did this to you and Earl just to get money!"

Her voice stayed soft. "When you see your own sin, you can forgive others when they sin against you."

"Oh Delilah, you just hit me right between the eyes!"

Her voice raised louder than his. "What?"

"I get what you mean. I'm guiltier than Nate. I've hurt you and Earl more than he has—and I did it all for money."

She reached over and touched his arm. "That's not what I was saying. I just meant, sins in general. I never meant to call you out on that."

Dave pointed to his glovebox. "Could you get my map out of there. We need to find another two-lane highway to take. I told Nate that we were gonna take highway 6 to Indiana. We'd better veer further south or we'll run into camera people again."

She fumbled with the roadmap of Illinois and Dave pointed to a line lower on the page. "What road is that?"

"It says highway 18."

"Good," Dave answered, "We'll take that backway to Indiana and get there by sundown. Your parents wouldn't want you out on the road with me at night."

She nodded. "They didn't want me to go to Indiana at all—because that boy they don't like lives there."

A twinge of jealousy pricked Dave's heart. "You won't try to see him, will you?"

"No." she shook her head slowly. "He wouldn't want to see me anyway."

She slipped back into her reading and toe wiggling while Dave's mind returned to painful memories of the other Delilah.

CHAPTER TWENTY-ONE

Losing the First Delilah (flashback)

Dave's mind went back to the other Delilah and the incident under the train. It had happened years ago, and he'd always blocked out the memories for some reason. Something about riding in a car with another Delilah and using that name again caused everything to resurface. The car rumbled over some bumps in the road and Dave remembered waking up under the railroad bridge to the vibrations of his cell phone. He recalled scratching his head and saying, "What?" into the phone.

"Where are you guys?" Nate shouted, his voice so loud it stung Dave's ear.

"We're down under the railroad bridge. Why?"

Nate didn't try to hide his frustration as he barked out, "Delilah's cousin had to go home, and she couldn't find you guys. Now we gotta take her home."

"Okay, sorry about that! We fell asleep. I'll wake up Delilah, and we'll head back right now."

Nate snarled. "Hurry up! Katie told me that Delilah lives over by Shipshewana. That's a half hour from here, and I've gotta be home by one a.m. or I'll be grounded for the summer."

"Okay, okay—we'll be right there."

Dave shook Delilah. She moaned and barely moved.

"Delilah—wake up."

She rolled onto her stomach, and he could hear her moan again and then cough. She tried to rise onto her knees and leaned over. He guessed what was happening and pulled her soft hair back as she vomited.

"Da-hang it," she muttered.

"Oh you poor thing—what have I done to you?" He picked her up in his arms and climbed up the rocky slope toward the tracks. She moaned a little as he stumbled on a railroad tie. Her hair hung over his arm and one of her hands flopped as he walked.

Nate stood beside his car with keys in his hand. "Come on, Dave! We've got to get her home and back to Goshen before one a.m. or I'm done for."

"I'm sorry, Nate," Dave said sincerely. "That wine hit us a little harder than we expected, and Delilah is passed out."

"You'd better get her sobered up before we drop her off at home."

Delilah coughed, and Dave lowered her to the ground as she threw up again. He helped her wipe her mouth off with a napkin and set her onto the backseat. He climbed in next to her and tried to fasten a seatbelt around her while she slept.

"Are you sober enough to drive?" Dave asked.

"Unfortunately, I'm completely sober. Or else I'd be in a better mood about all of this."

"Okay—good!" Dave said. "I owe you big-time. How are we going to know where Delilah lives, I'm not sure she'll wake up enough to tell us?"

"I have her address already typed into my GPS." Nate said, "Katie gave it to me along with that bag of Delilah's."

Nate squealed his car tires before Dave even had a chance to put on his own seatbelt. He brushed Delilah's hair back from her warm cheeks and tried to wake her.

"Delilah, wake up. It's time to go home."

She moaned and mumbled something in another language. He listened carefully, but her words were a mishmash of guttural sounds he couldn't understand.

"Open your windows, Nate. Maybe some fresh air will help her pull out of it?"

Nate didn't answer, but the windows came down and cool air flooded the backseat.

Delilah sat up and brushed her long hair away from her face and mumbled, "Where are we going?"

"We're taking you home," Dave answered. "Katie had to leave and asked us if we could take you."

"Okay," she answered, and her head rolled back again.

"Oh—crap!" Dave growled, "I can't take this poor girl home like this. What are we gonna do?"

"Don't worry," Nate said. "There's a McDonald's in Middlebury. We'll get her a cup of coffee and she'll be as good as new before we get to Shipshewana."

"I bet," Dave muttered.

She did come-to a little after she drank a few sips of coffee. Dave kept talking to her and brushing her long hair from her face. The cool wind seemed to help.

Nate's GPS announced, "Your destination is on the right."

Dave leaned forward to see out the front window. They turned into a short lane and a huge white farm-house came into view. A white fence lined the driveway leading back to a buggy shed.

"This can't be it," Dave moaned. "That's an Amish farm."

Nate shut off his car at the entrance to the lane. "Ask her—this is the address Katie gave me."

Dave gave Delilah another sip of hot coffee. "Hey, hun, wake up; we're home."

She reached down and unbuckled her seatbelt, popped open the door and started to get out. Dave jumped out of his side and hurried over to help her. He grabbed her bag that Katie sent along. She stumbled a little and he took her arm with his free hand.

"Is this where you live?"

She nodded, "Yep—that's my house."

Everything looked quiet and dark. Dave helped her walk up the drive, but he still didn't know if they were really at the right place. A farm dog started barking and ran at them.

"Da-hang it, Buster, be quiet!" she commanded. The dog stopped barking and came up wagging his tail.

"Good dog, Buster," Dave whispered. He leaned into Delilah. "Are you going to be able to get inside okay?"

"Yeah—I live here."

She took ahold of the door handle and headed inside without saying a good-bye. Dave set her bag inside the door and decided he might be doing her a favor to get out of there as quickly as possible. He ran to the car with Buster at his heels.

"Let's go!" he shouted to Nate as soon as he hopped into the car.

Nate backed out of the drive and revved his engine as they sped away.

"European girl," Nate teased. He laughed out loud. "So, I'm too much of a redneck to understand a classy European girl, according to you?"

Dave shook his head. "I can't believe she's Amish."

Nate laughed all the harder. "You'd better start believing it."

"But—she was at the pool—wearing a swimsuit!"

Nate flipped the car dome light on and off. "Wake up, Samson. Haven't you heard about Rumschpringa? Those Amish kids go wild when they're on Rumschpringa. You just got duped by a wild Amish girl."

"Shut up, Nate—she's not a wild Amish girl!"

"Okay, believe whatever you wanna believe. But it's as plain as day that she is. I bet those wild Amish boys love her!"

Dave smacked the back of Nate's head.

Nate only laughed harder. "Wait till I tell all the guys at school that our basketball team captain is in love with a wild Amish girl."

"You keep your mouth shut, or I'll tell everyone what happened with you and Mary Lou Hansen!"

Nate stopped laughing. "Geez, dude, I'm just teasing you a little. I won't say anything. And, besides, you already promised you wouldn't tell anyone about Mary Lou."

Dave slumped back onto his seat and tried to think. It never occurred to him that a girl named Delilah could be Amish, much less that an Amish girl could look so beautiful in English clothes. He remembered telling Delilah that he had never kissed a girl. He thought about the fact that she didn't say that she'd never kissed a boy. His heart ached with jealousy as he considered that he might be one of many boys she'd been with. Dave tried to imagine himself dating her, and it seemed impossible. Her sweet face came back to mind and he felt guilty about getting her drunk—and everything.

Nate's voice snapped him out of his thoughts. "Don't be so down. You had fun, she had fun—now forget about her."

After that, Dave was afraid to see Delilah again. Nate wanted to go to the park, but Dave made excuses. He couldn't stop thinking about her. He wanted to see her. However, he was afraid that Nate would say something berating about her and they'd get into a fight. Dave feared he would explode if anyone said anything bad about her, especially Nate.

Dave also feared that she would hate him now for a whole bunch of reasons. For starters, he got her drunk until she passed out and then she woke up sick and vomited. He dropped her off at her Amish parents' home, still intoxicated and wearing English clothes. She probably hated him for that alone. He winced when he thought about how he ran off without even saying good-bye. And then, he wasn't sure how she felt about everything that happened under the train trestle. He could only hope that she forgot about how he acted toward her or dismissed everything as drunkenness.

Other feelings came into his heart. What if Nate turned out to be right? Maybe she was a wild Amish girl? Dave poured over his memories of how she smiled at him in her tan swimsuit. He couldn't forget how desirable she looked in that. He remembered how easily they touched. She told him to put her on his shoulders within minutes of finding out her name. During those few days, Dave concluded that her easy-going way was a type of innocence. Her actions were almost that of a little girl. Unless, of course, Nate was right and being in close contact with boys happened to be something she felt comfortable with. His heart ached with a pain he never imagined possible when he thought of her being a toy for uncaring boys, Amish or not.

His fear of seeing her with an angry face—with any negative expression—was debilitating. And then there was more. He felt embarrassed that she was Amish. He felt ashamed of himself that he was embarrassed that she was Amish. He feared anyone seeing him with her. Partly because he knew they would tease him about her being Amish, and because he knew he'd be furious if anyone said anything mean about her.

All these thoughts swirled in his head. None of his questions seemed to have answers. He couldn't tell if his fears were founded or irrational. He kept thinking that he would try and see her again when his mind and feelings became clearer. Suddenly, he realized that he had waited too long to see her again. After so many days had passed, she would think that he was a player. That his kind words were all part of a trashy trick to try and get her drunk and take advantage of her.

Over the next few weeks, Dave tried to take Nate's advice and forget about her. He couldn't. He drove by her family farm a few times and thought about stopping in. He tried to imagine himself asking her dad if he could take her out. That was laughable. He tried to come up with a plan to sneak up to the house at night and maybe toss a stone at an upstairs window like boys do in movies. He didn't know which room she'd be in. He even thought about parking at the end of her farm lane to wait for her to come outside. That seemed creepy. A few months passed. He hoped that he'd feel less guilty, but he didn't. He started hoping that he'd forget about her. Gradually, he did start to forget what she looked like. The harder he tried to picture her face, the more it eluded him.

One Saturday, about six months later, Dave decided that he had to see Delilah again no matter what. He drove right up to her house, determined to knock on the door and ask to talk to her. What did he have to lose? Although, it seemed possible that they might call the police on him. He had grown weary of feeling heartsick, so he didn't care about that anymore. Buster didn't run up to meet him, but another smaller dog growled at him as he got out of the car. His heart pounded, and his hands were shaking as he tapped on the door.

An older Amish man came out of a barn a short distance from the house. "Can I help you?"

Dave swallowed hard. "Does a girl named Delilah live here?"

"Why?"

"I'm a friend of hers, and I just wanted to talk to her for a minute."

The man gave him a stern look. "Her family moved."

Dave took a step toward the man, less afraid now that he knew it wasn't her dad. "Can you tell me where they live?"

The man leaned toward Dave, and his eyes pierced right through him. "No—they asked me not to tell outsiders where they went."

"Okay, thanks," Dave said and hurried to his car.

He didn't realize he had started crying until he felt hot tears running down his cheeks. He scolded himself for being such a baby, but he couldn't quit sobbing. "I've gotta talk to my dad," he said out loud inside his car. He had to pull over first and wipe his eyes so he could see before he raced home and found his dad out in the garage. He knew his dad would give him loving advice.

"I can't believe I thought she was European. I know it's no excuse, but I wouldn't have brought the wine and let everything else go the way it did if I had known she was Amish."

Dave's dad nodded. "I understand how it seems different. It's not though, because every girl is precious in God's sight. Sometimes a first impression of a person dictates how we think of them and what we expect of them. It's important to really take time to perceive who they are. I'm gonna start praying that you can find her and ask her to forgive you."

CHAPTER TWENTY-TWO

The Idea

Illinois, like Iowa, seemed to be an ocean of corn. An occasional farmstead with barns and out-buildings appeared like islands in the sea of cornstalks. They passed smaller seas of soybeans and hay from time to time. When pastures with cattle came into view, Dave alerted Earl, and he stopped playing with his plastic horses long enough to take in the sight. Once in a great while, Dave spotted a lone horse and shouted the news. Earl's face beamed with joy as he echoed Dave by yelling, "Horse!"

"I have an idea," Dave said to Delilah. "I'm going to stop at the next town and find a place with a Wi-Fi connection."

She wrinkled her forehead. "What's a *why fly*?"

Dave chuckled. "A wireless connection to the internet. So I can post something online."

"Whatever," she said and returned to her reading.

They came into a little town with a few gas stations and a bar. A little coffee shop sat nestled in the heart of town. Dave parked in front of the coffeehouse and got out his laptop. Earl and Delilah watched while he pulled up his Facebook page and logged in. "My dad started this page to help sell his books. I took it over after he died and post things as "Samson." He got out of the car and faced his laptop toward an open field across from the coffee shop. "Hey Delilah, would you do me a favor? Do you see this little button on my laptop? When I tell you, push it."

Delilah looked at the laptop and prepared herself to push the little button. Dave hurried out into the open area and said, "Okay." Delilah did as she was asked, and an almost silhouetted sideview of Dave appeared on the screen of his computer.

"Did I just take a picture of you?"

He came back near Delilah and the laptop. "Yep, I hope you don't mind. I just wanted to show you something." He studied her face and she didn't seem upset. "I want to ask you to let me take another picture just like that one. It won't show our faces, just our silhouettes. Would that bother you?"

"I guess not." She looked at Dave as if confused.

"Earl, would you be willing to push that little button on my computer when I say to?"

"Yes!" he nodded with a smile.

Dave told Delilah, "Let's go out there and face each other, like on the cover of the book."

She smiled and followed him out to the open field. They stood a few feet apart and faced each other, reenacting the cover of the book. He looked into her eyes and felt a spark of electricity flash between them. He called to Earl, "Go ahead." They gathered around Dave's little laptop and looked at the silhouetted picture. "I'll show you what I want to do," Dave said. He clicked on the photo and typed these words with the picture.

This is a picture of the real Samson and Delilah, hiding from the media.

Hello from the real Samson. All of you Delilah fans know something media giants don't. You know the real Delilah. I found her working at a restaurant just like the Delilah in the book. She is exactly like my dad described her. Anyone who has read Samson and Delilah knows that she wouldn't meet up with a guy at a hotel and then sneak off. Delilah wants to hide from the media, and I am helping her. Do us a huge favor. Please boycott any magazine that takes a photo of Delilah. If we all agree to that, they will give up and leave her alone! If you love Delilah, you will help me protect her. If you agree to boycott any magazine that shows a picture of Delilah, click "Like" and "Share." Let's see how many "Likes" and "Shares" we can get. Let's send a message to those media giants.

"Would you be okay with me putting this on Facebook for the world to see? I think it may solve our problem. If enough people refuse to buy their magazines and pictures, they will give up on it. All they want is money and sales. They don't care about us."

"I . . . see." She looked at the picture for a moment. "Sure, you can put that picture on. It's worth a try, isn't it?" She wrinkled up her nose with a smile. "Actually, that's a really smart idea!"

"I'm not that smart," Dave said and winked. "I prayed about it while you were reading the book. God must have given me the idea."

She gave him a knowing smile and they all three got back into the Mustang and sped down the highway. A bridge came into view and Dave began to groan.

Delilah stopped reading and looked at Dave. "What's the matter?"

"Here comes another bridge."

"Just look at the road straight ahead and don't even think about it being a bridge," she suggested.

Dave tried to take her advice. He studied the road closely and it worked until the pavement gave way to a see-through wire. "Hey, hey—Delilah! Take the wheel—Delilah!"

Earl began to chuckle.

"I can't drive a car!" she shouted.

Dave covered his face and growled through his teeth, "You have to—I can see right through this bridge!"

Earl's chuckle grew louder. The Mustang's tires made a strange rumbling sound on the wire mesh.

Delilah shouted, "I can't—I've never driven a car!"

"You have to," Dave groaned through his clenched teeth.

Delilah calmly said, "Okay—you can speed up now."

He peeked through his fingers and saw her hands on the steering-wheel. "What?"

"I said you can give it some gas. We're only going twenty miles per hour."

Earl's belly-laugh deepened to a point his voice went hoarse.

"Are we almost over?" Dave asked.

Delilah let out a sigh. "We'd be across by now if you would just give the car a little gas."

Dave pressed the accelerator.

"A little more," she instructed.

He pushed a little harder.

"That's good. We're over it now."

Dave looked past Delilah's hands on the steering wheel and saw a solid roadway rolling out before them. He let out a long, slow breath. He took the wheel, and she picked up her book and resumed her reading. Earl went back to farming with plastic horses.

After a long stretch of reading, Delilah put the book down on her lap. "Why did your dad tell people that there was a real Delilah?"

"Because he was getting criticized about Delilah's character in his book. Everyone said that the character was too 'perfect' and didn't have any flaws."

"Un fa shdendich," she blurted out. "I have all kinds of flaws."

"Like what?" Dave asked, not being able to think of any right off the top of his head.

"Well, for starters, I use the expression, un fa shdendich, too often."

"That is not a flaw," Dave said.

"It is by Amish standards. Our ministers preach against members using slang phrases." She answered as though that explained everything.

"What does un fa shdendich mean?" It hadn't occurred to Dave that it may be a cuss word.

"It means something like, 'I can't understand it' or 'unbelievable.'"

Dave scrunched his face. "And what is bad about that?"

"It's not the word that is so bad, it's repeating it often and using it the way a worldly person would use a swear word. That is what our ministers are against. And now, everyone in the world knows that I do that. Do you have any idea how embarrassed I am? I've been trying so hard to keep myself from saying it and it's difficult."

He smiled and looked into her innocent eyes.

"I used to say, 'da-hang it' all the time." She returned Dave's gaze as if appalled at herself for such wickedness.

Dave laughed. "Okay, so there is one glaring fault. What else do you have?"

Delilah folded her arms and looked away.

He nudged her shoulder. "Oh yeah, you bite your fingernails when your nervous."

She looked at him and her mouth dropped.

He lifted a finger. "Oh, and you wiggle your toes when you read."

A giggle spilled out of her. She pushed a hand against his arm. "Really, I have lots of other faults. I'm terrible with math. They won't even let me use the cash register at DJ's because I've made so many mistakes. Oh, and one more thing—I talk too fast."

Dave raised his eyebrows. "I've never noticed that."

"It's when I'm speaking Pennsylvania Dutch. English is my second language, so I speak it more slowly. When I'm speaking Dutch, I rattle it out like a windmill in a storm." She looked at Dave with a serious face and raised her eyebrows as though she had won an argument. Dave laughed, and Delilah furrowed her brow. "What is funny about that?"

Dave nudged her. "Just that It's cute, like all of your other faults. Like when you wrinkle up your nose every time you get a compliment."

She wrinkled her nose. "No, I don't!"

"I think I agree with the people who criticized my dad. You are almost too perfect to be real." Dave laughed after he said it.

Delilah folded her arms and looked away as if she were mad. "I'm not even close to being perfect," she muttered.

Dave laughed louder and looked in his rearview mirror and noticed Earl giggling too. "You Amish people look so innocent in those clothes."

"We don't wear these clothes to fool people. What am I supposed to do? Wear a scarlet letter?"

He laughed. "A scarlet letter? I can see in your eyes that you are way too innocent for that to be true."

Delilah narrowed her eyes and her voice sounded angry. "Okay, well, I'm not trying to deceive anyone, but that doesn't mean that I shouldn't try to put my best face forward."

"Whoa—take it easy here." Dave spoke calmly to try and settle her down. "I don't know why you're so upset just because I told you that you look innocent."

She folded her arms and turned away. "I'll tell you something that will show you I'm not even close to perfect—if you tell me your secret."

"Like the real Samson, there is a way to discover my secret. Shave off my beard."

She gave him a sideways glance. "What?"

Earl interrupted their conversation with a series of Pennsylvania Dutch words. He had been so well-behaved riding in a seatbelt all day. His patience seemed to be at its limit. He pulled on the belt and wiggled in the seat about as much as his tooth wiggled in his mouth. He didn't out-and-out cry, but he moaned and looked so sad that Dave couldn't stand it.

"What does Earl need?"

Delilah looked at Dave. "Earl says he's hungry and wants to stand up for a minute."

Dave shrugged. "We should stop even though we are only a few hours from your cousin's house."

"I think Earl is trying to stretch out our trip because he likes being around you," she said with a smile.

He glanced at her with a smirk. "I'm kinda guilty of the same thing. I'm gonna miss you both."

She giggled and almost flashed her eyes at him. They rounded a curve in the road and Dave noticed a short lane shaded by a large grove of trees. He pulled in sharply.

"This little spot might be perfect to stretch our legs for a moment," Dave said. "We need to get Earl out of this car, and nobody will see the Mustang from the road, so we don't have to worry about camera men finding us."

Delilah leaned forward, looking over the dashboard. "We could have a little picnic down by that creek."

CHAPTER TWENTY-THREE

A Surprise in the Woods

Dave parked the Mustang where nobody would see it, and they all got out and stretched. Delilah brought out her box of goodies. Dave laid a blanket on the grass and reclined on one side, watching Delilah cutting up apples and cheese. Earl hurried down to look at the creek. He called to Delilah in Pennsylvania Dutch, excited about something he found in the water. Dark woods stretched out on the other side of the creek as far as they could see. Golden evening light cast a magical hue on everything around them. For a moment life seemed like a fairy tale. Rushing water sang a melodious tune. Birds flew back and forth above them, joining their sweet songs with the brook's sonata.

Dave told Delilah, "Lay back and watch these clouds."

She let herself flop onto her back. "Oh, those clouds look threatening."

He teased with a growl, "Naw, that storm is passing to the north of us."

Earl came running back to where Dave and Delilah were stretched out on a blanket. He spouted off an excited row of Dutch words.

Delilah sat up and looked across the creek. "Earl says there's a treehouse across the creek and he wants to know if he can go play in it?" She gave him a handful of cheese and apples to put into his pocket and take along.

Dave stood up and followed Earl to the creekbank. A large tree just beyond the water filled up the sky with its massive branches.

"There!" Earl pointed.

"I see that," Dave said. "That's a pretty cool treehouse."

Creek water rushed past, gurgling with a fairly strong current. However, the water didn't look too deep.

Dave picked up Earl under his arms and spun him around a few times while the little guy let out a squeal of delight. After he set him on his feet, Dave squatted beside him. "Go ahead but be careful you don't fall out of the tree."

Earl chuckled and rushed through the quick current. His little bare feet digging into the muddy bank on the other side. Dave watched as little Earl half-climbed a tree. He made some use of a ladder of boards that had been nailed to the trunk for children that didn't know how to climb. It seemed Earl's bare feet were almost like a second set of hands as he scaled the trunk and conquered the challenge of entering the fort.

The massive oak's trunk divided into four smaller, but still huge, trunks. Someone saw the oak's potential as a perfect treehouse tree and built an elaborate fort within its limbs even though there were no houses anywhere nearby. Not only did this treehouse have a roof, but it had sidewalls with large, open windows.

Earl poked his head out of one of them and waived. "Hi David!"

"Hello Earl David!" Delilah's voice surprised Dave, he didn't realize she had gotten up and stood beside him.

They both waived at Earl.

"Should we go over there and check out that treehouse?" Dave asked.

Delilah shook her head emphatically. "No thanks! That creek is a little too wide and its current looks too strong for me." She cocked her head and gave Dave a wide-eyed expression. "You go right ahead and join Earl if you want. I think I'll stay on this side and watch those clouds."

Dave looked at the creek again. "Yeah, you're right. I'd have to take my shoes off if I wanted to go over there. You'd better tell Earl to call to us before he tries crossing back over. I wouldn't want him to slip in that quick current.

She cupped her hands to her mouth and called, "Earl!"

His smiling face reappeared at the window again. She used her octave-lower Dutch voice to explain that he needed to get her attention before crossing back over.

Dave followed her back to their picnic spot. They took their places on either side of the blanket with the food box between them. Delilah stretched out, gazing at the storm clouds off to the north. Dave watched her. She picked a long, thin blade of grass and nibbled at the white end of an otherwise green stem.

It seemed so ridiculous to Dave that a battle went on inside him between two Delilahs. For one thing, neither of them would really want to be with him. He doubted he would ever see the first Delilah again. He prayed that he would get a chance to see her just one more time, so he could tell her how sorry he was. As he watched this Delilah, he smiled about how methodically she had stolen his heart. Every little curl of her lips and singsongy line of sweet words gently gripped another piece of his heart.

The clouds billowed up into impressive domes. Lightning flashed within their interiors, giving them a majestic and surreal look.

"It looks like it's raining up north," she said.

He only grunted an agreement, picked up an apple, and bit it with a crispy crunching sound while he watched her mouth play with the blade of grass.

She took it out and said coyly, "Tell me more about the girl you liked in high school."

"What should I say? I mean—she was pretty and nice. You remind me of her in some ways."

"What's her name?" Delilah asked.

Dave coughed on a bite of apple and she sat up to see if he was okay. "Eh—I'd rather not talk about it," he said.

"Did you think she was the one for you?"

"I don't know. I never really looked into her eyes," he said.

"Why do you say that?"

"My dad told me that I'd know when I found the right girl if I looked *into* her eyes and not just *at* them."

She gazed at him as if daring him to look into her eyes. He couldn't bear to do it. The innocence in her eyes stung his heart too much. He didn't need to try it anyway. He had already looked into those eyes on the first day he met her at the diner and knew she was the right girl on so many levels. He just didn't feel like he was the right guy.

Without looking away from him, she asked, "Did she end it or did you?"

He lifted the apple and waved it in the air. "It's really hard to explain. Let's just say the whole thing ended badly."

"You need to find her and talk to her."

Dave took another bite of apple to give himself time to think of what to say. He spoke around the apple in his mouth. "I don't think she would want to talk to me. I was—mean to her. I feel awful about it, but I'm sure she would rather not see me again."

She sat up, pulled her knees to her chest and tugged her dress to keep it modest. "I disagree with that. I think you both would feel so much better if you found her and told her that you're sorry. Then, you'd be able to move on."

He let himself look into her eyes for a moment. Deep kindness and concern for his welfare glowed in them. A pain pierced his heart, and he had to look away. It was as if he could see right into her soul through her eyes. Kindness, innocence, trust, and a sweetness that almost seemed like sadness emanated from them. He feared that she might also see into his soul if he let her look into his eyes.

"Maybe you're right," he said. "That's a bridge I need to cross, but I don't know if I have the courage to do it."

"I'll pray for you. That God will provide an opportunity for you to talk to her, and that you'll have the courage to say what you need to say."

"I have a question for you," Dave said. "Did you ever have a time of Rumspringa?"

"Not really. I spent a week at my cousin's place when I was about seventeen. She was doing the whole Rumschpinga thing and talked me into dressing in her English clothes a few times." Delilah stretched out on her side with one arm propping up her head. Her eyes glazed as if remembering. "I didn't like who I was in those clothes."

"You *are* who you *are* no matter what clothes you have on," Dave corrected.

"Not true!" she glanced at him for a second and then gazed off as if remembering again. "When I put on those English clothes, I felt like another person. It brought out the worst in me."

"Like what do you mean?"

"Before I put on those clothes, no boys ever seemed to notice me. When I dressed in my cousin's English clothes, I got a lot of attention from boys." She hesitated. "Well, especially from one certain boy."

Her eyes rolled over to check on Dave's expression and then away again. A smile curved onto her lips. "It was very tempting to put on clothes that made a boy notice me, and he was so handsome. I have to admit I was stunned when he first spoke to me. It's so flattering to a woman to have a man swoon over her. I was so surprised at how attractive he seemed to think I was in those clothes. It did something strange to me too. I acted bold and confident. I felt almost—sexy."

Her face got red and she hid it with her hands for a moment. She recovered and continued. "It was very tempting to see the effect those clothes had. They made him crazy for me. I don't think he would've looked at me twice if I'd been wearing an Amish dress."

Dave listened intently, his heart astounded by her words. He thought of the other Delilah and how her clothes tempted him to think of her in a sensual way. It had never occurred to him that it might also be tempting for a woman to find herself alluring. He wondered if he would have been attracted to that other Delilah if she would have been wearing Amish clothes when he met her.

She laid back on the blanket and picked up her blade of grass again, working it with her lips. "Is this part in the book?"

"No, I don't think so," he said.

She let a smile stay on her lips as she watched the clouds. "I'm surprised how much the book keeps being so similar to our trip."

Dave felt the color leave his face. Fortunately, she didn't see him go pale. "I wish you'd quit reading now. You've already found out the important things, and I don't think you'll like the ending."

"Why? What happens?"

He scratched his head and tried to think of what he could say. "Well . . . there's an accident and Earl gets hurt."

She sat straight up and looked first toward Earl and then at Dave. "Does he fall from a tree?"

Dave laughed. "No, a car accident on a bridge."

Delilah lay back, relaxed again. "I guess not everything in the book is exactly like our trip. But I have to admit it's strangely similar."

"I know, it's kinda freaking me out," he said.

Thunder sounded with a mighty clap and made them both jump. Delilah stood up and gathered the food items. "It looks like we'd better clean this all up before it starts raining on us."

They worked together folding up the blanket and loading everything into the Mustang before heading over to end Earl's fun. Another rumble of thunder sounded, and big fat raindrops began to fall. Delilah called to Earl, and they could see him descending from his treehouse. She ran ahead, holding one hand over her Amish covering to keep the rain off. She gathered up her dress and apron in the other hand as she ran. Dave couldn't help but smile at how cute she looked. Suddenly she stopped as if she had seen a bear. Delilah turned to Dave, her eyes wild with fear. "The creek's gone full!"

Dave ran up and gasped. "Oh no! What were we thinking?" He cupped his hands and yelled to Earl, "Don't try crossing over!"

Earl finished climbing down and ran toward them. His eyes wide as he surveyed the crisis himself. Water rushed between them in a torrent, creating white-tipped rapids and making an eerie roar. Dave's mind raced as his eyes searched the area, trying to think of a quick solution. Sheets of rain pounded on them, making it even more difficult to think. He turned to look for a log or gate he could throw over the water as a bridge. And then he heard a splash and Delilah scream, "David!"

He flashed a glance at Earl, who still stood on the opposite bank pointing into the water. Dave sprinted to where Earl pointed and saw a blue dress surface in the torrent. He yelled, "Delilah—*Delilah*!" and ran full speed trying to get ahead of where he last saw her dress and jumped. The cold water pushed him down hard, and he hit the bottom. As he came up, something banged into him and he grabbed it with one arm. The unmistakable warmth of a body pushed against him, and he held onto her for dear life.

They rolled and tumbled for what seemed like an eternity, however, only a few seconds passed before they worked together and stood. Dave drew in a deep breath, having held his before jumping. Delilah, on the other hand, gasped and choked. Just before they were pushed down by the raging current, Dave caught a glimpse of Earl, standing on the bank holding out a small stick. Dave's hand instinctively reached for it, but his mouth shouted, "Stay back!"

The heavy water pushed them without mercy. Both of Delilah's arms hugged Dave tightly around his waist. A thought flashed into his mind. *This is how people drown!* Yet somehow, the fact that she held onto him worked to his advantage. It freed up his one arm to flail for something to grab on to while his other arm clung firmly around Delilah's body.

As they spun out of control, a solid object punched Dave in the back. He grabbed at it with his free hand and held on. He didn't know what it was, and he didn't have time to process that information. All he could do was use the water's momentum to swing Delilah around him and throw her limp body toward the bank. As he did, he saw Earl pulling on her arm. Dave held tightly to the object with one arm while he used his feet to finish shoving Delilah's body onto solid ground.

A sense of relief flooded his whole being, to see her on the bank. He wrapped both arms around the solid object and tried to catch his breath before attempting to climb out of the torrent himself. Water, whether from the rain or his hair or the splashing current, continued to hit his face and enter his lungs as he tried to draw in oxygen. He coughed and spit and looked up at Earl. The little boy knelt beside Delilah, pushing her as if trying to wake her. The sight shot a final burst of adrenaline into Dave's aching body, and he made a frantic thrust toward the bank. He felt himself clawing at the mud with primal fury.

He didn't remember how he did it, but he suddenly realized he had not only made it up the bank but had reached Delilah's side and rolled her over onto her stomach. He pressed on the small of her back and watched her spit out water. He did it again and wondered if he pushed too hard. She coughed more water and moaned. He rolled her onto her back and pressed his mouth over hers, breathing in life, if possible. Once again, she coughed up water. Her face was dripping wet. Her lips looked blue and cold. Once more he covered her mouth with his and gave her a puff of air. This time she moved. First an arm lifted. Then she curled up in a fetal position and coughed and moaned. Her Amish dress clung to her, soaked and dark.

Dave looked at Earl. "We need to get her out of this rain!"

Earl pointed to the treehouse.

Without knowing how he'd get her up into the tree, he hoisted her into his arms like a child and ran. As they covered the ground between where they crawled out of the creek and the treehouse, Delilah stirred and began crying, "Earl— where's Earl?"

"He's right here behind me!"

She moaned again and slurred out the words, "Earl—where are you Earl?"

Dave tried to speak soothingly, "Earl's fine. He's right here with us."

When they reached the tree, Dave looked down at Earl. "You climb up there ahead of me. You can help pull Delilah up like you did at the creek."

Earl instantly rushed up the trunk and reached for her.

Delilah came to herself as Dave adjusted her in his arms to climb. She began to writhe. "What are we doing?"

He set her down, because of her struggling to get out of his arms. "We're trying to get up in that tree with Earl." He tried to sound calm and pointed to Earl.

She looked up at Dave with sweet eyes. "I . . . see. I'm sorry I fought you."

"It's okay," he smiled. "We want to get you out of the rain."

She reached up and let him take her into his arms. He lifted her toward the wooden ladder that was attached to the trunk. She took hold of a board and he cupped his hands and let her stand one foot in them. He lifted her like a person hoists another onto a tall horse. She must have had experience with that because she immediately knew how to use his help. Earl remembered his job and reached one hand down to her, while using the other to hold on to part of the treehouse. Seeing Earl obviously filled her with new hope and vigor, because she climbed the final steps into the shelter and held him in her arms.

Dave followed her up and flopped down, belly first, on the wooden floor of the treehouse and moaned.

"What happened?" Delilah looked from Earl to Dave and then back to Earl.

"We took a little swim," Dave said, allowing a smile to curve on his lips.

She looked at him curiously. "I jumped in the flooded creek to get to Earl, didn't I?"

Earl spoke to her in their own language for a moment.

She raised one eyebrow. "Earl says you jumped in after me and saved me."

Dave nodded slightly.

Delilah winced as if afraid to say the words. "Earl says that you kissed me."

Dave covered his eyes and laughed. "Please explain to Earl about mouth-to-mouth resuscitation."

Her eyebrows raised in recognition. "I . . . see. I didn't think that you really kissed me."

She and Earl had a conversation while Dave let his exhausted mind and body slip into a short nap.

CHAPTER TWENTY-FOUR

The Tree House

Sometime later, Dave awoke to the sound of rain on the roof. He listened to the peaceful sound for a few moments and then realized his face was pressed against a plywood floor. His eyes fluttered open and Delilah sat across from him on the floor. She made herself comfortable in the small room's corner, with her legs off to one side like a mermaid. Her dark hair, parted loosely, following the contours of her face; Silky and straight around her cheeks, both sides meeting under her chin. From there, her hair flowed in dark waves over her shoulders and fell around her arms to her waist.

He lifted himself slightly. "Delilah, what are you doing here?"

"I'm letting my hair dry."

He pushed himself up until his arms were straight and turned into a half sitting position. "Is that really you?"

She smiled a little, but her eyes gave away that his words almost offended. "Do I look that different?"

Earl moved, and the motion caught Dave's attention, reminding him of where he was and how he got there. The little guy sat in the shadowy insides of the treehouse without a shirt, beside Delilah.

Dave stood up with a jerk and a pain shot up his back. "Ouch," he groaned and rubbed his neck.

Delilah moved to stand up. "Are you okay?"

He motioned for her to stay seated. "Ooh, yeah, I think so, but I feel like I've been through a car wreck."

"I'm so sorry." The waves of her hair flowed as she shook her head. "I was afraid Earl wouldn't wait for us to get to him. I thought I could cross the creek."

He leaned down and looked into her eyes. "Are you feeling okay?"

"Yeah—why?"

"I'm worried that you might get a fever after taking in all of that water," he said.

She shook her head and her hair tumbled around. "I actually feel fine."

Dave slowly lowered his body back into a sitting position across from Delilah and Earl. He studied her face. He couldn't believe how different she looked with her hair down. Her eyes looked so much darker and bigger. Since Dave met her at the restaurant, her Amish dress had done a good job of concealing her figure. At this point, having been soaked in the creek, it clung to her, failing to hide her curves. Everything about her brought back memories of how she looked as a teenager, when he first saw her at the pool.

She gave him a questioning look as if wondering why he looked at her like he did.

He tried to pass if off by asking, "Do you even know how to swim?"

"No. That was dumb of me to try going in after him, wasn't it?"

Dave shrugged. "Actually, I was thinking it was pretty brave of you. I wish I had a sister that loved me like that."

"It was pretty brave of *you* to come in after me," she said.

Dave laughed. "If I were a little smarter, I wouldn't have to be so brave. Why didn't I think about what was going to happen to a creek with a downpour upstream?"

Delilah giggled. "I should have thought that far myself."

"Did the creek go down yet?" Dave asked.

She shook her head, hair falling around her. "I don't think so." She paused then asked, "I thought you were afraid of water?"

"No. I don't like bridges, but it's not the water I'm afraid of."

He gazed at her. She looked so beautiful with her dark tresses curling around her face and falling around her shoulders, as far down as her waist. He shook his own wet hair and scratched his head. "And, of course, I parked my car in such a way that nobody will see it and send us help."

Delilah smirked. "I . . . see. And, I suggested that you mail your phone. Now we can't call anyone."

"Don't feel bad," he said. "It would have been ruined when I jumped into the water anyway."

Earl chuckled at that.

Dave leaned out through the window for a moment. "It looks like we might be spending the night in a treehouse."

"Good," Earl said.

Delilah scoffed. "It might be good if we had dry clothes or a blanket."

Her words made Dave think about how nasty his shirt felt, stuck to his back like a washcloth.

"*Coom*," Delilah said as she motioned to Earl. He scooched closer, and she pulled off his suspenders and took his pants down. "Let's hang these inside here for a while before the evening gets cool." She motioned to Dave. "You too. Get that shirt off and hang it on this nail beside Earl's."

Dave started to unbutton his top button and eyed her nervously.

"What's the matter Samson," she said. "Are you afraid I might see your muscles?"

Earl could hardly contain his laughter. He flexed both arms and said, "I'm Samson."

"What are you going to do, Delilah?" Dave half teased, half worried about how cold she would get if she tried to sleep in a wet dress. "Maybe Earl and I could go stand under the treehouse for a while and let you air out that dress of yours?"

"Never mind," she said. "I wrung it out while you were sleeping and it's drying while it hangs over my knees. Besides, I don't think you'll find much cover under this treehouse. It's built in the fork of four large branches."

Dave nodded. "Oh, that's right."

Earl pointed to Dave shoulder and spoke in Pennsylvania Dutch.

"He says that your skin is coming off," Delilah explained.

Dave craned his neck to see his shoulder. A large flake of dead skin hung where his sunburn had been. He slowly pulled it up and off. Earl watched with wide eyes. Dave scratched another flake up and gently pulled it loose. "Do you want to try it, Earl?"

Earl scooched up closer and let his tongue turn as he pinched a little skin and gave it a tug. His fingernails, though tiny, stung a little as he worked hard pulling off pieces of dead skin. Earl spent the next half hour pinching and scratching edges of dead skin off Dave's back. Delilah sat in her corner and watched with a smile on her face. He had a feeling she wanted to try it too, but it seemed too awkward to invite her, and she seemed too shy to join in.

When Earl finished pulling off all the dead skin he could find, Dave took off his shoes and wrung out his socks.

"Let's do the rabbit," Earl said.

"Oh, you want to try tying my shoes?" Dave held his shoe on his lap and went over the little memory verse. "The rabbit goes around the bush and down into his hole. Now pull him out by his ear!"

Earl's chuckle came out of his little round belly, which shook. "Grab his ear." The richness in Earl's voice gave away his smile, even in the darkness of evening in a treehouse.

"Now you do it," Dave said.

Earl pulled one shoestring and untied the shoe. He straightened out the laces and curved one into a loop. "The bush," he announced. "The rabbit goes around the bush . . . and the hole!"

"Pull him out by the ear!" Dave said.

"By his ear!" Earl repeated with a deep chuckle.

Delilah laughed as she watched them. "You're learning better English being around Dave."

"David," Earl corrected her.

"Oh yes, I mean David." She gave Dave a knowing look.

After Earl practiced tying Dave's shoes for a while, he said, "I'm hungry."

Dave leaned out the window and looked at the creek. "It's still about as full as it was when we went swimming."

"Swimming," Earl repeated with a laugh.

"I can see my Mustang and the box with apples and cheese."

Delilah sat up and tried to see out the window. "Oh Samson, please won't you swim across that river and get Delilah an apple?"

"And blanket," Earl added.

"My, you *are* speaking English," Delilah said, looking at Earl.

"Get Delilah an apple," he repeated.

Dave shuffled his feet and gathered himself to head out into the rain.

Delilah scrambled toward him and grabbed his wrist. "You are *not* going to get apples!"

"If Delilah wants an apple, Samson will get her one," Dave teased.

She pushed Dave's shoulder until he fell back to where he had been sitting. "Delilah doesn't want to be responsible for Samson drowning. I already almost killed you."

They all three laughed, and the sound filled up the little one-room treehouse.

Earl hummed for a moment and then sang. "Ain't no river wide enough."

Dave took the cue and started the song. "Listen baby . . . ain't no mountain high enough."

Dave and Delilah sang it through several times, and Earl laid his head on Delilah's lap and let his eyes go shut while he listened.

Delilah gently shook Earl. "You'd better put your shirt and pants back on before you fall asleep."

The little guy's eyes were half shut while Delilah buttoned up his shirt and pulled on his small pants. She leaned back in the corner and let Earl nestle up against her. Earl spoke in Dutch, and Delilah translated. "Sing that song one more time."

Dave and Delilah went through it again. A pang stung in Dave's heart, and he realized that he was gazing into her eyes while he sang and she into his. Earl's breathing grew deep and slow. Suddenly Dave noticed Delilah's mouth trembling. He crawled over the wooden floor and took his shirt off the nail. "What's the matter, Delilah?"

"Nothing. I'm fine."

He buttoned up his shirt and leaned closer to her. "You're shaking. Are you crying?"

"No, I'm fine."

He reached over and touched her sleeve. "Oh Delilah—you're freezing."

"I'll be okay."

"Are you scared of me?" he ventured to ask.

"No, I trust you completely."

He scooched near her. "If you trust me, then let me sit next to you and keep you warm. I'm worried about you—that you're gonna get sick if you shake like that all night."

"Okay," she said.

Dave scooted up beside her and she leaned in, trying to warm up.

She giggled, then said, "If a girl wanted to get away from you, all she'd have to do is run across a bridge."

He elbowed her side. "Yeah, but don't jump into a flooded creek or I'll come in after ya."

They laughed together for a few moments. Frogs began to sing an evening song. Dave's thoughts returned to the moment he gave her mouth-to-mouth. He remembered the taste of her soft lips. He felt guilty for thinking that way and tried to push it from his mind. A moment later, he realized he was replaying the scene again, smiling as he placed his mouth on hers.

Delilah moved her head slightly against his shoulder. "What are you thinking about?"

"Oh nothing," he said, then felt guilty. He confessed, "Well, I was thinking about what happened earlier. Do you remember any of it?"

She laid her head back on his shoulder. "I remember stepping into the water and calling your name." She hesitated for a moment. "I also remember when you grabbed me in the current. I felt safe when I realized it was you and I held on with all my might."

He laughed. "You trust me too much. I almost lost you. It pretty much was a miracle that we didn't both drown."

He could feel her looking up at him. "What would have happened to Earl if we both washed away?"

"I can't even think about it," Dave said.

She let out a sigh. "What happened next?"

"We were tumbling underwater, and somehow I caught hold of a branch or something. The power of the water swung you around me, and I used that momentum to toss you up onto the bank. Earl was right there helping the whole time."

She snickered through her nose. "He saw you give me mouth-to-mouth."

Dave imagined her wrinkling up her nose even though he couldn't see it because of the angle of her head against his arm. "Yeah, it didn't cross my mind that he wouldn't know what I was doing. I hope he's not mad at me for kissing you."

She giggled and pressed her forehead against his arm. She spoke in her lilting, higher-pitched English voice. "I think he liked it. He said with a big smile, 'David kissed you and you came back to life.'"

Dave smiled in the dark. She moved to get comfortable and ended up with his arm around her.

He rubbed the sleeve of her dress. "Oh, Delilah, your dress is still wet, and you're freezing."

"I'm okay," she said.

"No— I'm worried about you two. Let me wrap my arms around you and Earl to keep you from catching your death of cold. That is—unless I'm scaring you?"

"I'm not scared of you at all," she said. "After all, you just saved my life."

Dave cleared his throat. "If you keep reading that book, you'll be scared of me."

"What are you talking about?"

He groaned. "Something bad comes out about me in the book."

She leaned away from him enough to look in his eyes. "I don't believe that! For one thing, you're a very kind man. And another thing, your dad wrote the book. He wouldn't put something bad about you in his book."

He let air out through his nose as a short laugh. "Remember, everyone thinks it's a novel. Nobody else knows that Samson is actually Sam's son."

She sat silently for a moment. "But, he didn't know that we'd really take a trip like this together. How can part of it be true?"

"I don't want to talk about it. It's embarrassing."

Delilah nudged him in his side. "Just tell me."

He felt his throat tighten. "No! I'm not joking around. I don't want you to ever read the end of that book. I want you and Earl to like me and trust me. I'm afraid you'll hate me if you read the ending."

"I could never hate you."

"Oh yes you could," he insisted.

She giggled, "What happens? Do we fall in love?"

Dave let himself laugh for a moment. "Maybe."

"Does he kiss me in this part?"

"No," he said with a chuckle.

She let her elbow nudge his side again. "Why not?"

"Because he didn't think you'd want him to."

She took her turn snickering through her nose. "He can't read me very good, can he?"

She looked up at him, and he studied her mouth in the dim light. He wanted to kiss her so badly that he could taste it. He would have leaned in immediately if he didn't fear what she would think after reading the rest of the book.

"I guess nobody would want to kiss me."

He hugged her against his shoulder. "Are you kidding. Sweetness bubbles up out of you and comes sparkling through your eyes."

"Is that a line from the book?"

He laughed. "Maybe there is something in there like that, but I just said it because I meant it."

She gazed at his face in the darkness. "I like how you said it. Better than what your dad wrote."

She didn't look away and seemed to be waiting for a kiss. Suddenly, a thought crossed his mind. *I'll lean toward her a little and make her come in for the kiss. That way she can't think later that I forced myself on her.* He moved his face ever so slightly toward hers and closed his eyes. Instantly, he felt her soft lips meet his. They tasted as sweet as he remembered. She pulled away for a moment and then he leaned into her for another. She willingly let him.

Earl stirred and mumbled something, and both Dave and Delilah giggled in the dark. He didn't try to kiss her again.

They cuddled, all three of them, in the darkness. Night sounds began to grow all around them. Crickets, frogs, and cicadas chirped continuously in the background while Dave listened to Earl's deep breaths. Warmth began to generate as he wrapped his arms around both Delilah and Earl. Delilah's breathing seemed soft—not that of a sleeping person. It made him wonder what she had on her mind.

"Tell me what happened with you and that girl," she said, giving away her thoughts.

He let his arms tighten around her in a gentle way. "You don't want to know."

Her hand touched his accidentally, and she quickly withdrew it. "Does it come out in the book?"

"Yep."

"Un fa shdendich! You know you're just making me want to finish reading it all the more." The sound of her voice gave away a smile.

"I know," he said. "My life is ruined already. Someone will tell you what happens even if you don't read it yourself."

She lifted her head away from him in an effort to see his face. "How does that ruin your life?"

"Because, the last thing in the world I want is for you to hate me, and you will."

Her body sank back into his. "I . . . see. Should I be scared of you?"

"I don't think so." He hesitated before adding, "But, I don't think you'd let me kiss you or put my arms around you if you had read the whole book."

"Un fa shdendich," she whispered.

He held her in the darkness until her breathing grew deep and slow. Savoring every moment, he imagined what life could be like if he married her. He knew how attractive she looked in English clothes. He knew for a fact that this was the girl he had fallen head over heels for in high school. The image of her beautiful dark hair falling around her sweet face, freshly stamped into his memory, matched that of his first love.

However, Delilah made it crystal clear that she had no desire to leave the Amish. Besides, something about her Amishness made her who she was. It wouldn't be good to change one thing about her. He tried to imagine himself Amish, and he let out a chuckle accidentally.

Delilah stirred, and he wrapped his arms around her tighter. She nestled in sweetly. He let his cheek lay against her soft hair. A smile developed on his lips without his planning on it. Sleep didn't come to him right away. He felt so restored, as if part of his own soul had been missing and had returned to him. He knew that if she had been awake, she surely would have felt the love in his embrace. Sooner or later, she would figure out that he was the boy she met in the park, and the affable relationship they had built over the past week would shatter.

Dave contemplated how changed her personality seemed and how different she looked in Amish clothes. He struggled to reconcile in his mind the astonishing contrast in her behavior from the first time he met her in the park to the day he met her at the restaurant.

A guilty feeling pressed in on Dave for not telling Delilah as soon as he realized that she was the girl. But, telling her while they were trapped together in a tiny treehouse with Earl would have been cruel. There wasn't any way to know how she would react, and he feared the worst. He expected that she would have a few harsh words for him at the very least. She seemed so forgiving and gentle. Yet, she also seemed completely oblivious to the fact that they had met before. Because it didn't make any sense to tell her at the moment, he let himself drink in the pleasure of holding her in his arms. Nothing in the world could feel more healing than to just hold her. He doubted she would ever allow him to be that close to her again. He promised the Lord that he would reveal his true identity and ask her for forgiveness before dropping her off at her cousin's home.

CHAPTER TWENTY-FIVE

Looking Deeper

Robins began to sing joyfully at the first glint of light. Their gentle song woke Dave from a sweet slumber. He suddenly realized that his back had gone numb and his arm that held Delilah tingled with a thousand pins. He started to move but then looked down and saw her sleeping peacefully with her head on his chest. Earl sagged comfortably on her lap. He decided that he could endure almost any pain to hold Delilah in his arms for as long as possible.

A few moments later, Delilah sat straight up and looked around the small room of the treehouse. She gently rolled Earl onto the floor and stood up. Dave let his eyes go shut just enough to make her think that he was still sleeping, so he could watch what she would do. She adjusted her dress that had become slightly twisted at her waist. She carefully gathered her long hair and wound it up while holding several hairpins between her lips. A pain pricked his heart as he watched her beautiful locks slowly disappear. He doubted he would ever see her with it down again. One by one, she used the hairpins to secure her hair and then carefully put on her covering, pinning it in place. She shook her apron and reached both hands behind her waist to tie a neat bow.

With everything perfectly in place, she brushed her hands all along her dress, front and back, smoothing out any wrinkles. She turned from side to side, examining herself to be certain everything looked right, and then she spoke matter-of-factly, saying, "Earl, it's time to go."

Dave moaned as he tried to stand. "Oh man, I'm sore from all the swimming we did last evening."

Earl's eyes popped open and he chuckled deeply. Delilah didn't laugh or meet Dave's eyes. He instantly worried that she regretted letting him kiss her. She gave Earl all of her attention, and the awkwardness of it overwhelmed Dave. He decided to climb down and check on the creek. He pulled up his damp socks and began tying his shoes.

"Let me," Earl said.

He moved his foot toward Earl. "I'll tie one and you tie the other." He watched as the little boy struggled with his shoelaces.

"Around the bush—in the hole—pull his ears," Earl said.

"You got it," Dave exclaimed. He glanced at Delilah, but she didn't look at him. "I'm going to go check on the creek. Let me know if you need help getting down from here."

"I'll be fine," she muttered.

Dave could hear gurgling water as he climbed down the board ladder. Rushing water noises rose up from the creek as he drew closer. He stood on a grassy ledge surveying the banks on both sides, searching for a good place to cross. The water level had dropped considerably. However, he didn't feel certain that Delilah and Earl would be able to withstand the remaining current.

Further down, near where he had pushed Delilah out of the water, he discovered a place where tree roots grew out of the bank and looped back down into the bank below. He concluded those roots, and God's providence, were what saved him and Delilah from a certain death. Just beyond the roots, he spotted a large rock protruding from the gushing water.

"We can cross here," he said to himself.

He headed back to the treehouse just in time to see Earl descend like a monkey. Delilah's bare feet and blue dress emerged, and he stepped back and turned his face away to give her privacy. She carefully felt each step below with her toes before moving down.

"Can you help?" her voice rose sheepishly.

Dave looked up and realized her dress had snagged on one of the boards and pulled tight against her legs, locking her in place. He laughed and reached up, unhooking her dress. He took her by the waist and spun her around, setting her feet on the ground.

She giggled, even though she seemed determined not to. "Un fa shdendich!"

Earl's rich chuckle echoed in the woods as he put his hands on his little belly.

"I found a place we can cross," Dave said, pointing to the spot.

They all three gathered at the bank and Dave explained, "I'll hold onto this root with one hand and stand on that big rock. You can take my other hand and I'll help you step onto the rock and on over to the other side."

Earl reached out immediately and took Dave's hand. He didn't hesitate to jump onto the rock and over to the other side. Delilah wrung her hands and looked at the water fearfully.

Dave held up his free hand. "I understand how you must feel, but trust me, you can do it."

She took his hand and pulled back. They met eyes and she pleaded, "Don't let me fall in there again."

"I won't," he assured her. He feared it was a promise he couldn't make.

She counted, "One . . . two . . . three . . . and then stepped onto the rock. Instead of using her momentum to jump to the other bank, she tried to stand up straight and lost her balance. Dave let go of his hold on the tree root and grabbed her waist with both hands, almost throwing her toward the other bank. His focus stayed fixed on her feet until he saw them touch the ground safely, and he felt himself submerge under the current again. He only rolled a short distance underwater before he managed to get to his feet and scramble up the bank.

"Oh David, I'm so sorry," she cried.

He jumped onto his feet and slapped his hands against his wet jeans. "No worries, a good morning swim is always refreshing."

Earl doubled with laughter and even Delilah let out a giggle. Dave popped open the back door of his Mustang and dug through his suitcase.

"I'm gonna hide behind these trees and put on some dry clothes before we leave," he announced.

Delilah took Earl and they stood with their back to Dave while he quickly peeled off his soggy clothes and dried himself with the picnic blanket. He yanked on a dry set of jeans and clean shirt.

"My turn next," Delilah said.

She scrounged through her things and pulled out a deep plum-colored dress. Dave and Earl turned to face the car while she hid behind them and changed. He noticed a reflection in the car window. He could see her bare back, but he quickly forced himself to look away. However, he had to wonder if she had noticed the same thing when he changed.

Dave put a hand on Earl's shoulder. "How about Earl? Do you need dry clothes?"

He met eyes with Dave and shook his head.

"I guess you didn't get as wet because you didn't go swimming with us," Dave said.

Earl nodded and let his happy chuckle out in full force. As soon as they were all situated in their seatbelts, Dave reminded them, "We only have a couple more hours before we reach your cousin's house. But we'd better stop and get some breakfast first."

Delilah picked up her book and began reading. The pages seemed to turn more quickly than they had before. Dave thought about her eyes. He wanted to peer into them so badly. He would have been happy if she would have given him a knowing look or smile, to acknowledge what happened last night. She gave him nothing. Not even a glance. He imagined that she might have figured out who he was and already hated him.

When he couldn't take it any longer, Dave touched her sleeve. "What's the matter, Delilah? Are you sorry we kissed?"

"I'm ashamed of myself," she said. "I've learned some hard lessons in life, and I've repented of my sins—and then I went and kissed you."

"Don't be so hard on yourself. I think it's my fault," Dave confessed.

She shook her head. "I pretty much asked for a kiss. I know when I'm guilty."

"Delilah—you are a good person. What happened wasn't that bad."

She waved her hand and refused to look in his eyes. "You don't know the whole story about me."

He didn't tell her that he probably did know the whole story. He would have blurted it out at that moment if Earl hadn't been

in the backseat. Delilah turned another page and focused completely on her book. Her toes wiggled on the dash as she bit her
nails.

Dave alternated between watching her, little Earl in the mirror,
and the road that rolled out before them. Every time he checked
his speedometer, he realized he was driving too slowly. He didn't
want the trip to end. Yet, he feared Delilah would finish the book
before he dropped her off. He tried to work out a way he could
gently break the news to her about who he was. Maybe it would
be best if she figured it out for herself by reading the book? He
knew it was inevitable. However, it would hurt less if he didn't
have to say the words himself. He couldn't resist watching her
toe wriggling and nail biting. As if she could feel his stare, she
turned her head in his direction without meeting his eye.

He whispered, "You can keep that book and read it later if you
want."

"Un fa shdendich, you are afraid I'm gonna finish it while
we're together, aren't you?"

"Yes, I am," he confessed.

She finally looked him in the eyes. "I'm sorry, but I *have* to
know the ending. It can't wait."

Dave didn't try to hide his disappointment. "Whatever. Are
you to the point where they have the accident?"

"Yes—on the bridge," she said with a nod. "I'm to the part
where they're on their way to the hospital, and the ambulance
driver tells her that he needs Earl's parents' permission before
they can treat him."

Dave slumped down in his seat. "Okay, get ready to hate me."

"Why would it make me hate you?"

He looked out the driver side window to avoid her eyes. "The
truth comes out about me. I'm not as good of a guy as you think
I am. Some things come out about the girl I liked in high school
and how I treated her."

She shook her head slowly. "I'm surprised your dad wrote about the accident happening on a bridge. Didn't he know that you don't like bridges?"

"It's because our family had an accident on a bridge when I was about Earl's age," Dave explained. "My dad liked to use real stories in his books."

She turned her whole body in Dave's direction. "Your family had a crash on a bridge?"

"Yep—almost exactly like the wreck in the book."

Delilah reached over and laid her hand on Dave's arm. "I'm so sorry I teased you about being afraid of bridges. No wonder they bother you."

"It's okay—I like it when you tease." He winked at her and she blushed.

While passing through a small town, Dave noticed a diner about the size and style of DJ's. "Let's stop in this little restaurant and get some breakfast."

"We could just eat apples and cheese," Delilah suggested.

Dave shook his head. "After all the swimming we did—and spending a night in a cold treehouse—I need bacon and eggs!"

Earl let out a hoarse belly laugh. Delilah smiled as Dave parked the Mustang.

Everyone in the tiny diner stopped eating and talking as Dave, Delilah, and Earl stepped inside. An attractive blond waitress met them at the door and led them to a booth. As soon as they were seated, the breakfast crowd stopped watching them and resumed their eating and conversing.

The waitress handed out menus and asked, "Can I get you some coffee? I just made a fresh pot."

Dave smiled at her. "I'd love some coffee!" He looked at Delilah and Earl. "Do you two want milk?"

Earl nodded, "Chocolate!"

The waitress walked away, and Delilah glared at him. "Did you see her blouse?"

Dave smirked and whispered, "Yeah—she needs to button that top button."

After they studied their menus and put in their orders, Dave took a sip of the coffee and spit it back into the cup. "Ugh—this coffee is horrible."

"Let me taste that," Delilah said.

"I don't think you want to after what I just did."

Delilah pushed a hand at Dave as if his words were silly. She took a sip and poured a bit of her chocolate milk into his cup. She added a teaspoon of sugar and stirred it in. "Here—try it again."

Dave gave it a taste. "Huh, that's good."

They all ordered eggs, bacon, and hash browns. When the blond waitress set their plates on the table, she leaned over Dave, and her blouse hung down so much that it embarrassed him.

Earl got busy eating. Dave met Delilah's eyes and tried to ask her without Earl noticing. "Does that waitress know her top button is undone?"

Delilah nodded. "She's working you for a better tip."

The waitress stopped back at their table and batted her eyelashes at Dave. "Is there anything else I can get ya?"

"Do you have cinnamon rolls?" Dave asked.

The blond touched Dave's shoulder. "We sure do! How many would you like?"

Dave looked at Delilah. She shook her head and held onto her stomach as though full.

"Just give me two of them," Dave said.

As the waitress leaned down to set the rolls in front of Dave and Earl, Dave asked, "Who makes these?"

She flashed a big smile at Dave. "A local bakery makes them fresh twice a week. Enjoy!"

Delilah looked from the blond's blouse to Dave's eyes with a cold expression. Earl tried to stick a fork in his roll and couldn't. Dave broke off a chunk and dipped it in his coffee to make it softer. "They must be going to make fresh rolls again tomorrow because I know they didn't today."

Delilah had to catch a swallow of chocolate milk in her napkin as she splatted out an unplanned giggle. When Dave came back to the table after paying the tab, he laid a few dollars on the table. He didn't want to offend Delilah by leaving the blond a good tip.

Delilah let her mouth hang open. "Is that all you're giving her?"

An older woman interrupted their conversation. "Excuse me—but could you people stay here for a few more minutes. My son works for a newspaper, and I told him that Samson and Delilah are here at the restaurant. He's coming as quick as he can to get your picture."

Delilah's mouth fell open.

Dave waved a hand. "I'm so sorry ma'am but we really don't want our picture taken. Please don't take it personally."

Dave pulled a few more bills from his wallet and tossed them with those already on the table and took Earl's hand. He opened the door for Delilah and realized she had stopped to pick up the tip off the table. She headed toward the door but paused near the waitress and handed her the money and whispered something in her ear.

They all three jumped into the Mustang and charged off before the newspaper guy could get there.

"What'd you say to that waitress?" Dave asked.

Delilah gave Dave a coy smile. "I just said, 'I think your top button accidentally came undone.'"

CHAPTER TWENTY-SIX

Crossing the Real Bridge

For the next few miles, Delilah intermittently read from her book and paused from time to time, letting out a sigh as if something bothered her. Earl quietly hitched up teams of plastic horses on his lap. After driving on a long stretch of road that seemed more like a tunnel because of the tall cornstalks flanking the road on either side of them, Earl interrupted the silence with a series of Pennsylvania Dutch words.

Delilah looked at Dave. "Earl needs to take himself away."

"Take himself away?"

Delilah smiled. "Bathroom."

Not far ahead, another small town came into view. Dave searched for signs of a fast food restaurant or gas station so Earl could use the restroom. Just as they came into town, a city park appeared. Once Dave found a shady spot to park the Mustang, they all climbed out and stretched.

Delilah handed Earl his hat. "You'd better wear your hat."

Earl's little legs scrambled toward the restrooms. Delilah didn't bother to put on shoes. She meandered through a grassy area and around a tree. Dave followed her. She leaned against the tree-trunk, staring off into the distance. He noticed her toes fidgeting in the grass. She nibbled on her thumbnail for a moment and opened her mouth as if planning to speak.

After drawing in a deep breath, she looked directly at Dave and said, "I was thinking about something—something about me that I should tell you."

Her words were interrupted by Earl's pitter-patter racing toward them. Dave picked Earl up under his arms and swung him in a large circle while the little boy chuckled loudly. Dave lowered him down and he hit the sod running. As he ran, he pointed to a large playground sprawled out behind the building. Big maple trees shaded swings, slides, and other equipment.

Delilah called to him, "We'd better tie your shoes or you should take them off!"

"I tie them," Earl said with a grin. His loose tooth sideways in his smile. "Rabbit goes around a bush and down his hole," Earl announced as he tied the shoestrings.

Delilah stayed on her knees beside him. "Then let me try and pull that tooth."

Earl stood, proud of his tied shoes. "Let David."

She glanced up sideways. "David doesn't want to pull your tooth."

"I don't mind," Dave said.

He knelt beside Delilah, and they both looked at Earl's tooth. The little boy moved it almost completely around with his tongue.

Dave lifted a finger. "Let me see how loose it is."

Earl opened wide and Dave popped out a little white tooth with a flick of his wrist. He held it up and showed Earl.

Earl pushed his tongue through the open slot with a grin and a hint of blood. "Can I play now?"

Delilah looked at Dave. "What do you think?"

Dave stood and snatched Earl off his feet, swinging him in a semicircle. "Of course you can! You tied your own shoes and let me pull out that tooth. Go have fun."

Dave barely got the words out as he lowered the little boy to the ground and Earl's legs churned, sprinting toward the playground. He stopped to pick up his hat that toppled off as he ran. He smiled at Dave and Delilah and said, "Thanks!" Then he resumed his mad dash toward the swings, holding his hat on with one hand.

They followed Earl, who had already climbed onto the seat of a swing. Pulling back on the chains, Dave released Earl and the little guy squealed with joy.

"Push!" Earl called.

Dave grabbed the chains. "I'll give you an underdog!"

He pushed hard, running under the little boy's seat and coming out the other side. Earl giggled and called for more. Dave pretended to lose track of where Earl was when running past. He looked around and called, "Earl David, where did you go?"

"Here I am, David!"

Dave jumped out of the way at the last second, just as Earl's swing came back, almost hitting him. That lasted for a good fifteen minutes. Delilah hung back and watched and giggled as much as Earl. Another boy about Earl's age came along and the boys decided they wanted to push each other on a merry-go-round. Even though the boys barely understood each other's words, they found a way to communicate.

When Dave turned back to say something to Delilah, he realized she had snuck away and found a seat on a picnic table that was near a privacy fence, under thickly leafed trees that provided so much shade it was almost dark. She didn't sit with her legs under the table but facing out toward the playground. He strolled over and took a seat beside her and they watched Earl playing with his new friend. He glanced at Delilah. Her face seemed distraught and she was biting her nails. He assumed she figured out who he was. If she hadn't yet, he knew that this was the moment he should tell her.

"What's the matter?" Dave asked.

"You were telling me that everyone thinks I'm such a good person, but it's not true. I have a dark secret."

Dave realized he was making an astonished face and tried to soften his expression. He assumed she was preparing herself to tell him about the boy she met at the park and he'd have to let her know that he was the guy. "You are a good person," He said.

"I confessed this at Church years, ago. We believe in confessing our sins to our Church. Once we do, it is forgiven and never mentioned again."

"That is amazing that your people are so forgiving and supportive," Dave said.

"Well, it is not mentioned in public, but people don't forget easily. They still remember what I confessed. That's the real reason that Amish boys don't ask me on dates." She glanced at Dave out of the corner of her eye.

Dave could feel his heart beating within his chest. He wanted to hear what she was going to say, and yet, he felt like running away and never having to hear another word. It didn't seem likely that boys wouldn't date her because of what happened between them. He sat frozen in time, staring at her.

Delilah leaned over and rested her hand on Dave's arm. He could feel her fingers trembling as she whispered into his ear. The quivering of her hand transferred into his arm and on down to his stomach. He felt his own heart pounding. Her warm breath tickled his ear, but her words fell into his heart, cold, as if she had stabbed him with an icicle. He wasn't sure he heard her right.

As cruel as it seemed to ask her to repeat it, he had to be certain he understood. "What did you say?"

Delilah leaned close and laid her trembling hand on his arm again. She whispered clearly, "Earl is not my brother."

Dave's whole being shuddered as he stood up and paced in front of Delilah. His mind raced, and he reached for the table, afraid he might lose his balance. He didn't know if he was hyperventilating or if he had stopped breathing completely. He didn't think to check if Earl was watching or not. He walked away for a few moments and then came back very close to where Delilah was sitting at the picnic table. He glanced at her for only a second. Her face looked blank, as if mystified by his response.

Dave fell to his knees on the other side of her to keep her body between him and Earl. She was close enough he could hear her breathing. Reason came to him for a fleeting moment and Dave thought to look for Earl before saying a word. He could see both little boys still playing on the merry-go-round.

"Is his dad Amish?" Dave asked without looking at Delilah.

"No," she said and paused. "English."

"Oh Delilah—I'm so sorry that happened."

"I've forgiven him," she said.

Dave tried to breath. Her words twisted the icicle dagger deeper. "I don't forgive him," he said, "I can't." He looked up for a split second.

Delilah's mouth gaped open. "What? why?"

"Tell me that you hate him," Dave said without looking up at her.

"I just don't," she said. "He was young and a little drunk, but I could tell that he was usually a really nice guy. I let him kiss me and then things got out of control."

"I'm sure you hate him for what he did to you? For Earl's sake, for your family's sake. Look what this has done to you. Tell me that you hate him, and I'll believe you. Tell me that you hate him, and it'll be easier for me." Dave was bent over, kneeling beside her with his face in his hands, mashed down on the picnic table's wooden seat.

"What is happening?" she said. "I don't understand what's happening right now." Her voice sounded far away and distraught. "I should have tried to stop him," she confessed.

"You shouldn't have needed to try and stop me." Dave's words felt sharp in his throat and stung as they spilled out. His heart throbbed within his chest. He covered his head with his hands and writhed in pain. He blurted out, "I hate myself. I hate my sin." He shook with sobs as he leaned on the bench and let all the guilt and shame that had constantly weighed heavy on his heart pour out through tears. He groaned from the deepest part of his being, "Please, God, forgive me—and take away this terrible feeling."

Everything went silent for a long moment. He wondered what expression she had on her face—what he might see in her eyes. He couldn't bear to look. A gentle breeze blew, and Dave felt his hair move, so softly at first that he assumed it was the breeze. Then he realized Delilah's hand lay gently on his head, softly running her fingers through his hair.

"I'm glad God let our paths cross again," she whispered.

Dave looked up. He couldn't see clearly through his swollen eyelids, but he thought he could see kindness in her eyes and tears running down her cheeks.

Her soft voice continued, "I didn't know how much it would mean to me to hear those words from you. It means everything." She didn't make any attempt to wipe her face dry but let her tears run down her cheeks, drip off her chin, and fall freely.

"You don't hate me?"

"I never hated you," she said. "I knew it was partly my fault."

Dave shook his head. "No, it was all my fault. I won't let you take any of the blame."

"That is not up to you but up to God to decide. Either way, He forgives us both." Her voice was as soft as an angel. "I'm glad we got to spend time together. Earl and I both like you." She pulled on his arm. "Come sit here beside me again."

He struggled to the bench and sat holding his aching head with his hands. He glanced over to see how Earl was getting along. "I'm amazed that Earl didn't come over here while we were talking."

"God must have sent that little friend along to keep him busy. He knew we needed to talk," she said.

Dave nodded in agreement. "God must have planned this whole trip because He knew we needed to talk."

"Did you know all along?" she asked.

"No—I didn't." He glanced at her, still too ashamed to look into her eyes. "Ever since that night, I've been tormented with how I treated you. My dad was such a kind Christian father. I went to him and broke down, confessing everything. He asked what I knew about you, and I told him that I found out you were an Amish girl named Delilah. I told him I went to your house to see you, but the people living there said your family moved away and were asked not to tell anyone where."

Her eyes showed surprise. "Did you go to my old house and ask about me?"

He nodded and finally let his eyes meet hers briefly. "Yeah—about six months later. I wanted to tell you how sorry I was about what happened."

She let out a sigh. "How did your dad find us?"

"It must have been the Lord," Dave said. "When I started going to college up at Rapid City, my parents came up often for visits. Dad always loved to drive around Amish communities and look at the farms and horses. He found out about the little town of Falls and always wanted to drive around that area. He told me about a diner down in Falls that had amazing cinnamon rolls." Dave looked at Delilah, and they smiled at each other. "He also mentioned that there was an Amish girl named Delilah who worked at the restaurant. He thought you were the nicest girl he had ever met. He told me about meeting your family—and about Earl."

Dave looked at Delilah, and she studied his face, waiting to hear more.

"I think he did the math and figured out that Earl was born after your dad's accident. He never came right out and said it, but it was obvious that he suspected Earl might be his grandson. All of this happened about the time Dad started writing his book, *Samson and Delilah*."

"And then he brought you in to meet me after that, didn't he?" she asked.

"Yeah, he did. He wanted to see if I thought you were the girl I told him about."

"What did you say?"

"I was sure it wasn't you. I guess because you were older and had changed so much, I didn't think it could be you. And you looked so different in Amish clothes." He gave her a quick smile. "I was super disappointed because I wanted to see you again. And, at the same time, I felt relieved that it wasn't you because I feared how that would go. Truthfully, I just couldn't deal with it. Seeing you made me feel guilty. My dad hinted about Earl being my son, but I was in denial. I couldn't let myself believe that it could be possible."

"Becoming a mother changed me a lot," she said.

He shook his head and started to speak, but Earl came running up to the picnic table and spouted off a long string of Pennsylvania Dutch words. He was smiling and excited. His cute face looked so different because of his missing tooth. Delilah rattled off a whole sentence in her lower-pitched Amish voice, while Dave tried to guess what she was saying.

"Earl wants to know if we are leaving right away or if he can play for a little longer," she interpreted. Earl's eyes moved to Dave to see what his answer would be.

"I'm in no hurry," Dave answered.

He looked at Earl and smiled. He wanted to pick him up and give him a big hug. Something told him that would not be wise at this point. Delilah passed the words on, but Earl was already running away, no doubt having understood what Dave had said.

"Does Earl know that you are his mommy?"

"No, not yet," she explained. "Our ministers wanted it to seem like he belonged to my parents— so children in our church wouldn't be confused."

Another sharp pain filled Dave's heart. So much so that he held a hand to his chest and groaned.

She reached over and touched his arm. "God will give him grace when the time comes."

Dave nodded but the pain didn't subside.

She tried to meet eyes with Dave and gave him a sweet smile. "I wanted to find you when I realized I was gonna have a baby. But my parents feared it would only make matters worse—that you or your parents would try to take the baby. Or that you'd talk me into leaving the Amish."

He dared to ask, "So, am I the boy you were interested in once and your parents didn't feel good about it?"

She nodded, smiled, and raised one eyebrow. "Un fa shden-dich— so, I'm that girl that you always cared about?"

"Yeah . . ." he slurred out with a grin. "You're the one."

"Why didn't you come to see me sooner?" she asked.

"Selfish reasons." He winced. "I thought you'd have me thrown in jail."

"What? For what?"

Dave looked over to be sure Earl wasn't close by. He whispered, "For what happened under the train—or were you too drunk to remember what happened?"

She shrugged her shoulders. "I remember it—even though I had too much to drink."

"It's all my fault, Delilah. You probably thought I got you drunk on purpose."

She shook her head. "No—our bodies betrayed us."

"What does that mean?" He continued his slump, his shoulders hanging.

She leaned over to meet his downcast eyes. "We were in over our heads and the current pulled us under." She looked in Earl's direction, watching him play with his friend. "I shouldn't have kept drinking that wine, no matter how good it tasted. I should have dressed modestly. If I had, things might have been different." Delilah looked into his eyes and nodded as if asking him to agree. She added, "I shouldn't have let you kiss me. I should have tried to stop you. I'm guilty too."

Dave reached over and took her hand that waved as she talked. "No! You didn't deserve what happened. It's my fault for bringing the wine. I never thought about all that you might be going through. All I thought about was if I'd end up getting kicked off the basketball team. Or if I'd end up in jail. And I felt sorry for myself that I lost a girl that I was crazy about."

"I pitied myself too," she said.

"Delilah—you have every reason to feel bad for yourself. I never let myself believe that you had a child. Even if I did consider it for a moment, I never thought about what that might mean for an Amish girl. Because of me no Amish boys have asked you out. Ever since I met you, I've tried to protect you from anyone who might hurt you, but all you needed was someone to protect you from me."

She bit her fingernails and didn't look at him until he said the last sentence. Then she turned her face and her eyes held a sweet, sad expression.

Dave moaned again. "Not to mention what it did to your family when they needed you most. Just when your dad had a terrible accident, you got sick and then they realized you were pregnant."

She drew in a deep breath and leaned on one hand on the bench. "I did get angry with you for a while. When my parents found out I was going to have a baby, they had me talk to the bishop and ministers. They wanted me to confess my sin in church."

Dave touched her hand. "Ugh—I put you through hell."

Delilah looked in his direction, as if startled by his choice of words. She quietly continued with her story. "I told my parents that I couldn't confess because I didn't choose this. I let my heart put all the blame on you. I got angry with you."

He drew in a long, painful breath.

"Let me finish," she said. "My grandpa, whose name was Earl, helped me. He took me aside and explained sin. He taught me that God would never hold me accountable for sins that were committed *against* me or *to* me. He said, 'No person will be judged by God for something done to them. Only your own sins can separate you from God.'"

She met eyes with Dave. "I thought he was telling me that I didn't need to make a confession at church. And, I asked him if that is what he meant. He said, 'I want you to confess to Christ what you are guilty of—not what the boy is guilty of. If you do that, you will feel free. And you will be able to forgive him.'"

Dave asked in a whisper, "Is that how you were able to forgive me?"

She nodded and looked deep into his eyes. "Yes. When I stood to confess my sin, I still wasn't convinced my grandpa was right. As soon as the words began to leave my lips, I saw it—I felt it."

Dave hung on her words. "Felt what?"

"I felt my own sin. I instantly knew my part and confessed that I sinned—and I felt free. And from that moment on, I was able to forgive you. I prayed for you many times."

He dared to touch her hand again. "You are a much better person than I am."

She squeezed his hand in hers. "No, now that you have repented—right here today on your knees, before God and to me—you are just what I am: forgiven and washed by God."

"I can't believe we didn't recognize each other," he said. "Didn't you think I looked familiar?"

She shook her head. "God must have kept us from knowing each other until the time was right."

"He must have," Dave smirked at her with a grin. "You should have known me!"

She laughed. "No—your skin color used to be darker."

Dave nodded. "I always had a dark tan during my high school summers."

"Your voice used to be hoarse. I liked how you talked," she said.

He wrinkled his forehead for a moment. "Oh, I think I had a cold that made my voice sound raspy."

Delilah laughed. "I should have known. Now that you say that, I remember that I ended up with a bad cold that next week." She looked at him and tilted her head. "And your hair is longer, and that little beard changed your looks too." She paused and added, "Your personality changed as well. You used to be so bold and flirtatious. Now you are so mature and kind."

"I've been on my best behavior because I'm with that famous Amish girl."

She pushed a hand toward him. "I'm the same Delilah you met at the pool."

He nudged her shoulder with his. "I missed you so bad—you'll never know."

Delilah smiled and looked into his eyes. "I think I do."

CHAPTER TWENTY-SEVEN

End of the Book

D ave, Delilah, and Earl headed out toward the Mustang. A few girls ran toward them in the parking lot.

Dave sighed. "Here come some of your fans, Delilah."

She blushed and hid herself behind his taller body. The girls were out of breath yet smiling as they drew near. Two of them stopped short. The cutest of the three seemed the boldest. She held out a blank sheet of paper and a pen and handed it to Dave.

"Un fa shdendich—Samson, you're even taller and better-looking in real life!"

"Taller than I was in the book?" Dave asked.

The girls all giggled. The cute spokesperson corrected him. "No—the picture on Facebook."

"Oh good—did you girls see our Facebook post?"

They all three nodded. One of the shyer girls said, "Us and everyone in America!"

The third girl said, "Un fa shdendich—probably everyone in the world!"

A middle-aged woman came up behind the girls holding a copy of *Samson and Delilah*. The girls gathered around her and giggled. "Look Mom, it's the real Samson and Delilah, and even Earl!"

Their mother seemed as excited as the girls. She held one hand on a cheek and with the other held out her book. "Samson, could you sign this?"

He held the book but stopped short. "Did you all "Like" and "Share" our picture?"

They all nodded excitedly. The mom added, "And we'll boycott any magazine that puts a picture of Delilah on the cover!"

"Thanks a million," Dave said. He wrote, *To my good friends, thank you for helping me protect Delilah. All the best, Samson.*

The woman reached the book toward Delilah. "Would you please sign it too?"

"I'd be happy to," Delilah said. Her nose wrinkled, and her lips curved into a slight smile.

Dave watched over her shoulder as she signed her *Delilah* right next to his *Samson*, and below both of their names she added *and Earl*. When they walked away, Earl asked Delilah something in Dutch. She answered him and then turned to Dave.

"Earl wants to know how those people know us. He was surprised they knew his name!"

Dave knelt in front of Earl and adjusted his suspenders. "My dad wrote a book about us; you, me, and Delilah. A lot of people have read the book and loved it. Now they all know who we are."

Earl nodded, his little black hat bobbing along.

"I guess we'd better get going," Dave said.

They took their places in the Mustang and buckled in for the final leg of their trip. Delilah picked up *Samson and Delilah* and found her place where she left off. Her bare feet ended up on the dashboard, and her toes resumed their wiggling. Suddenly there were a few sniffles and then Delilah reached for a Kleenex and blew her nose. She put the book down on her lap and said, "When you asked for my parents' address, was it so that you could send a check like Samson did in the book?"

"Maybe," Dave said.

"I . . . see. Not as much as he did in the book, I hope?"

"Well, I felt like Dad was giving me advice. I'm sure he would have wanted me to give your family money. I get a percentage of all the book's sales, and that's how I have money for a restaurant. Now that we found your family, the very least we can do is share some of the profits with all of you."

"My dad won't cash a check for fifty thousand dollars," she said matter-of-factly.

"You need to tell him that the money came from the book, and that my dad has passed on to eternity. After reading the book, I feel sure that is what my dad would want me to do."

"It's too much—way too much," Delilah said and blew her nose again.

"That's what my dad wrote in the book. It's not too much. Besides, you shouldn't feel too bad for me. That photo of us on the cover of *Humans* magazine put more money in my account than ever."

"Are you going to get your money from Charlie Rose?" she asked excitedly.

"Nope, but all of that publicity drives sales. I'm sure there was another big deposit in our bank account after that magazine came out."

"And you begged people to boycott magazines that took pictures of me? When that makes more money every time they do it?"

"Yeah," Dave said, "But I learned from you and Earl that people, family, and friends are what really matters. I don't want to be like those paparazzi, making money at other people's expense."

"What about your little restaurant you want to start up?"

"I'll find a way. I just need to find an Amish girl who can make cinnamon rolls and coffee."

She gave him a coy smile.

"By the way," Dave said, "is this cousin we are heading to see the same Katie that came to the park with you years ago?"

She nodded and raised her eyebrows. "The same one."

"She'll be surprised to see me, huh?"

"Probably almost as surprised as me," she said.

Delilah dived back into her reading. Horsey sounds came from the backseat. Dave glanced over his shoulder. He could see Earl playing with his herd of plastic horses. Delilah's toes writhed furiously as she turned pages of her book. Suddenly, she began to sniffle.

"Are you okay?" Dave asked.

She nodded and whispered, "I'm reading the part where we realized that we really are Earl's parents."

She read for another minute and then turned the book onto her knees. Her shoulders shook as she leaned forward and placed both hands over her eyes and wept. He tried to think of words he could say. He laid a hand on her back and prayed silently. He finally choked out, "I'm sorry."

She looked up as her eyes pooled with tears. She shook her head and waved a hand, signaling that she couldn't speak but she wanted to say something. After a long moment, she blurted out, "It's just that it's so sweet."

He nodded. "The way the book has us talk at the hospital is a little different than how it turned out at the park."

"I liked how you said it in real life—better than in the book."

More tears ran down her already-wet cheeks. Dave reached out and rubbed the back of his hand against her soft skin to brush them away. He wished that he could kiss the tears off her face.

They both glanced back to be sure Earl wasn't paying attention to them. His herd of plastic horses were busy plowing a low area of the backseat. They seemed to be hitched in teams of four, and he spoke to them in a low guttural voice, occasionally calling out "giddyup" and "whoa."

Dave laughed. "In the book, I thought I needed to lie to the doctor and say that I'm . . ." He lowered his voice to a whisper, "Earl's dad."

She nodded with a grin. "That upset me in the book, because I thought you shouldn't lie, and I felt forced to blurt out the truth."

They both laughed.

Delilah fell silent, and after a pause she asked, "What were you afraid for me to read?"

"At first I was embarrassed for you to read a book about us falling for each other. Then, I worried about you reading my confession. I knew you would ask questions, and I couldn't deny that the story is based on truth." He looked at her until she acknowledged his fears with a nod. He whispered, "I couldn't even deal with the idea of you reading a book that suggested Earl was our son."

She wrinkled her forehead. "By the way—why did you say that I'd know your secret if I shaved off your beard? Is it because you have a cleft in your chin exactly like his?" she nodded toward the back seat.

He took her hand and slid her index finger through his whiskers. "Did you remember that?"

"Yes," she said. If you didn't have that beard, I would have known it was you. But you're even taller now, and you seem so mature. I honestly didn't know or even imagine it was you until we talked on the park bench. Now I can't believe that I didn't figure it out!"

He mouthed the words, "Did you name him David after me?"

She nodded. "I named him after my Grandpa. I gave him your name for a middle name because I wanted him to have something from you."

A tear rolled down Dave's cheek. He could see her eyes follow it as it rolled into his beard.

"Now I see why you didn't want anyone to think we're cousins," she said.

Dave laughed. "We are so distantly related it's not an issue, but it makes me uncomfortable when you say it."

"I won't bring it up again," she promised and shook her head. "How did your dad know this road trip would happen?"

"He didn't. I mean— I told him all about what happened. He knew how much I cared about you, and I think he wrote the book hoping you would read it and at the very least you'd know that I cared."

Delilah slowly nodded in agreement. "That was a sweet idea."

"Dad was planning to go up to Falls after the book got published. I think he was going to give you a copy, but then he got sick."

She smiled. "Your dad and I were good friends. I'm pretty sure I would have figured everything out when I read his book. His plan would've worked."

"What will your parents think when they figure out who I am?" Dave asked.

"I don't know." She shook her head and busied herself with reading again.

Dave looked into his rearview mirror and spoke up, "You'd better start looking out the window, Earl. We are getting close to

Nappanee, Indiana. From here on out, we are going to see a lot of horses and Amish farms. If Delilah doesn't mind, I'm going to drive to Katie's on backroads, so we can look at horses." Dave checked his rearview mirror, and he could see Earl was smiling by only seeing his eyes. Delilah rattled off a lightning quick phrase in her own language, and Earl smiled bigger.

Dave turned to Delilah. "Is that okay with you?"

"Yes, Earl wants to see horses," she said. "I'm almost done reading this book, and I need to finish it before we get there."

"Oh, you can keep that copy if you'd like," he said. She smiled but started biting her nails as she got back into her book.

Delilah turned the last page as they pulled into her cousin's drive. Dave parked the Mustang and watched while she finished the last paragraph. She suddenly gave it a shove and let it flop onto the floor by her feet.

"What's the matter?" Dave asked.

"I don't like the ending." Her eyes flashed anger. "You just drop me and Earl off at my cousin's house and drive away." She opened the door and got out, "C'mon Earl, we are here. Get your things."

Delilah's face was expressionless as she took a few of her cloth sacks and carried them to the house. Dave helped little Earl get his shoes on and put his black hat on over his bowl-cut hair. He knelt and straightened Earl's collar. He looked into Earl's eyes and said, "I'm gonna miss you."

"Will I have a brother?"

Dave searched Earl's face, trying to figure out if the little guy had discovered the truth. "What are you asking?"

"You kissed her. Will I have a brother?"

Dave didn't want to lie or giveaway more than he should. He answered, "A woman doesn't have a baby every time a man kisses her."

"Kiss her again," Earl said with a smile.

"I want to," Dave agreed. He put a hand on Earl's shoulder and said, "Please take good care of her, and tell her to call me if you need anything."

"Okay," Earl answered. He hugged Dave so tight that it hurt— not his neck, but his heart.

Dave stepped to Delilah's side of the car and picked up the book. He opened the title page to write his phone number for Delilah. He found a note he hadn't noticed, written in his dad's writing under the title.

> *To my only son, David*
> *I pray this book will help you find the real Delilah.*
> *Love, Dad*

Katie came out and took Earl by the hand. She looked at Dave and smiled. "Hello, David. Long time, no see!"

"Hi, Katie, your cousin has quite a story to tell you."

Katie nodded but her eyes looked concerned. "She looks pretty upset right now."

"I'm going to try and talk to her a little more before I leave," Dave said and nodded in Earl's direction.

Katie seemed to catch his hint. She pulled on Earl's hand. "Come on inside with me, Earl. I want to show you our toy horses."

After she led him into the house, Delilah came back to the car to get the few items that were left. Dave stood between her and the house so she couldn't go inside without talking to him first. She stopped and looked at Dave and then at her feet.

"This isn't the end of the story," Dave said.

Delilah glanced at him sideways, a tear forming in the corner of her eye.

Dave reached out and touched her hand. "My dad didn't write a sequel to this story. That's up to us."

"Sequel?" Delilah asked.

"The next book," Dave said. "A book that tells what happens next. You and I get to write that story together. We get to decide how the story ends." He handed her the book again. "I put my phone number inside the front cover."

Delilah took it and gave it a hug and Dave a smile. Her nose wrinkled a little.

Dave bent his long legs so he could look deeply into her eyes. He saw hope and love.

"My house is only about twenty minutes from here," Dave said. "I know my mom wants to meet you and Earl. And, when you two are ready to go back to Wisconsin, call me. I really want to drive you back home. Besides, I want to talk to DJ about buying her diner."

Her eyes gave away that she wasn't content with his words.

"Listen, Delilah, I don't know how we can make something work between us, you being Amish and all, but I'd be so willing to try."

The tear that had been forming in the corner of her eye trickled down her cheek. It clung to her chin until Dave touched it and brushed the stream off with the back of his fingers.

He tilted her face toward him until he could look into her eyes again. "You and Earl are my two favorite people in the whole world. You think about what you want. I will do anything you ask—just tell me what you want."

Delilah looked deeply into Dave's eyes without speaking, as if willing him to see the answer in them.

Dave started to sing in a whisper, "If you need me, call. No matter where you are, no matter how far. Cause there ain't no mountain high enough, ain't no valley wide enough, aint' no river deep enough to keep me from getting to you."

Her lips trembled, and she couldn't seem to speak.

He leaned down to get on eye level with her. "You don't have to say anything now. I promise I will never pressure you again.

Maybe you should talk to your dad or ministers. You can call my phone after you've had a chance to think things over.

Delilah stood staring into his eyes deeply. She didn't move. He wasn't sure if she was waiting for a kiss or if she wanted to say something.

He basked in the pleasure of gazing into her amazing and beautiful eyes. Without planning to say anything, words fell out of his mouth. "I love you, Delilah. I've loved you since the day we met."

She breathed out, "Un fa shdendich." A sweet smile surfaced on her lips.

He wanted to kiss her so badly, but he didn't know if it was appropriate in the driveway of an Amish farm. She rose to her tiptoes and tilted her head up with puckered lips. Dave met her halfway, drawing her in with his hands on her waist. She kept it short, but it was as sweet as any kiss could be. He accepted her intuition as a guide. When he released her from his embrace, she turned and sprinted toward her cousin's house. He watched her bare feet going and her apron strings bouncing. She stopped on the porch and looked back at Dave, who hadn't moved.

Cupping her hands to her mouth, she called, "Check your messages as soon as you get home!"

Dave ran to the Mustang and revved it up. He spun out in the gravel, but after he turned onto the pavement, he slowed enough to wave good-bye. He could see Delilah and Earl, both waving, with big smiles on their faces. He punched his accelerator and shouted, "Come on horse car—let's get home and see what she says!"

The Mustang charged off with a roar.

For a list of books by Thomas Nye, check his website: amish-horses.blogspot.com

You can find Thomas Nye on Facebook, Instagram, and Twitter as "Amish Horses."

Or, write: Thomas Nye P.O. Box 495 Kalona, Iowa 52247